ALICE – F...

SURREAL

Chimera (ki-mir'ə, kī)
A creation of the imagination,
a wild fancy, an impossible dream

CHIMERA
books.co.uk

Alice – Fallen Angels first published in 2010 by
Chimera Books Ltd
PO Box 152
Waterlooville
Hants
PO8 9FS
United Kingdom

Printed and bound in the UK by
Cox & Wyman, Reading.

ISBN 978-1-903931-97-4

This novel is fiction – in real life practice safe sex

ALICE – FALLEN ANGELS

Surreal

Chimera *(kī-mîr'ə, kĭ-)* a creation of the imagination, a wild fantasy

Hughes' bulging dome forced open her anus, and sank rapidly within. He stroked her bottom cheeks, scrutinising the welts. 'You know what I'm going to do?' he asked.

Alice laid her flushed cheek to the table, the pain in her rear finally subsiding.

He withdrew slowly. 'After I've fucked your arse, I mean. I'm going to take you back to the dorms, just as you are.'

He thrust. Alice whimpered.

'Naked except for your suspender belt and stockings.' A rapid withdrawal executed, he sank again. 'Except I'll add a collar and chain. I'll chain you to a locker at the end of Ruth's dorm. A lesson to all those girls.' He sped up, his cock ploughing in and out, the tight circle of anus about his shaft entrancing. 'The humiliation will do you good, Alice. It will teach you your place in the structure of things.'

Prologue

In a few short months ill fortune ripped an intelligent, hard working, if naïve young woman from the bosom of privileged security, depositing her amidst the chancers and jaundiced predators of a hardened and indiscriminate post-war society.

Unable to come to terms with her sexual liaison with Richard, Alice fled, the discovery of her illegitimacy consuming her immediate existence. *The Hope*, by name if little else, seemed to proffer an opportune stroke of good fortune. In reality she had been ensnared, tempted and lured toward a pernicious way of life that would have appalled her a few months earlier.

The mental, perhaps spiritual struggle worsened. An exhausted and confused Alice slowly gave ground, surrendering to the debased urges that rarely let her be. Dreams intermingled with reality, Alice unsure as to which was which. With no one to turn to for sound advice she would be used, abused, and entangled in a world of sexual depravity.

Alice would slide further into that netherworld, powerless in defence, before kismet would smile again upon that philanthropic innocent.

Chapter 1

A brisk northerly rustled hosts of fragile amber and bronze, dying leaves that bowed before that implacable emissary of a skulking winter. Once impenetrable stone walls towered imposing, the ragged gaps and holes rent by time, war and pilfering. Uncertain on its promontory, torn but still dignified, whispers from a thousand years touched and ruffled a demoralised spirit.

A solitary trail, softened by an incoming tide, scored the mud and stone shore. Footprints, thrown rather than laid, led to the seat of that once noble fortress. High on a tower, silhouetted against the setting sun, perched a woman, her gaze settled upon a crimson-tinted ebb tide.

Strands kicked by the wind harassed auburn hair and wind-burned cheeks, pained emerald eyes. Alice held her coat collar tight about the neck, twitching with spontaneous shivers.

Much had been weighed that Sunday afternoon: her future, her past, her plans and aspirations. Regret appeased conscience. Loathing squeezed the heart. The realisation she could trust no one slowly saturated her cognizance. Reflection bawled that not one participant in the pantomime of her life had proved beyond reproach.

Alice suffered deception, her loving parents transpiring to be loving substitutes.

'Liars. They bore false witness.'

'Why not?'

'Why not, what?'

'Blame them for everything. After all, they only saved you from a bleak and loveless childhood. They only made the ultimate sacrifice, and provided you with the best education affordable. Don't look to yourself will you? I mean, goodness gracious me, you are perfection.'

A smile briefly flickering, the teenager glanced down. He leant on a tumbled wall, studying the blood-red skyline, that ever-present pipe sliced between sucking lips. Hate rolled with respect, drifted toward an unhealthy infatuation. Alice had thus managed to stay out of his bed, though the desire burned remorselessly.

Alice scowled. *'What is it with you? Why do you affect me the way you do?'*

6

'Power. Psychological strength. He holds the key to your dark side, that sexual energy you find irresistible. That is your incomprehensible desire, to drink from the fountain of debasement.'

Alice shivered, a pang of truth vitalising her crotch.

'Loosen the shutters. Let a chink of enlightenment filter through. Be awakened and stirred by what lurks there.'

'You are the devil and you tempt me with falsehoods. You're trying to trick me!'

'Fear at what you are? I am no devil. You know that. You also know what you are, and already recognise the electrifying future that awaits you. All you have to do is cast off the fetters of indoctrination, open your eyes and heart to what hails you.'

A week had passed since Richard's dramatic performance. She'd heard no more from the loathsome creature. His whip marks had dwindled to mere ghosts, albeit haunting spectres that raised the bogeyman with startling regularity. Hughes, she believed had sold her, or at least leased her body. And yet she did nothing, her mind refusing to reach a conclusion.

Hughes glanced up as if in response to the girl's animosity. 'Yes, you know, don't you? You know *me*. You comprehend with unfathomable empathy. Opposites attract. I'm under your skin as much as you're under mine, aren't I?'

Her words lost to the wind, Hughes raised his pipe in mock salute. Alice ignored the gesture, her mouth set, contempt in possession. Head lifted, she resumed that analysis of past, present and future.

She had showered after Richard's mauling, just as Hughes suggested. Washed? Or cleansed? *Scrubbed.* The surge of needles struck like purification, slicing without mercy, torturing further her tormented body. Wherever the scourge had cut and struck, so her flesh screamed its submission. Welts smothered her backside, cursed her sex and embroidered her chest.

She watched in utter silence the vague disrobing, the shadowy disencumbering beyond the shower curtain. She feared, yearned for, abhorred the prospect. Anticipation bred an indescribable need, the dementia of a seawater thirst.

He lingered to announce his authority, his prerogative to do just as he pleased. Brazen, Hughes posed with hands on hips, the hazy image of his privates threatening, announcing their intent.

Her whipped buttocks found the cold hard tiles, that traumatised flesh remoulded. Hughes stood before her, chilling, exciting her beyond reason, unbridled confidence his aura. He offered no smile, no words.

Alice trembled, the man's presence peeling her inhibitions, invoking the devil that lurks in all. Just as she had savoured the slash of leather on her naked body, she longed for the man's touch. She would never request, nor suggest. She would fight; try to repulse his sinful invasion. But she accepted she would fail.

Breaking eye contact, Hughes raised a hand, forefinger hovering. Alice covered, protected her breasts. 'They thrill, don't they, Alice?' he stated, quiet voice harbouring menace. Alice remained entranced by expectation. Green eyes riveted she could offer no reaction. 'The marks of the whip, I mean.' He smiled. 'Oh, your tits too. Yes, your tits excite. It's the combination, Alice. Welted, firm tit flesh.' He nudged her hand away, a wet breast available.

Alice jerked to his forceful grope, the man's fingers probing, digging deep. 'Whipped tits.' Lips licked, Hughes manipulated. 'So Alice, have you worked it out yet? Can you understand what drives a young woman like you? Can you comprehend the insanity that makes you want the lash? Why you love the pain; the scorching kiss of punishing leather. And why, Alice, does your fanny run wet at the sight of these laurels awarded?' A nipple pinched between finger and thumb impressed the point.

Feet shuffled, legs parted, thighs gave to the pressure. Hughes' fingers thrust, toyed, stroked her pussy lips. 'Ask that pious conscience why you want my cock inside you, Alice. No, worse than want. You yearn for this hot shaft stuffed between your legs, don't you?'

Alice met those unfeeling eyes, the irises as black as Satan's heart. Entranced, she waited, strung by his whim.

She responded to his foray with a rapid intake of breath, the man's finger probing deep, her vagina reciprocating with nauseous favour. Hughes shook his head. 'You know, when you first strolled into my office I would have bet on you being unsullied. A bit of a disappointment finding you aren't. So, how did you lose it? What was it, Alice? Eh? Vegetable, mineral, or a thrusting probe of male beef?'

Alice looked away, shamefaced.

Hughes withdrew the digit, returning immediately with three. Alice gasped, the stretch uncomfortably enthralling. 'Who was he?' Hughes pressed. 'Who did Miss Prim let in below? Who found the key?' Hughes smirked, his anger masked. 'Not that bald-headed, bespectacled prat, surely!'

He stepped back, fingers removed. Both hands settled on her upper arms, the man gazing disbelieving. 'Tell me it wasn't. Alice! Tell me that wanker didn't take your virginity.'

Incensed at the question, guilty of that coition, she blurted, 'No! Not him. What do you think I am, for God's sake?'

Hughes grinned. 'God's sake? I would have thought you cared little for him. After all, isn't Satan your master?' His arms encircled her waist, pinning her. Pulled close, her breasts, her belly, her groin pressed to his, his fingers playing with her welted bottom.

'Ask me,' he said.

Alice shook her head.

'You will in time.'

'Maybe,' she replied, unsure. 'And there again...'

'I like the unattainable,' he divulged with a sinister air. 'It's something to chase. To catch. And I will catch you.'

'Maybe,' Alice voiced, hesitant. 'Maybe you won't always want it. When you see it for what it is, then you might find it abhorrent.'

'Tell you what, Alice. I will show you abhorrent. I will demonstrate loathsome and how I treat it. *O'Leary!* In here. *Now.*'

Surprised, unprepared for the eventuality, Alice gazed stupidly at the newcomer. Curtain eased aside, a naked, curvaceous Ruth O'Leary made her demure entrance. She eyed the pair with suppressed aplomb, a dark arrogance inadequately masked by subservience.

'Well, Ruth,' Hughes grunted. 'Ask.'

The young woman curled fingers about his erection, begging in a sensuous tone. 'I want you. I want you to fuck me any way that pleases you.'

Hughes kept his eyes on Alice. 'Watch, girl. Watch me fuck this bitch, then tell me honestly you don't want the same.'

Released, Alice backed to the wall. Hot water still rained, all three crammed within the tiled confines. The steam, heat, closeness of naked bodies ignited a cauldron. Glistening flesh, sensuous wet skin, the audacious airing of intimate parts fanned the flames. Alice watched. Alice regaled in the taking of the blonde.

Hughes urged the young woman over, hands settled on her flanks, his piece gathering strength. The lift and expansion of incited cock impressed, enraptured. Unable to look away Alice witnessed that stem stiffen, distend to a breathtaking conclusion. 'Oh, sweet Jesus!' she gasped beneath her breath.

He exposed the plum, the massive head glistening with pre-come. Buttocks dimpling, Hughes gripped O'Leary tighter, fingers delving the flesh of her hips. The tip of his erection pressed, parted and slid unimpeded, stretching the girl's cunt to capacity.

Ruth cried out, the trespass excruciatingly agreeable. Alice spun between envy and revulsion, Hughes' arrogant smirk implying much.

Embarrassed, Alice diverted her gaze, that plunging organ possessively seductive. The flagrant crudity and explicit vaginal penetration played an irresistible euphony on her sex strings. Face to the wall, eyes covered by a wavering hand, Alice couldn't escape the pair's indulgent grunts and gasps. Then an impatient Hughes seized her neck. He pulled her from the wall and forced her over, to witness the pump of oiled cock in strained pussy. Pride closed her eyes.

Alice recalled her flight, sliding over Ruth's wet back, Hughes holding her, his left palm as effective as his right. Those whipped flanks heaved to his shocking slaps, Alice issuing cries of pained anguish in seconds.

Yanked back she dared not refuse him his wish. With contrived reluctance she followed the thrusting giant. The formidable breadth of that cock stirred. The division and awesome spread of Ruth's fanny drove heated stilettos deep into her own burrow. The mighty pods bloating their captive sac, swung beneath that staggering torpedo, the coming squirt gathering force.

Without breaking his rhythm Ruth frenzied in climax, he stooped to tease, to intimidate, to probe for intimate secrets. 'You're frightened of the pleasure it will give, aren't you Alice? To a good catholic girl being fucked

11

can never be enjoyable. Please thy husband by pretending to savour his despicable passion.'

He held her so close his hip brushed her facial cheek. 'Listen to Ruth. Hear those guttural moans? That's called ecstasy. Her cunt is alight. Tell me that's wrong, Alice. Convince me she is not entitled to wallow in her own body's consuming tide.'

Alice studied the girl's distorted down-turned face, the crease of forehead, the wrinkling of nose, the biting of lip. She perused the swing and lurch of fleshy breasts. She refocused on Ruth's buttocks and that enticing union. There was something compelling about the submergence of the male stem, the manner in which it penetrated, protruded from that most intimate place.

'I have plans for you, Alice,' the man cajoled. 'I have chains, iron manacles and coarse ropes. I have a fancy to see you act like a whipped bitch, naked with collar and leash, your body striped from shoulders to knees.' He dragged her about, so Alice bent alongside Ruth. Without losing pace he forced a hand between her legs. Fingers inside her, he goaded. 'Mine to do with as I please. Mine to whip, fuck and abuse as I want. Much like this rag here.' He dealt a hefty slap to Ruth's buttock.

Regardless of her severely flagellated bottom, Alice experienced the pang of urgent need. That impossible dilemma returned, hovered, teased her.

'Shall I whip this bitch, Alice?' Hughes enquired, pinching a handful of Ruth's bottom cheek. Ruth cried out, her body in spasm.

'Ha!' the principal whooped, withdrawing his cock. He turned the redhead, forcing her to her knees. 'Between your tits.'

Alice probed the gathering darkness, dull red clouds scudding the horizon. Why? Why did she accommodate his crude demands? Why did she embrace his stiff cock between her wet breasts?

The recollection repeatedly nagged. Even then that image resurfaced, still thrilling, still electrifying. His highly excited shaft pierced her cleavage, thrust between her generous breasts, which trembled to his impetus.

Then Ruth launched her assault, Alice reciprocating. Lips met, kissed. Tongues raided. The blonde's hand groped that lustful union of lunging stem and jostled breasts. Alice ungrudgingly partook of the pair's antics, beyond caring.

'Mad! I lost it. Lost all reason.' She glanced down at Hughes. 'If you only knew,' she voiced, knowing he couldn't hear. 'You could have had me that day. I was never more ready. I was aching for it. The urge was too much.'

She glanced back out to sea. *'Yes. I would have ridden your prick with the greatest pleasure.'*

As a substitute she ate greedily of his erection. She seized it, suckled it until the juices flowed, and then swallowed the secretion. Desperate lust? The act of a novice. An attempt to please both sides – saint and tart.

Legs drawn up, parted, Alice stroked her panty-covered pussy. *'I wanted him. I wanted his cock inside me. Is there a difference between a shagging you want and one you don't? He's a pig.'* Alice smiled. *'And he's magnetically attractive.'*

'And, he knows you, Alice Hussey. He reads your lusts and despair. He has no need to ask, he can taste your desperation.'

Alice lay her face in upturned hands. *'What have I become? How do I control this outrageous longing? Is this my inheritance? Is this why Rose Hussey was locked away?'*

'Are you going to stop up there all night?' reached her ears. 'It's getting late and bloody cold,' Hughes carped.

'Go back if you don't like it,' she shouted back.

'What?'

'I said go back to the Hope. I'll follow shortly.'

Hughes buttoned his coat and lifted the collar about his neck. 'How long?' he bellowed.

'Don't worry, I won't run off. Can't, can I? Not with these things on!' Alice lifted her arms in demonstration, the rattle of chain inaudible.

She scowled to the man's laugh. 'Just a game, Alice. I thought you'd appreciate a game.'

Hughes turned and wandered across the unattended lawns. Alice lowered her hands, the steel cuffs cold against her skin. Her eyes followed the snaking chain to the parting in her blouse. Beneath, unyielding metal links gripped her waist, a padlock securing it and the chain from her cuffs. Other links explored the division between her buttocks, and ground against the sensitive slit of her vagina.

The tyrant had forced her to fetter herself. While he stood leering she'd donned and secured the chains. Dressed but braless, she handcuffed herself and secured the short length to her waistband.

Alice descended the eroded tower, stepping lightly from stone to stone. Hughes waited, his figure clearly visible beneath the orange glow of a street lamp. 'Will this be the only way I get to go out?' she enquired peevishly. 'Am I a prisoner too, now?'

Hughes placed an arm about her shoulder. He leant close and kissed her neck. 'I have a mind to watch you,' he whispered.

'Watch me what?' she asked, baffled.

'Tease yourself.'

'How?' Alarm bells rang, the girl wary of where he tried to steer her.

Hughes delved her coat, his hand lifting her skirt, fingers settling lightly on a naked buttock. 'Don't you

14

like the game?' he asked nonchalantly.

'Taken out in chains? No, it's humiliating.' Intrigued by his question she sought clarification, not knowing whether she really wanted to know. 'Why do you want to watch me?'

Hughes stopped and faced the young woman. 'If you were fettered for the safety of the public, then yes, you might be inclined to humiliation. But you're not.' Hughes held out the keys. 'Take them off if you want. Toss them in the hedge. It really is of no consequence.'

Alice took the keys, releasing her wrists.

'To the layman those would be pure pain, pure annoyance. But to you, Alice… to you.' His hand wandered, cold fingers brushing against her crotch. 'They are a source of excitation.'

Alice winced, Hughes pushing aside the links, his finger sinking inside her.

'You see? Right, aren't I? The harsh steel, the pinch and grab of links, the probing of intimate parts…' Hughes held up the intrusive digit, moisture from her sexual well glinting in the streetlight.

Ignoring his argument Alice loosed the chain, the rattle of steel hitting the pavement alarmingly loud. She smiled. 'You don't know me. You think you do, but you're wrong. And I won't be your slave or prisoner.'

'There is a room back in the Hope. A very, how should I describe it? Yes…' he lifted a finger, pointing skyward. 'Hostile. It lies directly above the main boilers. Those that provide heating and hot water…'

Alice interrupted. 'You mean the hot water the girls never get to use?'

'Precisely so. Would you have me change that, Alice? Say yes and it will be done. It's only a matter of a cock or two.' Hughes smirked. 'You know. Stop cock.'

'Is that the price?'

'Nothing comes free in this world.'

15

'This room?'

'Hot. Even a naked body would sweat profusely. A chained, trussed and tormented naked body. Glistening, running with perspiration. Interesting?'

'Is that a direct probe? Do you mean *my* naked body?'

The man took her hand and pressed it to his crotch. 'This is a probe.' He glanced casually about. 'Here. Right now. Up against the hedge. Skirt around your waist. My cock in your cunt. That would excite, would it not?'

Alice shivered. *'It would. I would come in seconds. The moment this Goliath opened me I'd orgasm. Take me now.'* Alice shook her head. 'I don't think so.'

'Your body tells me a different story.' He raised an eyebrow.

The man's tone simmered with rapturous promise. He entranced. He charmed. He drew on her poison, on that corrupt disposition. He goaded and stimulated. 'Unbutton my flies. Get my penis out.'

Alice tried to ignore Hughes and the inner turmoil. Mental barriers defending virtue ground to a standstill. Dark whispers beckoned, sin enticing – like coke to the junkie.

'That's a direct order. Disobey me and I will put you over my knee and bare your arse.' His smile lacked warmth. 'You know I will. Undo me, Alice. Get my cock out.'

Heart racing, body shaking, Alice obeyed. Her gaze riveted on him. Her eyes transfixed by his wickedness, she flicked the buttons, opening the vent.

'Now, put your hand inside.' She felt his mass immediately, the man's underpants barely covering it. 'Ease it out, Alice. Grip the shaft. Hold it tight.'

Still she refused to look, her fist tight about his hot girth, Hughes' erection exposed but shielded by their closeness.

'Now lift your skirt.'

She shook her head in defiance.

'Yes, I know, people might see. But not clearly. They may guess but they won't be sure. That's the thrill, Alice. Now lift your skirt.'

'You're not fucking me,' she spat, unyielding. 'Not here, not anywhere.'

Hughes yanked her coat apart. 'Bare your pussy, girl!'

'No.'

Hughes ripped her blouse apart, baring her breasts.

'You pig!'

His temper flared. 'I'll show you the pig, you obstinate sow.' He spun her, pushed her hard against the privet hedge, twigs scratching her breasts and belly. He expertly and swiftly bound her wrists with his tie. 'It's a quarter of a mile to the Hope. You can walk it as you are, tits hanging out,' he spat angrily.

Alice lashed out with a foot, catching his leg.

Hughes grabbed her by the hair and shook her. 'I can rip your fucking skirt off as well if you like.' He lifted her. 'Do you like?'

'No,' the girl whimpered, close to tears.

Hughes let her go, stepping away as he did so. He pressed a hand to his forehead, expression stressed.

The approach of an old man walking his dog prompted Alice to turn toward the hedge. He passed suspicious, but offered no more than, 'Evening.'

'See how you let opportunity pass you by,' Hughes whispered.

Alice shot a scowl over a shoulder.

'You could have made his night. His week, maybe. But you hid your charms. You chose not to.'

'What are you?' Alice hissed. 'Demented?' She glanced down. 'And your flies are undone.' Hughes made the necessary adjustment. 'Local prison governor seen with half dressed young woman. That should do

17

your image the power of good.'

'I should have used that tie on your gob.'

'So what now? Are you going to risk your position just to teach me a lesson?'

Hughes folded his arms. 'You really do have the loveliest pair of boobs.'

'And you want the whole town to see them? I thought you'd want to keep them for yourself.'

Hughes pressed a finger to the left breast. He drew his nail across the flesh before flicking to the right one, clawing that too. He licked his lips. 'There's something about a welted bosom.' Alice tilted her head to one side, expression quizzical. He stroked the soft skin. 'Perhaps a birch,' he suggested, to intimidate.

'For what?' Alice demanded.

'I don't need a reason. You only need reason because you're indoctrinated. Because you can't let yourself go.'

He moved closer. 'Come on, Hussey, admit it. You'd be in seventh heaven if I trussed you and birched your tits.'

'You know it all, don't you? And you're so irresistible, too. It's Geoffrey Hughes' cock, so I must want it. It's Geoffrey Hughes with the whip, so I *must* want flogging. Well, sorry, but you're not that alluring.'

Hughes huffed. He untied her wrists. 'Do yourself up, young lady. You're an embarrassment.'

Hughes stopped two hundred yards short of the Hope gates, his eyes settled on a figure lit by the yellow haze of a streetlight. Cigarette smoke wafted up, blended with a mist drifting in from the sea.

'Someone you know?' Alice enquired, following his gaze.

'Maybe.' Hughes sucked on his pipe. 'Or perhaps it's just a Halloween ghost.'

'A what?'

18

'Halloween. American thing. Witches and ghosts.'

'He looks real enough to me. A bit like Humphrey Bogart in that hat and raincoat.'

Hughes smiled. 'Always the dramatist, Dennis Scrubbs. Plays it for effect.'

'You *do* know him then.'

'Questions. I've a few myself.'

The couple closed the distance, Scrubbs extinguishing his butt with the heel of a shoe. 'Hello Geoffrey,' the man greeted, his accent clearly Welsh.

'What do you want?' Hughes demanded, refusing the offered hand.

'Well now,' he said, admiring Alice. 'That *is* pretty. An improvement over the dogs of war, eh, Geoffrey?'

'It's been nigh on eight years.'

'I'd have looked you up sooner,' Scrubbs replied. 'But I've been doing for her Majesty, you see.'

'And now?'

'Now?' Scrubbs responded with intimation. 'Now I've got time to look my old army buddy up.' He put a hand against Hughes' shoulder. 'Now I've the time to sort out a few debts. Haven't I, *boyo*?'

'It's late. Where you staying?' Hughes eyed the man with a mix of uncertainty and contempt.

'Lost my wallet, Geoffrey. On the train, I guess. Need a room for the night. Thought being such an old inti*mate*, you might help.'

'It's a women's penitentiary, Scrubbs.'

'Do me the courtesy of calling me Dennis, Geoffrey. And I know the difficulty. Your Mavis has explained it to me.'

'Then you already know it's impossible.'

'Mavis said you have the authority.'

Hughes glowered. 'Did she now?'

'Is this the girlfriend, you lucky blighter?' Scrubbs ran his eye over Alice.

19

'This is Miss Hussey, *Dennis*. She is one of my key personnel.'

Dennis offered a hand. 'He always had a way with the ladies, did Geoffrey. Pleased to meet you, Miss Hussey.'

Alice felt her cheeks warm.

'Now I've embarrassed you.' Dennis rummaged in a pocket. 'Here, smoke?' He offered the packet. 'Lucky Strikes. American.'

Alice took one, Scrubbs striking a match, lighting it for her. 'Something sexy about a woman with a cigarette, don't you think, Geoffrey?'

Hughes pulled his coat collar tight about his neck. 'It's cold. You can bunk in my house, Dennis. Away from the women and temptation.'

There were questions Alice wanted to ask, answers she dearly wanted to hear. She could sense an air between the men. Dennis harboured menace, Hughes suspicion. But Hughes dismissed her. He pointed at the Hope as they passed. 'See why Mavis is still here, Alice. I'll be over in due course.'

The redhead unlocked the main door, then bounded up the stairs to the second floor. She quickly advanced on Hughes' study, stopping outside, face puzzled. She heard voices, Mavis and someone else, that other very familiar.

Unable to place the owner, Alice stepped in. 'Mavis,' she began, 'Mr Hughes wondered why...'

'Alice! I don't believe it! It's Alice Hussey!'

Stunned, the redhead gasped. A friend from the not too distant past rose from a chair. A wealthy and glamorous young woman still wearing the pompous mask of socialite breeding offered a hand. The raven-haired beauty shook her head, expression disbelieving.

Mavis moved close. 'You *know* this young woman?'

Hughes interrupted them. 'More an Aphrodite, I'd

say.'

'I thought…' Alice began.

'Scrubbs can settle himself. Now where did this delicacy come from?'

Alice stammered. 'Carters. She was… Jesus Christ! How have you come to this?'

Hughes prodded Alice's shoulder. 'So, is this the Second Coming?'

'What?'

'Jesus Christ is a woman this time around, yes?'

'No.'

'The way you carry on I thought perhaps you have invoked her.'

Gathering her wits, Alice explained. 'Hazel was the senior prefect at Carters. She reported directly to Miss Lake.'

'Huh! Just when I was about to kneel.' Arrogance courted arrogance, Hughes perusing the young woman. 'What I meant was, who delivered the package?'

'One Hazel Sweet, petty theft and prostitution,' another face entered, Hughes turning and offering a hand.

'Cyril! I had no call.'

'Does that mean I'm not welcome?'

'Of course not. Mavis, go.' Secretary fleeing, Hughes circled Hazel. 'So what did you nick, Sweet?' he asked from behind.

'I was framed,' Hazel replied indignantly.

'So yer didn't do nuffink then?' Hughes scoffed.

'As it happens…'

'Amazing how many *not guilty me lord* there are in English prisons. Cyril, what's up with your bobbies, always nicking innocent girls?

'Nice suit.' Hughes came full circle. He felt the cloth. 'Expensive.'

'I couldn't see any harm,' Cyril began.

'No harm done,' the principal assured. 'I'm sure we have a suitable uniform. It won't be ermine or silk, though. Might be a bit rough on the aristocratic hide, Miss Sweet.

'Where were you intending to stay tonight, Cyril? Hotel or my house?'

'I have to get back.'

'Shame. You'll stay for a spot of dinner, though? I could induct Sweet, and then join you.'

'It'll have to wait.'

Tone adamant, Hughes insisted. 'You're tired. Alice, would you be so kind as to escort Cyril to my quarters, and see to his immediate needs?'

She took the keys from Hughes. 'Of course.'

'Sorry, Geoff, I really can't. I have another prisoner to collect first thing in the morning.'

'Initiation, Sweet.' Hughes perched on the edge of his desk, legs stretched before him, ankles crossed, arms folded. 'What's your definition of initiation?'

Hazel shrugged. 'A ritual,' she offered, bemused. 'Why?'

'I understand the lags have a quaint ceremony for new arrivals, that's all. Best to know these things, don't you think?'

'What sort of ceremony?' the teenager asked, concerned.

'If you find their notion of a welcome not to your taste, then by all means feel free to complain. I have tried to discourage that sort of tribal outrage, but if I'm not kept informed there is very little I can do. Perhaps with your grounding as a head prefect you understand the importance of supporting a superior?'

Suspicious, the girl declared. 'I'm not sure I understand you.'

Hughes ignored her. 'How good a mate was Alice?'

22

'We shared the same circle of friends, classes and dorm.' Again she shrugged. 'What can I say? We weren't bosom buddies, but we were good pals.'

'You know what to expect if you don't toe the line?'

Shoes catching her interest, she whispered, 'Yes. It was explained.'

'So as a prefect, were you expected to punish less important mortals?'

'I was expected to dispense discipline for minor violations.'

'Cane?'

'If necessary. But it could also have been detention, lines or maybe the slipper.'

'Ever cane Alice?'

'No, I don't think she was ever punished.'

'Were you?'

'The head prefect took a dislike to me when I first started.'

'She caned you?'

Hazel nodded, the memory obviously unpleasant.

Hughes stood. 'Right. Shower. Uniform. Dormitory. How old are you, Sweet? Seventeen?'

'Eighteen, sir.'

He led her downstairs, collecting the regulation issue on route. 'Did you bring a suitcase?'

'Yes sir. I left it in the lobby.'

At the reception suite the principal signed the nervous teenager in. 'That's the paperwork done. Shower next.'

The admission area received a supply of hot water, the lack of in the dormitories always a shock to new prisoners. A tiled open rectangle eight feet by six proffered three showerheads. Hughes pointed to a nearby stool. 'You can stack your clothes on that.'

'Okay,' Hazel said, waiting for the principal to leave, or at least turn his back.

Instead Hughes leant against a wall. 'I'm waiting.'

The realisation dawned that he intended to stay, observe her disrobing. Indignant, she challenged, 'I'm not taking my clothes off with you watching. What sort of place is this? Is there no female officer?'

'Firstly, you refer to me as Mr Hughes, sir, or governor,' he warned. 'You present an image of being well to do, and yet you lack the basic courtesies.'

'So do you, *sir*. A gentleman does not remain whilst a girl undresses. That is a *basic courtesy*.'

'I am the man in charge of this establishment. I am the only official on duty. And I have to by law, supervise your committal to these premises.'

'Can't Alice stand in?'

Hughes sighed, his exasperation evident. 'You seem to have an attitude, girl. Let me remind you, you are a con. When you were convicted any rights you had went down the plughole. I have thus far been exceedingly patient.' His expression hardened, cold eyes boring into the young woman. 'Do *not* push your luck.' Hazel hesitated. 'Get on with it,' Hughes growled, Sweet twitching with shock. 'Any more of this insubordination and I'll etch the rebuke on your backside.'

Expression resentful, she sulkily removed an expensive cream jacket. Beneath the finery, he assumed, lay a consummate body. One he could peruse at his leisure. Fingers touched a strengthening poker, the indecorous deed concealed by a trouser pocket. He read her mood, the scowl of eyebrows, hatred openly vented. He swam in the heady euphoria of conquest, his victim helpless, her loathing merely aiding his cruel enjoyment.

Hazel's hands wandered to the blouse buttons, then dipped to the inch wide leather belt girdling her waist. No matter which she chose it would launch the humiliating unveiling of that which few men had ever seen.

Belt unbuckled, buttons released, the figure-hugging knee length skirt fell, Hazel reaching for the item, her face burning scarlet.

Hughes, head lolled to one side, greedily absorbed the cock-inspiring vision before him. 'How long were you at Kirkwood?' he asked.

'Three months, sir.'

Mesmerised by exquisitely developed legs, Hughes persisted. 'What sentence did the court pass on you?'

Tall, her finely balanced limbs rose from delicately sculptured feet. Graceful stocking-clad calves swept up to merge with subtle knees. Engaging thighs rose, broadening pleasantly, to kiss tentatively beneath a protrusive V of crimson lace, where hid the black curls of puberty, the mound beneath sensuously prominent.

Fingers begrudging every twist of button, Hazel slowly unfastened her blouse. 'Two years, sir.' Eyes closed in desperate ignominy as she pulled the blouse apart.

Hughes considered the revelation. Lace-veiled breasts thrust impressively, her thirty-four inch torso surrendering impressively to a twenty-inch suspender-girdled waist. 'Six,' he voiced, the word cast, not intended to strike home.

Hazel laid the blouse atop her skirt and jacket, all neatly folded. She raised an eyebrow in question, her natural pout innocently seductive.

'The minimum,' Hughes said, enjoying the vague taunt. He watched Sweet stoop, unclip a dusky stocking, the black ornate top a stirring contrast to the cream of her thigh. Notions and inspirations encouraged schemes, aroused wholly dissolute aspirations. 'Six strokes is the minimum, should you err,' he explained.

The stockings and belt lay over the chair, Hazel forcing the courage to reveal all. She battled ingrained propriety, deep-rooted modesty, and the convention that

25

a lady never takes her clothes off in front of a man, especially one unknown to her. She inhaled, her breath held. Courage bolstered, thumbs curled inside panty elastic, she pushed down. Jet shoulder-length hair shimmered, snaking tresses obscuring the fall and quiver of full, lace-encased breasts. Hazel straightened, her lower body naked, black pubic curls nestled between her thighs.

Hughes hovered in sexual suspension, a dozen maddened urges crowding rationality. Sweet would be a favourite, of that he was sure. Sweet would dance his indecorous tune, or wish she had never transferred to the Hope. Sweet could go far; maybe even join Alice on her precarious perch.

Exquisite, beautifully shaped breasts sprang clear of their lace harness. Hazel posed with no attempt to conceal her body, hand allowing the bra to fall. She watched Hughes with a childlike wariness, her large dark eyes uncertain, querulous. A Cleopatra to Hughes' rugged Mark Anthony, Hazel was the personification of that queen's presumed beauty.

Hughes nodded toward the showerhead, his anticipation extreme. Hazel would turn, show her back, and what he hoped might be the perfect backside. The man was not disappointed. His heart seemed to miss a beat, a vacuous sensation unsettling his gut. Desire, need, lust filed their demands, Hughes a puppet to his own urges.

The man's eyes engaged, riveted to the roll and quiver of the perfect arse. That 'sweet' derriere begged the hearty slap of eager hand, of strap, cane and leather whip. Sadistic hunger gripped, appetite irresistible. Excuses, schemes and sexual tension bombarded his psyche, the man impotent, the time not right.

Hazel squirmed beneath the shower, peculiar sensations, obscure overtones, lewd notions troubling her. That blanket of embarrassment had lifted, curiosity instead probed her loins.

Her black hair lay wet across her shoulders, her naked body lustrous, rivulets cascading, emphasising every rise, fall and trough of that spellbinding figure.

Nerves hollowed her belly, excited her groin. *His* presence effected a prickling of the skin, an acute awareness of her buttocks. The air of uncertainty, the knowledge *he* would use a cane on her bottom if *he* deemed it necessary threw open the gates of confused possibility. Hazel had never been so aware of her bottom. None had stood casually watching her every move. Hughes, seeing her naked, vulnerable and unable to do a thing about it, aroused her beyond definition.

The principal called time, tossing Hazel a large towel. 'Dry yourself,' he instructed. 'Then bring that belt from your skirt.'

She eyed him warily, her stomach flipping. She rubbed her body, her bottom flesh crawling with suspense, the sensation strangely alluring.

Hughes took the belt. The temptation to use it, to thrill at the crack of leather; to see that delightful meat heave and shudder, to indulge in the coloration, proved almost too much. He told her to turn and bend over, the belt doubled in his fist. Hazel waited anxiously for the whoosh and slap, the dreadful caustic sting, but instead she felt his hand between her legs, the forefinger tracing the slit of her sex. That digit stalled, spread her vaginal lips and dipped. The girl gasped as it probed deep.

The finger removed, he curtly told the young woman to dress, the urge to slap that flexed behind ignored. Even in a prison pinafore she managed to cut an enviable figure. Hughes knew her looks would draw unwanted attention, mainly from jealousy. But that night she would suffer the trials of initiation. O'Leary would ensure Sweet ran the gauntlet of dormitory savages.

Suitcase in hand, Hazel climbed to the top floor, spare prison clothing clutched beneath an arm. The scrubbed Hazel Sweet prepared to face the company of crooks, prostitutes and thugs, an ordeal that had proved disturbing at Kirkwood.

'Miss Hussey is in charge of this floor, Sweet. Best you keep in mind you're a thieving whore. I will tolerate no old buddy favours. Do I make myself clear?'

Hazel mumbled, 'Yes sir.'

'They won't be settled for another hour yet. Lights out is at nine. So there should be time to break the ice.' Hughes grinned.

The door hit a zinc bucket, the pail clattering across the floor. Silence and seventeen stony expressions met Hughes. 'Good evening whores, beggars and thieves,' he voiced, loud enough for all to hear. 'I have an addition to this growing band of incorrigible miscreants.' Expression suspicious, he looked about the room. 'Cookson, why are you in bed, girl?'

Blanket pulled up to her armpits the pale youth laid a hand to her forehead. 'Ain't well, sir,' she offered weakly.

'I see.' The principal casually closed the distance. 'And where might I ask is Davenport?'

'Toilet, sir,' barked O'Leary.

Hughes turned. 'Ah, I might have expected your input, O'Leary. I passed the bathroom, the lights were out.'

'Got cat's eyes has Maureen, sir,' Ruth lied. 'She can see in the dark.'

Hughes turned again, a finger pointed at Cookson. 'Keep your hands on top of the blanket. There is more to this than meets the eye.'

Hughes paced. 'Davenport, you have a choice. Show yourself now or receive one stroke for every second you

28

remain hidden.'

He turned and paced back. 'In fact, Cookson, you can share in Davenport's misfortune. Both of you, one stroke per second I am kept waiting. One...! Two...! Three...! Four...!'

Cookson glanced in desperation at the wooden locker beside her bed.

'Five...!'

Jenny Cookson cracked, her friend seemingly quite willing to chance her arm. 'For God's sake, Maureen!' the girl squealed.

Hughes posed, legs apart, hands clamped behind his back he stared at the locker. 'Six, Davenport... Seven, Davenport...'

The man strode deliberately forward. 'Eight... Nine... Ten.' He gripped the handle and pulled the door open. Inside huddled a naked Maureen, her clothes bundled in her arms. Hughes grinned. 'A round dozen, Davenport, and that's before I discover what made you hide in here.'

The man lunged unexpectedly, snatching back the coarse grey army blanket covering Jenny. She too wore nothing, the girl folding her arms to hide her breasts. 'Two vulnerable naked maidens?' He rubbed his jaw. 'Now nudity is not an offence as such, not in the dormitory, leastways. So why hide, Davenport? Why skulk in the locker?'

'She's ever so bashful, sir,' Ruth piped up. 'Was worried about you seeing her in the altogether.'

'Why was she expecting me? This is Miss Hussey's territory, not mine.'

'I guess she spotted yer, sir, and nipped in the locker.'

'O'Leary.'

'Yes sir?'

'One more word out of you and you will sleep facing down tonight. Understand?'

29

'Yes sir.'

Hughes sat on the bed beside a terrified Cookson. He ran his eyes over her slightly chubby frame. 'You haven't been to my study yet, have you, Jenny?' He laid his hand on her thigh and stroked, the girl flinching. 'You have a dozen coming anyway, Jenny. Now I can punish you, or I can crucify you. Have you anything you wish to tell me?'

Tears welling, bottom lip trembling, Jenny glanced at Maureen. Skin smothered in goose bumps, the girl shook her head.

'Shame,' he whispered, abruptly ramming his hand between the girl's thighs. She squealed as he pulled, his fist retrieving a wooden rolling pin. He sniffed at the end. 'Well, Jenny, how are you going to explain cook's rolling pin wedged between your legs?'

The young woman cracked, sobs racked her body, tears flowing freely down a freckled face.

Hughes stood. 'Complicity. Damn you whores. When will you learn? Every one of you, yes, every damn one of you will receive six of the hardest strokes Miss Hussey can lay to your miserable bare backsides. None of you will retire until the punishment has been dispensed. And think yourselves lucky it is not I thrashing you.'

He gazed at Cookson and Davenport. 'But you two; now there's a different story. You can have a taste of Victorian values. You may experience the bench and feel the wrath of the birch. Tomorrow. Nine a.m., in my study.'

Cookson curled, sobbing, a thumb rammed in her mouth. Jabbing a finger at Ruth, Hughes left them to contemplate. 'Look after this girl. Her name's Hazel Sweet.'

30

Chapter 2

Alice laid the cane down, the highly flexible six millimetre thick rattan tapping the polished wood of her dressing table. She had personally selected that rod from Hughes' collection. She had bound one end with twine to provide a firm grip and the other end with tape to prevent splitting. Hughes scoffed at her choice, suggesting she take one of his buttock ravagers instead. But her rod served her well.

Seventeen bums she had flogged. One hundred and two times that pliable length slashed and whiplashed about the miscreants' flanks. Every disciplined girl carried six purple welts, their seats etched and sore.

Alice opened a drawer and took out a pack of Woodbines. She perused the carton and then flicked it open. Inside nestled six cigarettes. *'Bad habit, Alice. Put them back.'* She shook her head, auburn hair dancing about slender shoulders. She lit one and drew deeply.

Smoke wafting lazily upward, she opened a bottle and poured a drink. Neat gin slid over her tongue, the spirit burning mouth and throat. She grimaced, coughed and then laughed. 'Hughes' chattel?' she muttered. 'Hughes' toy? Why don't I just say no? I'm supposed to be *working* here! Persuasive. The way he twists things…'

'He doesn't twist anything.' Alice frowned. *'He understands how to tug your strings. You can't say no. Why? Because he's exactly what you want. He can draw that other Hussey to the surface. The one you, the prim and proper Alice, doesn't want to recognise. The one you won't accept exists. You know this to be true. Well, sanctimonious prude, your day is closing.'*

Her expression hardened, Alice talking to her reflection. 'You'll go through with it, won't you? You'll let him whip you for no reason at all.' She stubbed the cigarette out, half-smoked. 'And when he finally loses patience and demands it, you'll let him do that, too.'

'Birched tits,' scurried from the mind's recesses. Alice shivered, an electric tingle travelling her spine, delving her sex. 'Birched tits.'

Arms lifted, expression intrigued, she studied the effect on her breasts. Head to one side she tried to imagine the trial. Shirt parted, breasts jutting, she loosed her imagination. Sensuous energy, corporeal indulgence warmed her. Face flushed, skin hot, she fell to that surreal realm of the sexual aspirant. Inspired, ingenuity fomented, the feverish drama gathered substance. Hands gripping an imaginary rope above her head, Alice saw, jerked to the lash and bite of numerous birch ends. She winced, sucked air, her mind's eye concentrating on another.

Lips parted, dry. 'Uh!' she gasped, teeth delicately nibbling the lower lip. 'Uh!' The girl jerked, proud breasts trembling, that impeccable flesh so sensually jounced.

A scream, barely audible, drifted down the hallway. 'Hazel!'

Her muffled wails came closer, Alice covering her ears. 'I can't help you. This you will just have to get through. So, so sorry.'

Alice paced, trying not to hear her old school mate's pleas and cries for help. She pushed the images of sadistic faces from her mind, all the while knowing exactly what they did, how they beat, humiliated, and scrubbed that poor innocent. A worn smile flickered. A memory returned. The upper crust but down to earth Hazel at Carters. They had it all. The funds, the lifestyle, the mansion built on a dozen acres. Sweet perfection they called her. Bright, responsible, honest. So what went wrong?

She could have spoken with O'Leary, told her no,

demanded she leave Hazel alone. But what would that achieve? Hazel's remaining sentence would be a nightmare. At least by enduring the initiation the inmates would accept her, and maybe even keep her out of Hughes' corrupt hands.

Alice opened the door and peered around the jam. As expected the mob trooped out of the bathroom towing a naked Hazel, her skin a sore hue. Alice sighed. Hazel had always been gorgeous. She matured early, that fabulous body a gift, not earned.

They would stripe her around the dormitories. Probably six strokes at each port of call, thirty-six in all. Alice had been saved from that, falling to a far worse fate in some ways. But Pierce was gone. Hughes promised her the custodian would not be coming back, and she believed him.

Curious, the redhead strolled barefoot the length of the hall, listening for evidence of what befell Hazel. The girl's anguished wail followed an almighty slap, Alice recognising the sound of broad leather striking bare flesh.

'So they're strapping her instead.' The memory of *her* first strapping came crashing back, Alice unsettled by the recollection. Richard had beaten her bare bottom with a strop. Her parents not cold in their graves and Richard had flogged her mercilessly.

Without thinking Alice opened the door. Six times that harsh leather had savaged the girl's naked bottom. Six times she cried out in agony. Six times her pitiful wails were met with laughter. Startled faces turned Alice's way, the mass of Drake lowering the weapon.

Alice strolled silently forward, inmates stepping clear. She stopped immediately behind the bent Hazel and perused her beaten body. 'You animals,' she sighed. 'Why did you have to…?'

She snatched the leather strap from Drake, the huge

33

young woman offering no protest. Alice prowled. She moved slowly, scrutinising con after con. 'You are all scum. You complain of this living hell, but who makes it so? You do. All of you. But you're too dense, too vicious to change.'

Cooper, a particularly hard case, voiced her unwanted opinion. 'I was done when I arrived, so why shouldn't this stuck-up bitch get hers?'

Alice momentarily regretted her reaction; as broad leather smacked noisily against Cooper's face she felt a pang of remorse. The girl doubled, hand held tight to the fired cheek. Jaw set, green eyes burning, Alice asked. 'Anybody else want to say something?'

O'Leary raised a hand in sarcasm. 'Said you might be a right 'ard bitch, didn't I?'

Alice stopped with her face an inch from Ruth's. 'It ends here, Ruth. No more initiations on my dormitories. I will hold you personally responsible. Now help Hazel to my room. And wait for me there.'

Geoffrey Hughes lit Scrubbs' cigarette and then his own cigar. 'Five years, wasn't it?

Dennis nodded. 'With good behaviour.'

'How did you find me?'

'It wasn't easy. No one wants to talk about Geoffrey Hughes, government man.'

'Times change. People change. What was is no more.'

'Debts don't go away.'

'I owe you nothing, Dennis.'

'I took the rap for you.'

Hughes shook his head. 'No. You took the rap for you. You got caught.'

'I kept your name out of it,' Scrubbs argued.

'My name never came into it. I was never suspected, never questioned. You didn't turn police informer. That's why you are alive today.'

'What about my cut?' he asked, indignant.

'The police seized it, didn't they?'

Dennis levelled a cold gaze on Hughes. 'Seems you're not grateful, that our friendship means nothing to you.'

'Oh, don't get me wrong, Dennis. It's nice to see you, especially out of prison. And I am grateful for you not squealing.' He offered a hand. 'Do call again, in say, ten years.'

Having donned a pair of regulation pyjamas Hazel preferred to stand, a hand gingerly gauging the tenderness. Elbow on a sill she gazed forlornly out of the window. Ruth stood behind, arms folded. 'You ain't escaped, yer know. It's just been postponed, that's all.'

'You're a bunch of perverts. God, I'm black and blue.'

'Not with all that padding, you ain't.'

'What padding?'

'Your arse, gel.' Ruth slipped a hand inside her pyjamas, hand travelling quickly over a hot buttock. 'Don't get me wrong. It's a truly sensuous fat bit of arse.'

Appalled, Hazel twisted, Ruth's hand pulled clear. 'What are you?'

'Queer, ducky,' Ruth giggled. 'If yer wakes up wiv some'at snuggling close, it'll only be me.'

Alice interrupted any further provocation. Advancing on the dressing table she said nothing. A finger traced the length of her cane, deep in thought. 'No point in thrashing you, is there, Ruth? It would have more effect saying I won't.'

'Ain't that a fact,' O'Leary retorted.

'I'll not wear it,' Alice continued.

'What? Oh, yer means favouritism.'

'What you do is barbaric.'

'An' every one of us has 'ad it. The respect yer gets

depends on how yer handles the pain. It places the gel in the order of fings.'

Ruth cocked her head to one side and grinned. 'And you, Al, you would have ranked as my lieutenant.'

Glaring, Alice nodded toward the door. 'Outside.'

Deliberating, Alice set the tip of her cane against her toecap. 'You can see how frightened the girl is. Can't you wave your damned initiation for once?'

'What is it, Al? Do you fancy her? Is that it? Cos I could understand that. I'd even join yer there.'

'No, Ruth, I don't fancy her. It's none of your business. I thought we had an understanding.'

O'Leary smirked. 'So that's it. Yer wants a favour. Why didn't you just say so?'

'Because I'm supposed to be in charge.'

'Tell yer what I'd really like. What I really wanna do.'

Alice smiled, tired. 'Don't ask me to have any sort of lesbian relationship with you.'

'Nah. Yer knows I don't fancy yer. Nuh, I'd really like to do what that crazy Scots bitch was offered. You see if you can get me a deal. You get me a starring part and your Sweet Hazel will be just fine.'

'Porn, you mean?'

'Yeah, if yer like. Don't matter much to me. Shagging, or lessie. If it's possible to do wiv my gorgeous, sensuous body, then I'll 'ave a go. And if they needs a girl who can take a strenuous whipping, then who better?' Ruth held her arms apart, grinning.

Dennis Scrubbs sipped a whiskey. 'A man could get used to this. Good cigar, nice malt. Yes, as I was saying. Plod knows I wasn't alone. And they won't let it be. Want the others, I guess. Visited me six times in prison, they did. Always on my birthday, too. No fucking card, though. Twisted bastards. Been around to see me a couple of times since I was released, too.'

Hughes sucked on his pipe. 'How long you been out?'

'Just short of a year, Geoffrey.'

'You'd have nothing to gain by helping the police now.'

'Oh, I wouldn't help them, Geoffrey. No, it's more a slip of the tongue I'm worried about. You know how it is. Lots of bloody questions. Confusion. Not keeping to the original story. Them catching me out.'

'And?'

'If I disappeared, and they couldn't find me, they might give up in time.'

'And?'

'A woman's prison, Geoffrey. Who would think of looking in one of them?'

'How long for?'

'Just until things go quiet. Mind you, I don't want to be a burden. No, Geoffrey, I want to be self-supporting. Say, a job and a few quid a week. That'll do me fine, that will.'

'What had you in mind? Gardener?'

Dennis smiled, smug. 'Mavis said you're short one officer. Eddie Pierce? He went abroad? I look good in a uniform. Right dapper.'

'No uniform here. Informal.' Hughes eased back in his chair. 'I'll think about it. You can stay at mine in the meantime.'

'Kind, Geoffrey. Very kind. Bit of a nocturnal animal, I am. Comes from watching your back in the twilight hours. Didn't sleep much at night. Sooner do that shift, old man, when you decide.'

'So, who's the visitor?'

'An old acquaintance.'

Bathed, Sheila studied her partner in love, lust and crime, in the mirror. She brushed steadily at lengthy tresses, lustrous blonde locks snaking over the white of her towelled dressing gown. 'I didn't know you had any,' she remarked absently.

Hughes sat on the end of the double bed watching her. 'I've given him Pierce's job.'

'Do you know him that well? What's his name?'

'Dennis Scrubbs. He's an army acquaintance.' Hughes settled hands on her shoulders. 'Tell you what, Sheila. Bed him. Find out where he's been and what he's been doing for the last few months.'

'Okay. Hello Mr Scrubbs. I'm Dr Doodney, resident psychologist. How would you like to sleep with me?'

'Needs a bit of work, but you've got the idea.'

'I've a better idea, Geoff. You bed him.' Sheila began dressing, slipping pants over her feet she hoisted them beneath her dressing gown. 'Why do you want to know, anyway?'

'Because he's not forthcoming.'

'You obviously don't trust him, so why take him on?'

'I'd sooner he was here under my watchful eye than elsewhere at the moment.'

'I'll try charm.'

'You do that.' Hughes watched the slide of gown over bare back with interest, Sheila donning a bra. 'There is one possible way.'

'Hmm?' Sheila replied, fastening her blouse.

'Hmm,' he mimicked, nuzzling her neck, pecking beneath an ear. To her sigh his hand flicked a button and slipped inside the blouse, fingertips kissing a nipple. A shiver traversed her spine. Hughes' touch retreated, his hands undid the blouse and nudged the cloth from her shoulders.

Sheila smiled uneasily. 'What's in your head?'

'Scrubbs. Arrange something. Entice him. If he's been without for a while he might well bite.'

'Oh, thank you very much! Why not just throw me at him? Here you are, Den, just stick a bag over her head. I

38

told you, Geoff, no. Ask Ruth. I'm sure she'd have him at the drop of a hat.'

'Pants,' Hughes corrected, pushing the sleeves from her arms. 'Dennis had a nickname in the army.' He settled his chin on her shoulder. Their eyes met in the reflection. 'Well Hung…

'What if I offered him *you* as wages?' he added.

Sheila suffered the queasy pang of uncertainty. Never completely stable, Hughes could be prone to acts of utter madness, none ever quite sure what his next move might be. 'Geoff, how many times? I'm not your *whore.*'

'No, of course you're not.' He fondled her breasts through the bra. 'I need your expert opinion, Sheila. I need to know I can trust him.'

'I won't sleep with him,' Sheila insisted.

Hughes bent to her ear. 'Sleeping was not what I had in mind.'

'Okay. I fuck him, then what?' She turned and faced Hughes. 'You accuse me of infidelity.'

'And you win again! You know what I'd do, don't you?' Hughes noted the subtle gasp, the gentle shudder. 'A complete stranger, Sheila. Imagine the thrill of a complete stranger. And a stranger with a huge cock, at that…

'What if you're caught in a compromising position?'

'Such as?'

'Supposing those bad girls tied you half naked to a chair. You know, as a prank or revenge. Say, skirt up around the tops of your thighs. They've nicked your knickers, too. Shirt open. No bra. Ropes biting into those lovely tits. I think Dennis would bite, don't you?'

Explicit needs lit her imagination.

'Tied tight,' Hughes whispered. 'Nothing between your fanny and Scrubbs' gaze.' Sheila's respiration increased. 'I think legs crudely tied apart. Your thighs

39

trembling as you fight to close the gap, to cover your
modesty…' Hughes' hands descended, fingers pushing
between her legs, thumbs rubbing her sex lips. 'Scrubbs
hangs back, doesn't rush to help you. You're squirming,
your bare backside against that hard wood seat. He can't
keep his eyes from what's between your legs, your cunt
slit. He's beguiled. Ropes digging into soft breasts do
intrigue.' Bra cups peeled clear, she watched the
kneading, squeezed flesh forced between spread fingers.
'He'd touch you, wouldn't he, doctor? He'd press his
fingers to your tits, because that's where the knots
would be.'

The woman listened, his words exciting her. She laid
her head back, eyes closed. 'Dinner at Henry's in
Chester.'

'That's the least I can do.'

Voices echoed, distant. Murmured accusations drifted,
insistent, soaring vaulted grey stone, making those
incorporeal utterances seem all the more sinister. Alice
listened, strained to make sense of the ranting.

'Devil child,' hissed, echoing about stark sunbeam-
illuminated pillars.

'Whore's spawn,' followed accusingly.

'Mad as a March hare,' shrieked another, from deep
shadows.

'Just like her mother,' knifed the girl's heart.

'She'll roast in the fires of hell,' voiced several
together.

'Unless…'

'Unless, what?'

'Unless she repents her sins. Unless we absolve her.'

'She's gone *too* far.'

'*No*. God is merciful. Her soul can be saved.'

'Yes,' Alice nervously called back, creeping toward
the voices, peering apprehensively into the gloom.

A demand from behind made her jump. 'She'll have to pay a heavy price.' Alice spun, trying to catch the spectre. A glimpse of white on black perhaps, but she could not be sure.

'Pain and humiliation,' turned her head again, the tone brittle and harsh.

'Pain? What sort of pain do you have in mind? And how do you propose to humiliate a whore?'

'Flagellation has always been beneficial. And the act, if self-administered before her adjudicators, will educate the wretch in humility.'

'You forget,' another joined the conclave, the voice familiar, chilling, 'this infernal instrument holds no fear for the bite of leather. It draws gratification from exhibiting its body. So how do you propose to punish it?'

Alice stabbed a finger into the air. 'You! You will never lay a finger on me again. That I vow before all that is holy.'

'Holy! What do you know of holy? You are not worthy of acquaintance,' the voice scoffed. 'Hear the degenerate that offers the temple of her body as a plaything for gratuitous pleasure. Hear the profligate that begs for divine punishment, so that she can satisfy her twisted carnal craving.' Richard moved into the light, Alice backing away in disbelief. He wore the robes of a cardinal, a shimmering halo inches above his head.

'No,' Alice hissed. 'No, this is madness.'

Four sisters of mercy emerged behind Barker, each holding a savagely barbed whip. They pointed at her as one. 'You are madness.'

Alice indicated Richard. 'It's him. He's the one that's mad, not me. He... he... he...'

That peculiar world spun, all caught in a supernatural vortex. Faces loomed, sneering, snarling. Miss Lake's

41

distorted features questioned. 'Why Alice, what is the matter with you?'

Jonathan's countenance, with raised eyebrow, demanded, 'Where's my money?'

A scowling Jenny accused, 'It was always you, not my Katy.'

Harris sneered and laughed. 'And to think, the master wouldn't listen.'

Alice awoke with a jolt. Blinking, she tried to make sense of her surroundings. A movement aided the flood of recollection. The warmth of another snuggled to her, an arm tossed over her waist. 'You awake, gel?' said Ruth.

Alice rolled onto her back and stared at the ceiling. 'Yeah. Had a weird dream, I guess.'

Hughes whistled tunefully, the keys to Hope spun by a thin chain on an outstretched finger. Leather soles clicked on cobblestones, the only sound disturbing the silence that night, the man's swagger indicative of his arrogance. His tongue wet the bottom lip, expression just short of a laugh. 'Poor Sheila,' he murmured. 'Perhaps I'll let her out in the morning.'

The gate groaned with its opening, Hughes glancing up at the top floor of the Hope. He stood a while, gazing at Alice's window. *Tomorrow, Alice. Tomorrow you can pay for the indiscretion. Do make the most of it.'*

Sheila lay face down, the living room rug rough against her naked skin. She eyed the dying embers in the hearth, a shiver climbing her body. She gasped frustrated, the mask of anger etching her face. 'You could at least have thrown a blanket over me,' she muttered. Then to an empty dark house she bawled, 'What if I need a piss, you bastard!' The echo seemed to mock. 'Why the fuck do I let him? Why do I trust him?' Sheila screamed with

42

exasperation.

Large one-inch iron links probed and nipped her skin, a length pulled tight about her waist and padlocked to another. The chain sank uncomfortably into her belly and crotch, linkage tugging at her pubic curls.

The woman gazed at the closed door. 'Are you out there, Hughes? Are you laughing your fucking socks off? Enough's enough, for Christ's sake! Let me loose.'

Sheila checked the time. *'Half an hour. Half an hour and my arms and legs are killing me. You'd better come back. You'd better let me loose.'*

She wriggled, trying to adjust her stance. Breathing laboured, a whining gasp indicated strained pleasure. The chain passed between her legs, engaging a rubber dildo pressed into her vagina. The final link terminated at a single set of stocks resting on her buttocks. Trapped hands fidgeted side by side, shoulders drawn back, arms and wrists continuously pressured. Her ankles were held parallel, either side of her hands, legs effectively splayed.

The inch thick, three foot long stocks wore rough and heavy on lathered buttocks, those cheeks neatly ravaged by fifty whiplashes. Crimson welts carpeted those lustrous dunes, the flesh raised from coccyx to thigh, hip to hip.

Cold crept into her cramped body, her butt the only source of warmth. Rough-hewn apertures chaffed sensitive wrists and ankles, the twitch and jerk of griping muscles worsening the discomfort. 'Geoff,' she called softly. 'I've had enough now.'

She listened, the silence worrying. 'Geoff. Look, you've had your joke.'

Nothing.

'Geoff. *Please!*'

Doctor Sheila Doodney called, shouted and finally screamed for a full hour before she accepted the truth.

She lay her cheek to the rug, discomfort worsened by fits of shivers. *'Oh, you bastard. You wait, Geoffrey Hughes. I'll fix you.'*

'How can you know that?' Alice demanded.

'I know a lot, see. I'm privileged.'

Alice chewed on the confounding piece of information. Unconvinced, she challenged Ruth. 'You're a con. How can you be privileged?'

O'Leary changed her tune. 'Don't mean that. Trouble wiv fancy words, ain't it? I meant, I gets to know a lot, bein' the top dog and all.'

Alice climbed on top of the blonde, legs straddling her waist. 'You can't know that. You don't just walk in on something like that. No, Ruth, there's more to this than you're letting on.'

Chapter 3

'Sleep well?' Hughes enquired, a cup of steaming coffee in one hand.

Sheila groaned. 'If I ever move again it'll be down to an act of God.'

'You exaggerate.'

'Listen you sadistic cunt,' she growled, 'I've been locked in this bastard thing for five Godforsaken hours…'

'There you go again,' Hughes interrupted. 'Must be a form of derangement.'

'What, trusting you?' the doctor riposted.

'Not at all.' Hughes chuckled. 'No one in their right mind trusts me. Look at that Scottish savage, Sandra. She sort of trusted me.'

The ensuing cackle disturbed Sheila.

'Perhaps it's an affinity with our beloved catholic martyr,' Hughes continued. 'This closeness to God. A personal mate at times. Anyway, Alice's attitude seems to indicate such. Bit of a bind, really.' Brow furrowed, Hughes concentrated. 'What say you, Doc?' he asked, nudging her naked hip with a shoe.

'Are you going to release me,' Sheila demanded, 'or chew the cud all day?'

'I like the way you are.'

'I can't stay like this,' she snapped. 'I hurt, Geoff. I really hurt.'

'I'd say you were a woman of your word. Yes?'

'Unlike some, I'm trustworthy. So what's your point?'

'I want you to look after Dennis.'

'I told you last night. I'm not whoring.'

'Did I say that? Offer him friendship. Find out if he would like to say, put you over his knee and spank your bare bottom. You could, if you could find it in yourself, give him a blow, or tender your arse. That wouldn't be sex, now would it?'

'Geoff, I'm a psychologist. All right, I suffer a quirk. But that's always been kept between thee and me.'

Hughes leant, easing hands beneath the stocks. He abruptly lifted, Sheila squealing in pain. 'Bollocks!' he barked. The woman dangled, pubes brushing the floor, wrists and ankles agonisingly pressured. Chains drew tight, embedding their links in her belly, groin and crotch. Tears welled, Sheila unable to endure.

Hughes let go, the woman dropping the six inches with a thump. 'Sheila,' he called in a whisper, 'will you help me?' he asked.

'I won't whore, aaaaah!' Hughes hoisted her again and teeth gritted, Sheila screamed. 'Yes, you bastard!'

The doctor winced as she hit the floor, breasts taking much of the impact. 'Excellent,' Hughes mused, unbuttoning his flies.

45

Ruth brushed her hair, blonde strands flicked over naked shoulders. She studied her reflection, the rope burns, imprints and welts. Her sexually satisfied hub lurched re-awoken, a flush of erotic tension urging carnal complicity.

Alice lifted an eyelid, blurred vision settling on the welted rump of Ruth O'Leary. Sordid shenanigans from the night before abruptly blitzed her drowsy mind. The solid thump of flexible rattan on compact buttock flesh spun an erogenous web, cooled embers reignited.

Ruth spotted Alice's interest in the mirror. 'Trouble wiv bein' this way, ain't it, gel? Yer needs the whipping to quell the lust, but the marks turns it all around again a couple of hours later.'

Alice reached out to examine, touch. 'Does my arse look like that?' she enquired fearfully.

Ruth shook her head. 'Nah, yours is fuller, firmer,' she grinned, 'and a damn sight sexier.'

Alice stroked the plethora of stripes, feeling the slight etch of tramlines. 'I meant whipped,' she explained.

Ruth turned, leant over the redhead. 'Not whipped to fuck, gel, more nicely simmered. Anyways, I'm more inclined to dining on your arse than whippin' it.'

Giggling, Alice asked, 'Just my bum?'

Cupping the redhead's breasts, Ruth became serious. 'I'll show yer the pleasure of caned boobs tonight, if yer like.' She drew her nails over Alice's nipples, the resultant sting and marks inciting an urge. Excitement bubbled, the redhead's breath taken.

'We could even have a competition,' Ruth suggested slyly. 'See who can take the most.' The girl raised an eyebrow. 'Loser gets it between the legs.'

Troubled, unsure, Hughes' suggestion on her mind, Alice rose.

'Just a suggestion,' the blonde offered, fearful of

offence.

'I have to go to work, Ruth. Hughes' cane strokes, as you know, are not always sensual.'

'He's got no right whopping staff.'

'Maybe. But perhaps I give him good reason. Perhaps it's what I need.'

Pain ground against pleasure. Hughes' energetic penetration; the forceful impetus of hard cock and the way in which he took her, thrilled beyond description. However, the excruciating hurt from numbed, chaffed limbs and the heavy wooden stocks digging into her lower buttocks dulled that enthusiasm.

Hughes had turned her over with little consideration for comfort. Hips propped by the wooden restraint, back arched dramatically and legs parted wide, she proffered an irresistible invitation for ravishment. The ring that held the dildo was of sufficient girth to encompass Hughes erection. With an internal diameter of two and a quarter inches and a penetrating flat of one, it prized Sheila's sex lips apart, opening the gates of her pussy. The feel of that steel about his shaft and the manner in which it fettered her crotch intensified his lust.

The acute angle of entry, Hughes thrusting downward, delivered a message that couldn't be ignored. Seeing that thick meat plunge, her cunny receiving, accentuated the boil of sexual tension. The capture of limbs, forcing a presentation of her sex, rendered her a slave to her own kink.

Animosity bred contempt, Sheila slung between adoration and loathing. 'Bastard!' she grunted. The mind-twisting pleasure strengthened, stirred her belly. Sheila grunted, his cock managing what others failed to do. Hughes cared little for her expectations, his only urge to fulfil a particular and immediate lust. Cock throbbing, balls pulsating, he tensed. Orgasm fired, his come flowed. Wad upon wad spurted haphazardly, Sheila receiving.

He withdrew, wiping the surplus on the woman's bush. He rose, tucking his piece away and re-buttoned the flies.

'That was premature,' Sheila complained. 'I was about ten seconds off coming myself.'

Hughes shrugged and suggested, unconcerned, 'Stick a finger in and finish it.'

'Once upon a time you at least pretended you cared.'

Hughes laughed. 'All fairy stories begin once upon a time.'

'Are you going to let me out now? You know, so I can finish what you started.'

Without another word he released her, and relieved, Sheila unfolded. Pained and cramped her anger resurfaced. 'You ever try something like this again and I'll cut your fucking nuts off.'

'Really?' he asked, black eyes chilling.

Sheila immediately backed off. 'An empty threat. I'm mad at you, that's all.'

Hughes picked up the stocks as she vigorously rubbed at arms and legs. She watched with trepidation as he set them down by her feet. 'Ankles in the apertures, please,' he instructed, tone uncompromising.

She shook her head. 'No, I've spent the last five hours in there. No more, Geoff.'

'It's not a request.'

She watched helplessly as Hughes re-fettered her feet, ignoring her protest. 'I've got work to do. How long this time?'

'Have a day off. Contemplate the folly of threatening me, and nurse your sore arse.'

'I need a pee! I'm desperate!' She frowned. 'My arse is okay now.'

Hughes removed his leather belt. 'Was, Sheila. Past

tense.'

He flipped her over, heavy wood stocks pinning her with legs wide apart. Kneeling beside the woman he raised the belt high over a shoulder. Eyelids squeezed, Sheila braced herself for the merciless crack of burnished doubled leather.

Dressed, Alice ushered Ruth back to her dormitory. There she checked on the new arrival, ensuring Hazel slept reasonably well.

'Tonight,' Ruth whispered as Alice was leaving.

'We'll see,' she replied, preoccupied.

'Nah, no "we'll see". Tonight, or she,' Ruth nodded at Sweet, 'gets it.'

'That's...'

'I know.' O'Leary grinned. 'It's your decision.'

Nails clawed the floor, Sheila squealing with every vigorous clap. Flying leather stoked her bum, whipped the flesh to a deep hot red. Hughes knew his 'victim'. He could simmer Sheila on a devilishly intense and passionate griddle, or spin her in a vortex of mind-twisting torment.

Ten blasting strokes passed in a blur of flying leather. Buttocks heaved, the flesh pounded, nerves stunned into fired incendiaries. Sheila twisted and writhed. No cry, no squeal, no contortion offered a modicum of relief.

Sufferance mitigated agony, Sheila pushing up, breasts clearing the floor, back angled toward beaten bottom. White hot embers seemed to smother those lambasted dunes. Gut churning pain mellowed, surrendered to an avalanche of overwhelming sexual stimulation. Masochism's trick induced the hunger, an unfathomable desire for unbridled flagellation.

Hughes had surpassed rationality. His sadistic madness paralleled Sheila's masochistic insanity. She

49

cared not what he did, as long as it involved a particular physical abuse, and he saw only the opportunity to lay his belt to the woman's vulnerable body.

Swaying, tremulous breast caught his eye. Dropping one half of the strap he stood astride the woman and wound several coils of belt about a fist. Sheila sensed his intention and held the position, crazed libido longing for the swingeing slap. Hughes obliged with a smirk of satisfaction.

The V-shaped end of his belt whipped a breast, the leather cracking like a bullwhip, her flesh stung. She sucked air asthmatically, the resulting burn both exciting and insufferable. Leather bit its twin, flesh jerked and stunned. The sole of Hughes' shoe forced her back down, held her against the floor, smarting breasts flattened.

'You're enjoying it too much, doc,' he taunted. 'Enough for now.' He thought for a moment. 'I'll come back for lunch… maybe.'

Fingers about the door handle, the principal glanced back. Sheila stroked her heated rump, fingertips caressing a mass of welts.

'I think it's time our catholic disciple suffered for the sins of *her* flesh.' He rolled his tongue against the inside of a cheek. 'A whisper has reached the Grim Reaper's ear. Lesbian shenanigans in the dead of night.'

'Ruth?' Sheila purred.

Hughes nodded. 'Oh yes, Ruth indeed.'

'What about Scrubbs?' she asked, disinterested.

'Should I send him over?'

'Only if he brings a saw, a pair of bolt cutters, or he can pick locks.'

'I do believe Dennis is an adept locksmith. Have fun.'

The door shut behind him, she groaned. 'You would too, you callous bastard.'

50

Alice leant over the second draw of a filing cabinet, Hughes close, trousers brushing against her skirted bottom. Nervous, she glanced back, the man's mood dissuading her from comment.

'Good night?' he asked, surprising her.

'Sorry?' she said.

'Not goodnight as in see you in the morning,' he explained sarcastically. 'More, was it a good one between the sheets?'

Shocked, Alice stammered, 'I... I don't know what you mean.'

Hughes continued to provoke. 'You smell sweaty.' Guilt climbed her spine. The prospect of him actually knowing sickened. 'Not revolting sweaty,' he added. 'More of a sexual sweat.'

'I'm sorry. I'll have a wash.'

Hughes took the advantage. Groin against her bottom he leaned to one side blatantly sniffing. 'Personally I find the aroma enticing.' Alice squirmed, uncomfortable. 'But if it worries you, you could use my shower.'

Alice stared at the door recalling the last time she was in there. Caught off guard, unsure how to answer, she replied hesitantly, 'I'll think about it.'

Hughes breathed heavy in her ear. 'You're quite safe. I won't take advantage of the situation, or you. You have my word.' He smiled enigmatically.

Sensing the press of something else, Alice wriggled clear. Perplexed she faced Hughes, studying his expression. A demand to know his intentions passed unsaid, the man intimidating, unpredictable and volatile. She eventually shrugged. 'If you think I should...'

A faint smile played on his lips. 'Did O'Leary insist?'

Stunned, she visibly jerked. 'Pardon?'

'Ruth O'Leary. Did she twist your arm?'

Her backside tingled, the flesh crawling. 'For what?'

Hughes folded his arms and leaned against the desk. 'We can play all morning if you like, Alice. You know, pretending nothing occurred when *I* know precisely what *did* transpire. The outcome will remain the same.' He stared icily, all amusement gone. 'Well perhaps not exactly the same. The more you prevaricate and lie, the worse it could be.'

'Who?' she asked, voice a whisper.

'Who told me? Do I need an informant? I have a full set of keys, don't I?'

Alice fidgeted nervously.

'You confess and I will consider quarter.'

Alice hesitated.

'Come on devout catholic, confession is good for the soul. Or is it a case of you thinking I might not know everything?'

Still she resisted.

'Fine, an incentive then.' Cane in hand he demonstrated the weapon's flex and potency. The cut of air dramatic, Alice's stomach flipped. Masochism is a capricious master, rhyme and reason lost to complex influences. The sudden threat of dispassionate chastisement could toss the coin of reaction either way. Fear and pain, or the flush of sensual consequence, might reign supreme.

Alice's hormones failed to spark. The threat of summary corporal punishment mortified. The rod pressed to a shoulder guided Alice over, bottom becoming the epicentre of her dilemma, awaiting the first intolerable slice of flexile rattan.

Hughes tapped her skirt-covered rump, the ripple of cloth suggestive of what lay beneath. He was in no hurry; the suspense all part of the entertainment.

Tired of his despotic attitude she blurted, 'Oh, get it done with. In fact, why not get that pervert Barker to do it? And then you could film it again, couldn't you?'

Eyebrows raised, Hughes sucked in his cheeks. 'Hmmm…'

Alice straightened. Pointing a finger at him she snapped, 'Don't even think about it!' Angry, concerns tossed to one side, she persevered. 'You have no right anyway. Who do you think you are? I'm an employee, not a slave.'

She hugged herself protectively, fingers squeezing upper arms. Then voice lowered, she threatened, 'I can leave whenever I like.'

'Do you want to go?' Hughes asked. 'Shall I take you to the station? Got any money?' He approached her. 'Have you any clothes?'

Alice wavered. 'What's in my wardrobe and what I'm wearing. And you owe me a month's money.'

Hughes escorted her to the office door. 'The clothes belong to the Hope, if you recall. I would like them left. And I owe you nothing. After deductions for bed and board, wear and tear on your uniform, and fines for lateness, inefficiency… I can give you a full list if you like.'

'You bastard…'

'Oh yes.'

'Well, I still have some of my old clothing. And I still have some money left from—'

'Put it all in the safe, did you?'

'No, of course I didn't.'

'Checked it's still where you left it? You do work in a den of iniquity, you know.'

Five minutes later Alice stared disbelieving at an empty purse and the last of her own clothing torn to shreds. 'Oh, you…'

'What's up, gel?' spun Alice about.

'Ruth!' Alice pointed at the rags. 'Who? Who would do that?'

53

'Someone who don't like you much, I guess.'

'Hughes is behind this.'

'Why?'

'To keep me here, that's why. And he knows about us. Someone spilled the beans.'

'Yeah. Guess who?'

'You know?'

'Your mate, Sweet. It were 'er.'

'Why would she? I don't understand.'

O'Leary shrugged. 'Who knows? But she's a snob, an' snob's think they're a cut above everyone else, if yer knows what I mean. She'd do anything to save her arse.'

'Ruth, he's got me where he wants me.' Alice leant on the sill and sighed dejectedly, gazing out over an early morning Flint. 'What will happen to Hazel?'

'Sneaks and backstabbers like her get what's coming to 'em.'

'Well?' Hughes enquired.

'You knew.'

'Knew what?'

'You had my money stolen and my clothes torn to shreds.'

'Bit of an accusation, that.'

'So cane me for it.'

Hughes smiled. 'I will, Alice. Oh, I will. But now I have things to do. Please excuse me.'

''Ello lamb, you're lookin' a bit sheepish.' Ruth ran a hand through Hazel's hair. 'Been at the grass 'ave yer?'

'That supposed to mean something?'

'It'll mean it's shearing season, if I find out you've blabbed.'

'About what?'

'I remember one snitch who had somehow managed

54

to keep her pubic hair. Bit like you, Sweet. She was shorn with paraffin and a match.'

'Is that a threat?' Sweet asked, unfazed.

'It added a whole new dimension to burnin' passion.'

Hazel took a blonde tress between her fingers. 'Nice hair, Ruth. Still, you've a pretty face, you'd probably get away with it.'

'Wiv what, humbug?'

Hazel opened a comic and began reading. 'You're beginning to get on my tits, O'Leary. I've had enough of your idle threats and childish behaviour.'

Ruth smiled. ''Ave yer now? Well this ain't no idle threat, gumdrop. I'm going to get on your tits big time.'

O'Leary walked away.

Chapter 4

A jar of face cream hit a mirror with disastrous results. Glass fragmented, cascaded to the surface beneath. Hughes lifted his head, a heavy paperweight narrowly missing it.

'You fucking shithouse!' Sheila screamed. 'All fucking day. Stuck in that thing *all* fucking day!'

Hughes ducked from cover, Sheila hurling everything she could lay her hands to. 'Piss-head!' A vase smashed against the wall, cut flowers and water showering the governor.

'Jesus, Sheila! I thought you'd appreciate it.'

'Appreciate? You shit-brained arsehole! I pissed and crapped myself waiting for you. How the fuck can anyone enjoy that?'

'Sheil,' he held his hands out. 'Come on. It's your rule, not mine. Never discuss the scenario, just do it. That's what you like; having no say. And anyway, it wasn't all day. That's an exaggeration.'

Slowly she lowered a threatened missile. 'Bastard!' she spat. 'Whip me to hell and back, but don't you ever leave me like that again.'

Hughes ran a finger down the woman's cheek. 'How long to get ready for dinner?'

'Where?'

'Charleys.'

'The rest of the afternoon.'

'Time for a fuck then.'

Pushed, Sheila fell backwards onto the couch, Hughes following. Two seconds later, erection released, Hughes sank his huge shaft between her legs. Lower limbs circling his waist, Sheila gratefully received. 'Ah, sweet fuck,' she gasped. 'Feeling *that* stretch almost makes up for the shit day.'

'Almost?' Hughes asked, thrusts lingering.

'I just wish that vase had hit your fucking head. That *would* have made my day.'

Alice took Hazel to one side. She gazed at the girl's attractive face, trying to think of the right words.

'What is it?' Sweet asked, concerned.

'Have you seen Hughes today?'

She shook her head.

'Last night?'

'No. Why?'

'Someone told him Ruth was with me last night.'

'So that's what the bitch was on about.'

'What bitch?'

'O'Leary. She's been making threats. Why would you think it's me anyway? After I left you I went back to that dreadful dormitory, and those awful girls.'

'Did you say anything to them?'

'Didn't have to. Apart from taunting me the main topic of the night was what you and Ruth were doing.'

Deep in thought, Alice paced slowly around Sweet.

'I didn't say anything to Hughes, or anybody else, Alice. Honest. You've got to believe me. I wouldn't do that. Not to you, not to anyone. Did I ever grass anyone up at Carters? Come on, did I?'

'Someone did. He didn't come anywhere near that floor last night, of that I'm sure. So how does he know I spent the night with Ruth?'

The couch lurched and groaned beneath their energetic antics, Hughes' hips rising and falling with rapid abandon. Sheila's naked body lurched, her breasts dancing erotically. Hughes held back, waited for Sheila's gasp of climax before releasing his seed. The woman eventually succumbed, her orgasmic convulsions startling him. Legs squeezing his waist, her fingernails feverishly clawed at his chest. Back excessively arched she rocked, face creased with the intensity of climax.

Pectorals stinging, Hughes enquired, matter of fact, 'Good one, was it?'

Sheila sighed, her body settling. 'Good one? It very nearly blew my brain away.'

Hughes clambered to his feet.

'See what happens when you treat a lady with consideration?'

Hughes grunted. 'Yeah. She has a far better orgasm than me.'

'Pig!' Wiping the excess from her vagina, Sheila asked, 'Did you catch up with our lesbian friends?'

'I had a chat with Hussey.'

'And?'

'I've clarified her position.'

Three o'clock that afternoon, Alice and Ruth stood side by side before a truculent governor. Both girls experienced the queasy roll of nervous bellies. Both guessed they were in for an uneasy time.

'I'm surprised at you, Alice,' he began. 'Isn't the act of sexual intercourse between those of the same gender forbidden by your faith?'

'I'm no longer practising, sir,' she replied, confused.

'I see. You stopped believing last night, so you could involve yourself in a disgusting entanglement with this vermin here.'

'I stopped believing when God saw fit to kill my parents, sir.'

'So you're telling me now you're a sceptic?'

'Yes sir.'

'Fine, as long as we know.

'I know lesbianism is not actually illegal, unlike homosexuality. But it is not something society wants their noses rubbing in. And it is a sordid act not only condemned by government guidelines, but outlawed in this establishment, and for very good reason.

'Ruth, I have punished you for much since you came to the Hope, but I have never done so for lying. I will say though, that whatever you admit to I will not treat it as seriously as Alice's involvement.'

The redhead frowned, events seeming to leap out of control. 'Excuse me, Mr Hughes,' she piped, exasperated. 'I thought I'd made my position quite clear. I'll not stand here beside a convicted criminal and be judged by you without evidence.'

'You won't?' He leaned back, smug. 'This is not judgement day, Alice. This is a preliminary hearing to allow the accused parties to state their cases. This is no game. This is serious. Either you listen and cooperate or I will have charges levied. Do you understand me?'

Uncertain of his direction, the girl fell silent.

'I am considering gross misconduct. You are the supervisor of the dormitory floor, a position of responsibility. O'Leary is an inmate, and as such vulnerable to the guidance and moralities of her immediate superior. Sleeping with her is...' Hughes took a deep breath. 'O'Leary, I'll deal with you later.'

Given her cue to leave the blonde closed the door behind her, immediately pressing an ear to it.

Hughes stood to one side of Alice. Hands sunk in trouser pockets he asked without looking at her, 'Did you sleep with Ruth O'Leary last night?'

Alice nodded.

'Thank you. I thought you no liar. At least I'm right on that count. Understand, even if by turning a blind eye you lay open the naïve and vulnerable to gross sexual acts, of what may later be a psychologically damaging experience, the Home Office will be deemed responsible. All criminals are considered either naïve or vulnerable, that's why they offend in the first place. You, Alice, as a bright, principled young woman with a responsible attitude, should ignore your inclinations, or at least keep them covert.

'Well, do you accept you're guilty of gross misconduct? Or do you believe you have the God-given – sorry, I forget, you're now a non-believer – do you consider your position in the Hope gives you a right to take such outrageous liberties?'

'Pierce used to... and you! I suppose your cock rammed between their legs isn't a psychologically damaging experience.'

Voice raised, Hughes berated Alice. 'I don't give a fuck about Eddie. He won't be coming back. Whatever he did he didn't get caught! And who have you seen me having sex with? Eh, Alice? Who?'

'Ruth.'

'Anyone else?'

'I've heard...'

'That is scandal. That is slander. Offer that to a court

59

of law. *I've heard.*'

'Everyone knows what you get up to.'

'You will not find one shred of evidence. You will not find one female in this establishment who will complain of sexual misconduct. And that is my point, Alice; it's not what you do, it's getting caught that matters. And for that you will pay the price. So next time you will cover your tracks.'

'I didn't get caught. Someone snitched.'

'Alice, either wield enough clout to silence your critics, or do what you desire well away from prying eyes.'

'So, you are going to punish me?'

'Justice must be seen to be done. The whole damn establishment now knows that Miss Hussey slept with *the* Hope scoundrel. They *will* be assured that audacious rascals, and indiscreet overseers, will be dealt with, swiftly and severely.'

She considered her position, her *faux pas*. Downright unfair came to mind, amid a jumble of other concerns. 'Will be assured,' she queried. 'Does that mean you'll make an announcement?'

'No.' Hughes knocked out the ash from his pipe. 'It means they will watch.'

The full horror of what Hughes intended struck, Alice's head swimming. 'No!' she blurted without thought. 'I'll not agree to that!'

Hughes leant forward, elbows on desk. 'What else can I do? You've left me with very little choice in the matter.'

'How will I be able to control them after that?'

'They'll admire you for your grit. Especially when they see you take it without flinching.'

'Like I would!'

'Of course, one answer would be to leave the Hope.'

'I can't. Remember?'

'Money and clothes are easily replaced.'

'What are you plotting now?'

'Call it motivation. You're wasting God-given – sorry, there I go again with the God bit. One is young, attractive and desirable for a relatively short period in life. You are advantaged. You possess qualities that if utilised could set you up in comfort for the rest of your days. You will be provided with a new and extensive wardrobe and the annex to my house: a decent sized flat of your own.'

'Porn movies,' she sighed. 'That's it, isn't it?'

'No. Stop jumping to conclusions.'

Hand squeezing hand, she demanded, 'What then?'

'Stills. Glamour. Schoolgirl. A bit of over the knee, that sort of thing. And I have an appreciative and select client base that would be interested. Nice people. Like to show their appreciation in pound notes. I make no demands. Do only what you're comfortable with, Alice.'

'And if I agree, you won't cane me in front of the girls. Is that it?'

'I have to. You *and* O'Leary. I have to maintain the status quo.' Hughes drummed his fingers on the desk. 'But I'll provide a pair of trousers to cover your modesty. A thin pair.'

'What was all that about just now then?'

'That was about after paying for your mistake.'

'What have you in mind?' she asked, dreading the answer.

He lit his pipe, deliberately building the tension. Puffing smoke, match tossed into an ashtray, he eyed Alice. A slight smile playing on his lips, he opened a drawer and tossed an implement at her. 'That.'

The girl caught the piece, the weight and feel horrifying. Gripping the handle she perused the polished, well-employed leather.

'Two and a half inches wide, sixteen inches long and three eighths thick.' Hughes recited the vital statistics. 'Pity you're not still into penance,' he added sarcastically.

'It looks a beast,' she remarked gloomily, trying to ignore the familiar inner battle, fear and intrigue vying susceptibility. 'And Ruth?' she asked.

'That's none of your business. Be concerned about your own backside.'

'I'll take your strapping. I'll give the other business a try.' She folded her arms defiantly.

'But?' Hughes said for her.

'You strap me in private. And we sign some sort of agreement before I do anything else.'

'That's your last word, is it?'

'It is.'

Hughes toyed with a pencil, continuously turning it in one hand. 'You drive a hard bargain, but I find myself in a difficult position. The animals scent blood and I have nothing to give them.' He snapped the pencil in half. 'Any suggestions?'

Alice smiled nervously, body fidgeting. 'You're not whacking me in front of that horde.'

'What I am offering,' Hughes paused for thought, 'you don't seem to realise what's involved here. I am trying to keep this within the Hope walls. I could, should, put the matter to my superiors. If I did we would not be talking about a smacked bottom. No, Alice, we would be looking at legal proceedings.'

Alice grinned. 'This is a set-up, isn't it?'

'What is? You choosing to sleep with an inmate and making sure the whole establishment knows? Do you really think I would go to, have to go to, so much trouble just to smack your backside? Is that it?'

'No, but that's not the reason, is it? You'll stoop to anything to get me involved in your racket.' Losing her rag she jabbed a finger at him. 'This is all about me being coerced.'

Face set, Hughes angrily returned, 'So you're accusing me of sending Ruth to seduce you. You're saying she's not your lover.'

'I don't know who snitched, but you *have* used this sorry business for your own ends.'

Hughes settled, calmed, as did Alice. Leaning on the desk he perused some papers. 'Okay, you win. Private flogging it is.'

'And the hordes?'

'I shall have to throw them Ruth, and perhaps Sweet as well.'

'Hazel? Why?'

'I understand she was in your room for some time before she returned to the dorm.'

'No, not really.'

'I want two behinds. Ruth's and one other. Either yours or Hazel's, I'm not fussed.'

Alice held his gaze, trying to read the man's mood, his intent. 'You're bluffing. I'll pay for my mistake, but in the way I should. In private.'

The man took a wallet from an inside jacket pocket, offering Alice twenty pounds.

'What's this for?' she asked warily.

'You'll do. I'll buy dinner tonight. And for Charley's you'll need an evening dress. That should cover it.'

Alice slammed the money down. 'What do you think you're buying with this?'

'Goodwill, I hope. You can keep it. It's yours. Go and catch a train back to where you come from if you like. But before you do, just think for a minute. That twenty is four weeks' wages for you. It's nothing to me.' Hughes took out another hundred in five pound notes and threw them at her. 'I have thousands, Alice, and I'm offering you a share. A sizeable share.'

'Alice, give your keys to Mr Preesal. He's going to look after the dorms tonight.' Hughes rested a hand on her buttock. 'You can stay at my house.'

Swallowing nervously, and unsure about almost everything, she accepted his pawing as a sign of things to come.

Black fabric clung and emphasised every curve. A plunging neckline displayed the thrust of a flawless cleavage, her back bared almost to the buttocks. The dress flowed over hips, forming tight about her pelvis, the restrictive cloth only easing at the knee.

'Fits like a glove,' Hughes had complimented. Poured on, sprang to Alice's mind.

She dispensed with the underwear, the presence of showing too clearly through the thin fabric. Stiletto shoes raised her, the effect on calves and bearing sensual.

With a shawl about her shoulders, Alice said goodnight to Preesal and headed for the stairs. A wolf whistle stalled her, Alice not surprised to see Ruth approaching.

'So who's going to pull you tonight?' Ruth asked sarcastically.

'No one,' Alice replied peevishly.

'So who yer trying to impress then?'

Alice glared at the girl. 'Understand, O'Leary: me supervisor, you con. Get back to your dorm or I'll ask Mr Preesal to take the necessary measures.'

'You gonna fulfil my expectations tonight?'

'I made no promise.'

'But I did.'

Alice eyed her with contempt. 'Ruth, don't get jealous on me. We've been caught. This time we'll get off light. I'm not risking a next.'

'Go on, go have yer fancy dinner. Go and play wiv

yer highflying mates. I should'a known you didn't mean any of what yer said.'

Alice smiled awkwardly. 'I do like you, Ruth. Honest.'

The blonde relented. 'Yeah, me you too.' She smiled grudgingly. 'All the same, if you don't come back, *someone* will fill your place.'

'You haven't been back to see me,' Sheila remarked, the pair strolling behind their male companions.

'No, time's the problem.'

'I'm always available, Alice. And I'm always willing to listen.'

Hughes glanced over a shoulder, ensuring neither of the women were in earshot. 'How was your first day?'

'Finding my feet. Sorting things out. You know how it is.'

'I'd prefer it if we didn't discuss past business in front of the ladies, especially Alice.'

'I won't,' Scrubbs replied bluntly.

Plied with wine and brandy before, during and after the meal, Alice left the restaurant a touch too carefree. Flushed, she stumbled light-headed to the car, inhibitions drowned, crumbling morals deluged by alcohol. Accompanied by Sheila the young redhead slumped inebriated on the back seat, her head on an equally drunk Miss Doodney's shoulder. Sheila responded, placing a comforting arm about the girl. The gentle sway of the moving vehicle, with the excess of drink, combined to prematurely close Alice's eyes. Sleep crept insidiously, bearing the ghouls and irksome phantoms of a troubled conscience.

While she dozed in a troubled, surreal world, another's eyes roamed, drank of her delectable charms, wallowed in the corporeal dips and surges of an irresistible body. Restraint beyond her, Sheila laid a tentative finger to the sleek feel of smooth breast, antagonising a fired libido. Lust fuelled by alcohol, dissolute tendencies surging unimpeded, Sheila sampled abandoned adventure. A wary eye on the men in front, she sank her hand between those inviting spheres.

'Is this the cleavage of a decently raised girl? Would a woman with the morals you promote have her breasts hanging out in such a fashion? I think not.'

Harris, Jonathan's butler, strolled casually about Alice. 'Integrity is sadly lacking in you.'

Alice pulled on the hem of her shirt, hanging level with the tops of her thighs.

'Sleeping with another female! And if that's not disreputable enough, that female happens to be one of life's wretched unfortunates. Are you suitably ashamed?'

Alice slowly nodded, her lower regions crawling in anticipation.

'Then why do you have designs upon *her*?' He pointed at Sheila.

The man stood directly behind Alice, inches from her naked bottom. His breath on her neck, the close proximity of his body sending shivers down Alice's spine. 'I haven't!'

'But you do nothing to stop her fondling you, do you?'

'I...'

Sheila nuzzled close, her hand inside Alice's dress, fingers playing with her breast. 'The question is, what to do with an immoral wretch who's always at it?'

That shirttail felt like gossamer. Awareness dominated all thought. Vulnerability gnawed at resolve, achieved humiliation. Pride fell in tatters, the spirit humbled.

'Take away the clothes and you bare not only the flesh.'

'Look inside her head,' advised the doctor. 'She may

have a screw loose. It's a hereditary complaint. Her mother was sex *mad*.'

Puffing on the ever-present pipe, Geoffrey Hughes smiled knowingly. 'Her soul, that's where the answer lies.'

'There are no easy answers,' boomed a familiar voice. 'She is damned. The devil rides her body. It is Satan's lust you witness. Any depravation will do, as long as it deviates from natural practices.'

'We know what it is, Barker,' Hughes scoffed. 'It's what we do about it, that's what we're concerned about.'

'How do I look inside her head, doctor?'

'We should insert a probe via her mouth. If stuffed deep enough it should *come* within reach.'

'And how do I access her soul, Mr Hughes?'

'That is in her cunt, Harris. You know where that is, I take it?'

'Satan will merely laugh at this psycho spiritual hokum. Drive him out, I say! Scourge the catalyst and the monster within will eventually wither.'

Harris unfastened his fly. 'I will seek her soul.'

'And I her mind.' Hughes advanced with a monstrous, swaying erection. He forced Alice to her knees, Harris lying between her thighs. The man sank his podgy fingers into the flesh of her hips, his rigid cock pressed to the gates of her sex.

'No!' Alice begged. 'I don't want to be examined. Not like this. Not with those monstrous things.'

Hughes held his erection to her mouth. 'I didn't suppose a queer girl would. Now open wide.'

Alice held her lips tightly closed, her face turned away.

'Have a look for her soul, Harris, while I see to opening her mind.'

'No!' she cried as thick hard meat pressured, parted

67

and then sank rapidly between her vaginal lips. Hair gripped by Hughes' fists, he jerked her head forward, her open mouth impaled. His extensive organ stretched, filled her, the stem forced to her throat.

'Can you see anything, Harris?' Hughes asked, hips mobile, his heavy bulb exploring every millimetre of that restrictive wet hole.

Harris thrust, his organ thickening, extending, sinking ever deeper. 'Only darkness,' the man replied. 'Seems her soul is as black as Satan's. What have *you* discovered?'

'Just a minute.' Hughes thrust, his cock forced deeper, Alice choking. 'As I thought; there's two faces to this one. They keep switching.'

Tough leather thongs lashed her backside, the tails cutting diagonally. 'One's Satan. Drive him out! They're joined by lunacy. It touches both, innocent and subverted. I tell you she's possessed by evil!' Lash after lash bit and scalded naked buttocks.

'I see no evil,' barked Hughes. 'Do you, Harris?'

Eyelids closed, the man grunted and gasped, his hips thrusting at a frantic pace.

'Feel it, Hussey. Feel the probe. It seeks not soul nor devil. It delves and stretches, arouses and stimulates. It delivers sensual turmoil, delights beyond your imagination, and pure unadulterated ecstasy.'

Richard fell to his knees. 'I will prove it. I will hook this beast from her tainted body. I will free her mind and her soul.' Her anus stretched, gave to the man's excitement, his shaft urged deep. Humid groin touched, pressed to soft buttocks, wiry pubic hair tickled bottom flesh.

'See, Hussey. I set your mind free and this is what you choose. The thrill and consummate pleasure of illicit penetration. Foul, lewd and depraved acts. There is no evil. It is you, Alice. It is the way God set your cap.'

The engine dying awoke her, bleary green eyes blinking, trying to focus. Alice raised a hand, pressed it to her forehead. 'Oh hell, I think I might be a bit woozy.'

Sheila giggled. 'I think you might be a lot woozy.'

Dawn Summers, an incurable who gave her body more regularly than she sold it, tapped Hazel Sweet on the shoulder. 'You're wanted.'

Immediately suspicious, Hazel asked, 'Who by?'

Dawn shrugged. 'Bossy knickers. Who else?'

'Where? Her room?'

Summers slumped in a chair, legs hanging over the arm. Picking up a copy of the Dandy she nonchalantly scanned the pages, a finger up her nose.

Hazel surveyed the dormitory. 'Where's Ruth?' Dawn ignored her. Hazel wrenched the comic out of the girl's hands. 'I said, where's O'Leary?'

Unimpressed, Summers pointed at the comic. 'Please,' she suggested, expression bored.

'Not until you tell me what's going on.'

'You're beginning to fuck me off, piss-head. The comic?' Summers held her hand out.

Hazel dangled it out of reach. 'Ruth?'

Whiskey bottle half empty, Hughes broached the subject he desperately wanted an answer to. 'Cards on the table: what do you want, Dennis?'

'Now that's beating about the bush, Geoffrey, isn't it now?'

'Not my style.'

'I told you, I just need to lie low for a while. Not for my sake, you understand. I've done my bird, now haven't I?'

Hughes nodded, suspicious. 'That's why I'm asking. What do you think I owe you?'

'You always was the doubting Thomas. You doubted me back then, and you're doing it now.'

'You were the only one to get caught.'

'So that proves a point, eh? I kept my mouth shut. You, Eddie and Charlie Weeks have had a good few years thanks to me.'

'Thank you for your loyalty, Dennis. Now when did you say you were leaving?'

'Shame you're being like this. See, I looked upon my silence as a sort of investment?'

'Investment?' Hughes scoffed. 'Not getting caught would have proved more lucrative.'

Scrubbs stood and ambled to a window. Hands stuffed deep in pockets he gazed out over Flint. 'Truth is, Geoffrey, I'm skint. I've nowhere to go and winter's rolling in.'

'I've got a violin somewhere,' came Hughes' callous reply.

'A few weeks and a couple of bob. That's all I need.'

Hazel proved no match for Summers. Although latterly phlegmatic, the girl had once controlled the feral wildcat packs that survived the bombed out shells of downtown Coventry. Hazel stared at her kneecaps, her arm so far up her back her fingertips touched her neck. She screamed with the pain, Summers psychotically impassive. 'You wanna see Ruth, piss-head. You can see Ruth.'

Dawn hauled the humiliated ex-prefect, ex-Carters girl by her long black tresses, Hazel's hands trying to ease the hurt. Summers' heel opened Alice's bedroom door, Hazel thrown in seconds later.

'She didn't fall for your crap,' Dawn explained with indifference. 'Don't know what you want with the bitch anyway.' She wiggled her butt. 'You got me, ain't you?'

Face down, Hazel lay pinned, Ruth's foot on her neck.

'Yeah, Summers, so why not wait outside in case I needs yer.'

'Fuck you.' Dawn left.

'Loose cannon, that one. Word is she done for a feller and got away with it.'

'You're all crazy in this asylum.'

O'Leary increased the pressure, Sweet squirming. 'Respect, Haze. I expect respect. Yer don't have to get to yer knees or nothin'. But when I asks yer to come, I expects respect, and for yer to come.'

'Dawn didn't say it was you. I thought Alice wanted me.'

'Nah, you just don't trust me, do yer?' Ruth removed the foot. 'On yer knees.'

Ruth lay back on Alice's bed, hands supporting her head. 'Reason for your summons, Haze, you've got a payment to make.'

'What for?' Sweet demanded.

'Protection. To stop me beating the shit out of yer.'

'Money?'

'Yeah, if yer got some. Or fags. Or booze.'

Hazel shook her head. 'I've nothing like that.'

'Shame.' Ruth studied the ceiling. 'Tell yer what, Haze. Yer can cough wiv yer body.'

'I can what?'

'Pay, Haze. We could be happy all round. The debt cleared. My body satisfied, my needs met, you educated.' Ruth studied her fingernails. 'Yeah, I reckon yer could do that.'

'Okay.' Hughes opened the parlour door and nosed outside.

Scrubbs spun on his heels. 'Is that "okay" as in I can stay here?'

'Don't you go giving the wrong impression,' Hughes warned. 'I'm not the benevolent type. You can stay

71

because I can use you.'

'Great.' Scrubbs shrugged. 'What will I be doing?'

'Taking over from Alice.'

'And Alice?'

Hughes smiled, Scrubbs grinned in return, then Hughes' smile faded. 'None of your fucking business, Scrubbs.'

'What are you proposing?'

'Voluntary instalment. I don't expect yer to get too amorous just yet. So I'll settle for a bit of friendly horseplay.'

'What do you have in mind? Leap frog?' Hazel asked sarcastic.

'Nah. More like,' Ruth produced a thin rattan, 'sting the titties.'

Hazel folded her arms, the suggestion unnerving, provocative in an unfathomable fashion.

'Bed and board,' Hughes offered. 'Plus four quid a week.'

'Fine,' Scrubbs replied.

'And as much cunt as you want.'

He failed to fully understand. 'Eh?'

'They will expect. They will demand. Whores every one. And your pecker will have to rise to the occasion round-the-clock.' Hughes paused. 'And talking of whores, where the hell are those sots?'

Constraints wiped by alcohol, Alice studied Sheila, the woman stood with her back to her. Her gaze settled on the doctor's behind, those buttocks snug in a tight-fitting skirt. 'You've a nice figure, Sheila,' she remarked casually.

'I thought you were asleep,' the woman replied.

'You once told me you caned out of duty, but did take

some satisfaction from it.'

'I did, didn't I?'

'Can I ask you a very personal question?'

'As we're both the worse for wear, and not likely to remember what we've said, I don't see why not.'

'Do you have any tendencies the other way?'

Sheila laughed. 'My, Alice, the other way? That *is* a very direct and personal question.'

'I mean unnatural inclinations, not…'

Sheila advanced on the young woman, expression wilful, amused. 'Do you mean sucking a Shire horse's cock is unnatural, my dear?'

Alice blushed. 'You don't…'

Kneeling on the bed, thighs straddling Alice, she smouldered. Eyes fixed on the redhead she suggested, 'Perhaps you should investigate.' Lips pouting, Sheila lowered herself, rounded backside thrust out and up. Body moving from side to side she tantalised, teased, used the touch of her breasts to incite the supine girl.

Alice reacted, confused. The rise of Sheila's skirt, her stocking-clad legs bared introduced trepidation, uncertainty and suppressed enthusiasm. 'There's a price to pay, though,' the woman warned.

No words were forthcoming, Alice not sure what to ask, and whether she even wanted to know.

'I feel the other way. Queer, homosexual, not exactly unnatural, but definitely a little gay. Must be the drink. Or perhaps it's you. But one thing is certain; I desperately need my pussy licked.' Sheila began unbuttoning her blouse. With the two top buttons to go, she paused. 'Shocked? Have I got it completely wrong? Is this where I die of acute embarrassment? Say something, Alice.'

'I'm not sure what to do, what to say,' Alice replied.

'Well if you're at all interested, there's nothing except what you see between me and my naked body.' She released the last buttons and pulled the blouse apart.

Hughes' belt marks caught Alice's eye, the girl reaching inquisitively, touching Sheila's breast. 'What's that?' she asked, stroking a fading mark.

'It's the answer to your question. Want to kiss it better?' she asked, the breast dangled flirtatiously. Inexperience and uncertainty spawned indecision. The moment lost, a gamble foundered. Embarrassment cut deep, Sheila's pride shattered. 'Don't tell me,' the woman presupposed. 'I'm too old.'

Alice smiled reassuringly and shook her head. 'Don't assume, Sheila. Don't take me or anything for granted.' There between a drink-sodden mind and percipient chaos, great clarity seemed to descend. 'I need another drink.'

'Either you find me attractive or you don't. What's the drink for, to bolster your nerve?' Sheila sense the indecisive turmoil, Alice still a servant to her indoctrinated principles. 'Thou shalt not fuck another woman. Which commandment is that?'

Puzzled, Alice replied, 'There is no such commandment.'

'So God hasn't forbidden the fruit of lesbian love. What's your problem?'

'This is one hell of a way to analyse me, doctor.'

'Analyse you, Hussey? I don't want to analyse you. I want to explore every inch of your gorgeous body. I want to lick, kiss and bite every intimate part. Hussey, I can do things to you that will turn you inside out.'

Impetuosity flared unchecked, and with no warning Alice threw her arms about the woman's neck. Her embrace fired smouldering embers, the engagement of lips more a melding of lusts, of sexual spirits. Frustrations, anxieties, years of inculcation evaporated on the wings of liberation, Alice closing her mind to the inconvenience of God.

74

Flares of ecstatic energy teased, amassed and besieged. Flesh burned with desire and expectation, needs intolerable, drowning commonsense, drawing the dark side to dominate. Resistance quelled, Alice succumbed to the older woman. Dress tugged clear Sheila swooped, teeth biting supple breasts, Alice incapable of choice, the illicit ravaging of her body throwing lucidity into turmoil.

Feverish passion spawned a rival flame, Alice replying with reckless abandon. The pair rolled, exchanging dominance, Alice on top, Sheila on top. Lips met, courted wildly, tongues entwined in a rhapsody of discovery.

Tangled in half-discarded clothing, sheets and blankets, the pair crashed to the floor. Alice rose, her legs astride Sheila, the woman gazing wildly. Alice giggled with the indecency of it all, Sheila's nails clawing her back, the woman's teeth sunk into a breast. She held her there, tongue raking a nipple. Alice tossed her head back, long red curls coiling down her back. And there she froze, unable to speak, unable to move.

'What the hell's going on?' Hughes demanded. 'For Christ's sake, Alice, is no woman safe in this establishment?'

Sheila let the breast go, an impression of her intended love bite painfully obvious. Sheepishly she looked up at Hughes. He sighed. Words failed him.

Alice pulled herself up, a sheet wrapped about her calves impeding progress. Mind fogged, she couldn't comprehend the hindrance. Breasts exposed and rousing, she pointed a finger at the principal. 'You!' The man glowered. 'You,' she iterated. 'You set this up. You told Miss Doodle, Doodney, to come on to me, to seduce me. You got me drunk. This is all about *you* getting what *you* want, isn't it?'

'I warn you, Alice. Mind what you say here.'

Alice struggled to her feet, finally working out what held her. 'So, Mr Hughes, what you after now? You've got the film and the stills. So what else can there be? You're going to thrash me anyway, so it isn't that.' She threw her arms apart. 'And come to that, what has it got to do with you anyway? Who do you think you are? Adolf Hitler?' She fell back onto the bed. 'Ah, I know. I know what Geoffrey wants. It's what he's always wanted.' She rolled over onto her front, attempting unsuccessfully to pull the dress up.

'Damn!' she swore. 'Can't get my skirt up, Geoff. Looks like Alice's pussy is off the menu tonight. Shame, cos I was going to let you have it. Get it over and done with.'

Alice looked back over a shoulder, eyes glazed. 'Yes, Geoffrey, I was going to let you shaft me good and proper. Blasted skirt won't come up, though.'

Hughes leapt forward, fists gripping the dress. Muscles flexed he was about to rip it from her, but Sheila grabbed his arm, her eyes warning him. 'No, Geoff, she's drunk. She's no idea what she's doing or saying. It wouldn't be right.'

Hughes shook off her hold. 'You heard her. She invited me.'

'And when she wakes up in the morning with no recollection she'll be inviting the police.' She let the words sink in. 'Can you afford them nosing around?'

He jabbed a finger at Sheila. 'She's got no respect.'

'She's drunk, Geoff.'

'She doesn't need drink to bad mouth me. She needs setting straight.'

'Fine; a thrashing she will most likely accept. But—'

'And what's your fucking game?'

'How do you mean?'

'You're confusing her. I *know* she's not queer, but all the time the likes of you and Ruth are playing with her

76

head she's not going to see that.'

'You cheeky bastard! It was you that wanted Ruth to sleep with her. You can't have your cake and eat it.'

'Yes, I wanted her unsettled not converted.'

'I think you've lost sight of your priorities. I'm beginning to think that having sex with this young woman is paramount to you. You have the pick of over a hundred girls and you want her. The unattainable, is that it? A major notch on your bedpost?'

'And I firmly believe you want Alice for yourself. What's up, tired of Ruth? Or was it three in a bed you was after?'

'I've never denied you anything!'

Hughes wrenched the cord from a dressing gown, and still irrationally angry he bound the sleeping Alice's wrists behind her back. He snatched another and snapped, 'Now you.'

Resigned, the thrill of the unknown and his unpredictability inspiring suspense, Sheila showed her back and crossed wrists. She winced to the bite of cord, Hughes deliberately over-tightening it. The possibilities were endless, the probabilities diverse and intimidating. Anything might happen; anything without moral restraint, without quarter and without consideration. That aspect chilled, frightened, launched a rash of goose bumps. Her head swam with anxiety, anticipation, the thrill of the unknown jangling every nerve in her body.

The strident slap of hand against flesh stirred her further. Another within seconds snatched the slumbering Alice from her dream world. Hughes towered over her. She couldn't move her arms, her wrists pained, her hands immobilised.

Hughes said nothing, explained nothing. Lifted by her hair, her blurred focus fell upon Sheila, the woman tied, naked breasts barely covered, noting her own breasts in an equally embarrassing state of exposure. 'What...?'

77

Alice managed, confused. 'Is this a dream?'

'It could be your fantasy come true,' Sheila suggested. 'Up to you, and how you ride it.'

Alice frowned. 'A rollercoaster, you mean?'

'Oh yes, I think Geoff can guarantee that if nothing else.'

Each held by their hair, Hughes steered them downstairs. Alice followed what she imagined was a dream, her expectations extensive. Sheila steeled herself for what she expected.

Asked the day before, and Hazel Sweet would have stated adamantly that she would never stoop to such depraved acts. But the reflection of mirror and window glass told no lies. They confirmed Hazel's unprincipled complicity.

She could plead that she could take no more, that Ruth would have striped her backside all night. She could defend her involvement as coercion, the two-dozen welts on her breasts evidence. She could point to the crisscrossed cane marks on her abdomen and groin, and cry duress. Ruth ensured the writhing Sweet endured several directly to her crotch.

Yes, Hazel could cry intimidation, could sob her heart out in another's sympathetic arms. But didn't those trophies of suffering excite? Didn't the vibrant product of the lash stir lascivious feelings? Worse, could the strait-laced Sweet ever admit that the accumulation of those stripes wasn't the torture she made it out to be? Could she concede, even to herself, that at least half of those severe strokes invoked the most implausible satisfaction she had ever experienced?

Torso rising and falling, whipped breasts bounced and jiggled, Sweet was unable to tear her gaze from that entrancing reflection. Every meeting of Hazel's rigorously beaten buttocks and Ruth's cushioning thighs

78

reminded of the savagery. It resurrected the defencelessness, her vulnerability, the ecstatic combination of nudity and domination.

Ruth felt her breasts. Her hands played and petted. She lay beneath Hazel, expression concentrated, her orgasm not too distant. Their union, a curved length of thick black rubber penetrated and pleased both. It stretched her sex, fulfilled an urgency for depravity, a lust for the unnatural. Fourteen inches of malleable rubber was coerced and manipulated until it fully penetrated. Hazel stared with mixed feelings at that protruding monstrosity, her near immaculate vagina penetrated with a crude cudgel.

Ruth had whipped her there, twenty-four strokes laid to her lower belly and groin. Hazel twisted and writhed as that rattan reaped havoc, while a manipulative inner voice urged more. She parted her legs, inviting the crucifying smart of that flexile rod. She grit her teeth and made no protest as Ruth, lost to a sexual frenzy, lashed her cunny lips. The ultimate sacrifice.

Ruth gasped. Her nails sunk deep into Hazel's breasts. Bleary eyes flicked open, pale blue irises gazing up at Hazel. 'Oh gawd, Haze, I fink that rubber must have reached me brain. What a fucking orgasm!'

'Shall I get off?' Hazel asked, unsure.

'You done then?'

'I'm fine, honest,' the girl replied.

'Gawd, look at the state of your tits.' Ruth studied the girl's breasts. 'Sort of turns me on. Yeah, I loves the way yer tits stripe. I think I might cane yer again, Haze.' O'Leary noted the twitch of approval. 'And even if I don't, there's plenty would grab the chance, as well as this brute between their legs.'

World a woolly, indistinct place, Alice sprawled over Hughes' lap. The man regarded those consummate buttocks, drooling over the perfect pitch and roll of divine arse. Sheila stood to one side, savouring what was about to happen and relishing what would come next.

Dennis Scrubbs sat in the next room, head swimming with the effect of whiskey, his eyelids drooping.

Hughes' hand determined to awaken, to snap Alice abruptly back to the real world. Drink addled her mind, the girl somewhere between reality and cloud cuckoo land.

Sheila waited with anxious breath, knowing what Hughes was capable of. It struck with speed and strength, the flimsily clad buttock flattened and brutally stung.

Torment slapped a befuddled head. Pain coursed through her body, the girl unable to determine why. Fire gripped her seat, the cheek stinging wildly. A second jolted her, setting her arse alight. Alice reared, Hughes' arm preventing escape. She cursed, swore as he forced her back down, his hand slapping.

Gripped by the continuous heave and lurch of stung cheeks, Sheila leaned against the door. Stirred, commonsense impounded by the disorientating effects of excessive Chablis, her high spirits gave to the black mood of jealousy, her sensuality to the lure of urgency.

Alice kicked and begged for a cessation. She sank her nails into Hughes' leg, the man responding with a fusillade of slaps. Still covered, that backside heaved to a storm of spanks, the girl yanked from the pit of intoxication.

Her naked breasts quivered with each hefty smack, pressed against Hughes' thighs. The girl's legs thrashed the air, the hem of her dress riding ever higher. Scarlet cheeks peeped beneath the hem. Embossed handprints etched her bottom. Tears filled Alice's eyes, droplets scattering on the carpet. Her bottom screamed at every explosion, the pain edging toward agonising.

Sheila checked the time. Alice had sustained for five long minutes, with the man's powerful hand pounding her buttocks. The redhead alternated between snatching deep breaths and squealing her acute discomfort. With her hands tied behind her back she could do little to fight, or defend her bum.

Hughes ceased, Alice sobbing. He peeled up the skirt to reveal two crimson moons smothered with finger marks. Then he lifted his focus to Sheila. 'Because you're older, and because you should know better. And more to the point, because I want to, and will thoroughly enjoy doing so,' he smiled, 'you can have ten minutes.'

Sheila pressed her body to the door, unsure her legs would hold her. She returned his gaze. 'And what precisely have I done to warrant such?'

Hughes stroked and massaged Alice's burning buttocks. His fingers slipped casually the length of the division, fingertips settling between her legs. 'You need to ask?'

'Ha!' Sheila eyed him with derision. 'That says it all, doesn't it?'

'I expect my resident psychologist to behave in a responsible manner.'

'I did!' The woman glowered. 'It's you that's acting irresponsibly. How dare you burst in on me anyway?'

'It was *my* bedroom!'

Alice shuddered, Hughes' finger probing her vagina.

'And you knew I was in there with Alice. A gentleman would knock.'

'And *then* catch you fucking hell out of a junior colleague.'

'I was not fucking hell out of her at all.'

'You weren't far off.'

Alice coughed. 'I feel sick.'

81

'For God's sake, let the poor girl be.'

'I might cane her yet.'

'I don't think so.'

'I might take it out on her arse instead of yours.'

'And what has become wrong with *my* arse, exactly?'

'You're being picky and stingy with it.' He laid a hand on Alice's bottom. 'This tortured rump is just begging to experience the slash and bite of a whippy rattan.' He patted the flesh, Alice wincing. 'Don't you think?'

'And her fanny could do with a thick hard cock, in your eyes. But that doesn't make it right.'

'Okay to stick your tongue in there, though. Okay to do what lesbians do. Unnatural sex is fine, gang, but straight functions are off the menu.'

'She wanted it, arsehole.'

'She's drunk, bitch. Something you were quick to point out back up there in the den of iniquity.'

'Fuck you. Go on, spank me. Cane me. I deserve it.' The brass doorknob turned against Sheila's buttock and she used her weight to prevent the door opening.

Hughes called, 'What is it, Dennis?'

'Just wondered where everyone is, that's all.'

'That's a broad spectrum, Dennis. Everyone.' Hughes raised an eyebrow.

'Forgot just how bloody pedantic you could be.'

Hughes rose, lifting Alice to her feet as he did so, and led the girl to the door. 'Tell you what, have a chat with Alice.'

Sheila scowled.

'Where is she?'

Hughes grinned as he took hold of the door handle. 'She's here with her bosom buddy, keeping abreast of matters.'

Sheila mouthed, 'Don't.'

He opened the door slightly and peered around the

82

jamb. 'She's a bit the worse for wear and feeling free and easy. Thought you might like to see her to the spare room.'

'Isn't that my room?'

Hughes smoothed Alice's skirt back down over her hips. 'It's a double bed.' He untied her hands and opened the door fully. 'Dress seems to have slipped a bit.'

Barely conscious, unaware of what transpired, Alice made no effort to cover her breasts, and taken aback Dennis made no move.

'Well come on, man, take her. Can't you see the girl's six sheets to the wind?'

'A practical joke, is it, Geoffrey?' Scrubbs sneered cynically.

Hughes leant against the door jamb. 'No joke, practical or impractical. Go test the water. Been quite agreeable so far.'

Scrubbs studied the man. 'I'm missing something, aren't I?'

Sheila put her head about the door, her naked torso hidden. 'Ignore him, Dennis. He's in one of his moods. Alice is drunk, and that's all. Alice needs to go to bed.'

Hughes opened his mouth.

'Alone,' Sheila insisted.

Hughes handed the girl over to the man and closed the door.

'You are incorrigible,' Sheila accused.

'Be a bit of a shock, wouldn't it? A lesbian waking up with nine inches of cock in her cunt.' Hughes drained his whiskey glass.

'Nine?'

'So I've heard.'

'You can't stand the thought, can you?' Sheila worked on the cord gripping her wrists.

'About what?'

'It's beyond Geoffrey. Geoffrey's stamping his feet, because Alice might just prefer someone else.'

'She's made her statement, with O'Leary, with you, and probably with Sweet. I just want her to know what she'll be missing.'

'You shit!'

'I might give him you as well,' Hughes suggested flippantly.

'I might prefer him,' Sheila riposted. 'Especially if the rumour is true.'

A scream from upstairs disturbed the stalemate. 'Seems Dennis took me at my word,' Hughes remarked, unconcerned.

'Aren't you going to…?' Sheila began, outraged.

Hughes laughed. 'Oh come on, Sheila, Dennis doesn't stand a bloody chance.'

The thunder of feet on the stairs followed, Hughes throwing the door wide. Dennis reached the foot first, Alice behind, hurling curses and anything she could lay her hands to.

'Misunderstanding,' Scrubbs grunted as he scurried past Hughes.

Alice reached the doorway, eyes bloodshot and still bleary. Looking passed Hughes she covered her breasts, hands hooking the dress straps back over her shoulders.

'Problem?' Hughes enquired.

Partly sobered, Alice asked, annoyed, 'Is this another one of your tricks?'

'I 'spect it's demons,' Hughes taunted, and Alice scowled. 'Perhaps you should avoid the bottle in future.'

'That man was in my room, trying to take my dress off.'

'And it wasn't a woman.'

Alice staggered by and deposited her bottom in an armchair, wincing. 'I know I'm drunk,' she admitted, 'but not that drunk. What are you up to, you devious shit.'

'Extending your options,' Hughes answered.

'What?'

'Hmm.' Hughes knocked the ash from his pipe. 'I thought all the female attention you're getting might be confusing you.'

'You're that petty,' she accused, 'that you'd let a man take advantage of me just to try and prove a fruitless point. All because you've convinced yourself I'm a lesbian.'

Hughes lit the pipe. 'Did he?'

'I told you, he was trying to get my dress off.'

'Can't blame him there.'

'You irresponsible…'

Hughes settled back, legs crossing. 'I suspect Dennis was just trying to make you comfortable.'

'That's not what you said just now.'

'I know Dennis. I know you. And I also know another man isn't going to taste the fruits before me.'

'That's not your decision.'

'It is under my roof. In my prison.'

'Then perhaps it's time I started going out.'

'You are free to do as you wish.'

'And not in chains.'

'As I said, you're a free agent.'

'Good. As long as that's understood.'

'I'd be careful about wearing that dress, though.'

'Why? What's wrong with it?'

'It makes a statement.' Alice waited on the punch-line. 'It says: if I'm without a companion, I'm up for a fuck.' Hughes pointed at a glass-fronted cupboard. 'Help yourself to a drink.'

'I've had enough. Enough alcohol and enough of you.'

'I'll decide that. Whiskey? Gin? Brandy? Help yourself.'

85

'I said no. I've had enough.'

'The dress states: look at my curvaceous body. Look at the way it hugs my tits and arse. It says: wouldn't you like me to wrap my legs around you while you give me a good fucking. Have a vodka... or a long, severe spanking.'

Hughes bordered on unstable, Alice never sure of what he could be capable of. 'Just a small one, then.'

'A large one.' Hughes sucked on his pipe, the embers dead. 'That do you, Sheila? A large one? Or are you already getting one?'

Alice looked around the empty room, puzzled. '*You* bought the dress for me.'

'Exactly. So I above all others know what it says. It incites me, Alice. Your saving grace is the amount of whiskey I've put away.'

Alice poured from the vodka bottle, her glass a third full. 'I really think I should get to bed.'

'Yours, mine, Dennis's, Sheila's or Ruth's?' Hughes crumpled a piece of paper, then rolled it between his palms.

'Certainly not yours.'

'No?' Hughes tossed the paper ball over the back of the settee.

Sheila opened the door and looked in, Hughes frowning in surprise. 'I'm going. Everything okay?'

'How did you get there?' Hughes asked, baffled. 'And where's Scrubbs?'

'He's outside. He's going to walk me home. And I popped out through the kitchen and backdoor, and came back in the front. Didn't think I was hiding behind the couch, did you?'

'Catch up with you later,' Hughes promised, his tone menacing.

The door left ajar, Alice was about to follow. 'Not yet,' Hughes directed. 'Not finished with you yet, or

that dress. There's a pair of handcuffs in that drawer.
Put them on. Hands behind your back.'

'And if I refuse?'

'I'll stand you next to Ruth O'Leary and strap your
bare arse before the whole Hope contingent.'

Chapter 5

Alice gathered her wits. She fought the effects of excess
alcohol and withdrawal to seek lucidity, and rational
argument. 'You're like Jekyll and Hyde,' she accused.
'I never know which one I'm talking to. Why did you
do that with Dennis? Why did you humiliate me like
that?'

'You suffer from a clash of character,' Hughes
replied. 'Probably more Jekyll and Hyde than you
realise.'

'Hang on a minute,' Alice protested.

Hughes held a hand up. 'Listen, I'm not criticising.
There are two sides to Alice Hussey. The proud and
independent individual. On the other?' Hughes winked.
'A tramp tending toward slut, who desires being treated
like a slave.'

Alice coloured.

'It's true, Alice. Don't try and deny it. You love it.
The subservient cap fits perfectly. I could tie you or put
you on a leash. Maybe chain you to a post. A very
public post. Maybe naked. Maybe freshly whipped. And
what would we find? Miss Hussey wet between the
legs.'

'I'm not...'

'Course you are, girl. No one's blaming you. It's the
way you're made. You just need to recognise and utilise
that part of yourself for your own enjoyment. For your

own sanity. Two sides, Alice. Play them both. Learn to be one and then the other. Keep the proud Alice for your work and daily routine, and use the submissive to ease the sexual tension, even to make yourself a little rich. Do you understand what I'm getting at?'

Alice smiled and nodded. 'Yes, I do. But I have to say you don't know me. You think you do but you don't. At times you're an arrogant shit, and right now is one of them.'

Sheila tossed her keys onto the kitchen table. 'So, Geoff was a bit of a wild bird during the war.'

'It made lunatics and nutters by the thousand. Geoff was no different to hundreds of others.'

'Do you like him?'

'Did, yes. Now? Times change. I've changed. Geoff's changed.'

'Did he shock you tonight, that business with Alice?'

Scrubbs smiled. 'Surprised me. Didn't shock, though. Past shocks I am, see.' He thrust hands into pockets. 'Damned pretty girl though.' Awkward, the man smiled. 'You too, Sheila. You're pretty too.'

'You don't have to say that, Dennis.'

'No, I mean it.' Scrubbs paused, thought, concentrated for a few seconds, then asked, 'Did Geoff give her a hiding before that?'

'Why do you ask?'

'I couldn't help overhearing.'

Sheila pulled a face. 'What can I say?'

'Her arse was a peculiar colour, too.'

'You...?'

'The scream. I didn't know she wasn't wearing any knickers. Just trying to do the right thing, you know. What'd she do?'

'Best ask Geoff.'

'Always was a bit sadistic, was Geoffrey.'

88

'How?'

'You name it. Tarts in Paris; punished them for fraternisation. Tarts in Belgium; the same. Then there was Holland. Didn't restrict himself to tarts, either. And when we went over the Rhine? Well that was the enemy, wasn't it?'

'What did he do?' Sheila pushed, curious.

'Worst? He tied some Fräulein to a clothes line post in the snow. He stripped her and whipped her, in front of the squad. Poor bitch.'

'Did he, you know, after?'

Dennis chuckled. 'Oh yes. We all did. All eleven of us. We gave her the fuck of a lifetime.'

Shocked, Sheila asked, 'You...?'

'No, don't be bloody silly. She was a fraterniser. A bleeding tart. A few deutschmarks, chocolate and fags and she would have sold her soul to the devil. Geoffrey did it right. He bought her, we had her, and then he punished her.'

'You condone what he did?'

'You think me bad?'

'I'm not a judge, Dennis.'

'Yes, I'd say the bitch got what she deserved.'

'I think you're in need of another drink, Alice. Gin or vodka?'

'No thank you.'

'I insist. Cigarette?'

'Release me and I will.'

'Ask me nicely.'

Thunder rolled across her eyes. 'Please release me.'

Hughes filled a glass with vodka. 'If you'd chosen diplomacy instead of being so righteously candid I wouldn't have to, would I? Now beg.'

'No. I'm no whimpering dog. I'll go without.'

Hughes lit one of the cigarettes and inhaled. 'You

89

didn't smoke when you came here. What changed?'

'I did.'

'You think you changed. This worldly, hard-faced strumpet is a façade. Beneath still lies the uncertain Alice Rose Hussey. Sweet, innocent and maudlin.'

'Not any more.'

Hughes grunted. 'Don't kid yourself. You've a long road to becoming a woman, let alone an adult with adult tastes. If you were to move on, another world, you'd immediately become that naïve girl that walked though those gates not so long ago. You would revert because you can't face who you really are. Least here you know the devil. At least at the Hope I have your welfare at heart. Out there who knows what trap you might walk into?' Hughes advanced. He put the cigarette to her lips. 'You need me, young lady.'

Alice dragged on the cork tip, then the smoke she blew into Hughes' face. 'And you, *sir*, are a self-righteous bully.'

Hughes held the glass to her lips. 'Ain't that the case. Drink.'

Alice sipped, Hughes tilting the glass. Neat vodka ran down her chin, dripping into her cleavage. 'Don't worry,' Hughes teased, 'I'll lick it off.'

She managed little of the glass, the spirit firing her belly, alcohol ravaging resolve. Hughes wiped the excess from her face with a handkerchief. 'I promised you the prison strap, I believe.' Alice glared. 'Tell me; would that change anything?'

'I don't follow you.'

'If I pulverise your backside will it stop you sleeping with Ruth, or Sheila, come to that?'

She shrugged, the effects of the vodka snowballing. 'I probably won't sleep with her again anyway. That shouldn't have happened. Sheila shouldn't have happened. It was... oh, I don't know. Misdirected, I suppose.'

'Before we go any further, I want you to appreciate just what is at stake.' Hughes picked up the strap. 'Now bend over, Alice. One to each cheek.'

Knowing there was no point in argument she did as ordered, her balance fragile. Hughes held the leather to her left haunch, Alice aware of its departure. It returned in full flight, annihilating all in its path. A blazing fury immediately followed the mighty crack, the blitzed buttock scalded beyond belief. Hughes offered no time for acquaintance. That hostile leather pulverised the right buttock. Alice straightened, cuffed hands rubbing at the sickening smart.

'Imagine twenty of those. I don't believe even you could stomach that.'

'W-what's the alternative?' she asked, sceptical. 'Your cock between my legs?'

'Ooch! That tongue has barbs. You're a shrew in the making. No, it's not your cunt I want.' He smiled calculatingly. 'Not yet.'

'Then, what…?'

'But you're not like him?' Sheila asked, thinking maybe he was.

Dennis shrugged. 'War makes one a bit indifferent. A whipped body is no more horrendous than a bullet-ridden one.'

'Was it sexual?'

'Now you're getting into personal.'

'I have taken the Hippocratic oath. I ask purely from a medical point.'

'Shame. There I was thinking you might be interested in my sexual bias as a woman.'

'Then you do have one?'

'What? A penis?'

Sheila laughed. 'A bias.'

91

Dennis's aura changed. The polite, unsung act evaporated. Sheila faced the confident seducer. 'Oh, I have a bias all right.' Dark brown eyes levelled passion. 'A disposition toward good-looking blondes, with certificates framed and pinned on the wall.'

'Now you're making me feel uncomfortable.'

Dennis moved closer, unrecognised pheromones bombarded her senses. He leant forward and sniffed. 'I smell fear. Fear of losing control, of loosing the reins. You're a single woman, aren't you, Sheila? You're not spoken for, though I can't understand why not.'

'That has very little to do with it.'

'Too soon? Don't know Dennis Scrubbs? Will I use you?'

Sheila stared into the man's eyes. 'None of that bothers me. Do I want to? That's all that comes into the equation.'

'Do you?'

'Answer my question and I'll answer yours.'

'Yes, I got a hard-on watching that bitch tied and stripped. My bollocks fair tingled seeing that dress torn from her body, with her arms above her bead, her back and arse soft, inviting and naked. A superb bit of tit, too. And I thought: I hope Geoffrey whips that tit. And when Geoffrey did whip that tit, even though I'd been up that Fräulein's skirt, I got even more turned on.'

The heat of sexual tension, of uncertainty, emanated from both. Their bodies gave to the aroused state of excessive warmth and an undue appeal.

'If I wanted something a bit different…?' Sheila enquired.

'Like some of what Alice got?'

The woman sighed. 'That might do for the aperitif.'

'I work wonders with a simple kitchen stool and a length of rope.'

Sheila's belly did a double flip. 'And how would you

feel about caning a girl in school uniform?'

'You have such?' Her expression answered him. 'Make it a date. Now, do I have to ask permission to take down her panties?'

Sheila pressed fingers to her groin. 'I wouldn't have thought so.'

'I want to witness a devout Christian seek forgiveness from her God. Not through an intermediary.' He wagged a finger. 'No, through direct communication.'

Alice sank in the mists of a Russian-brewed blur. He rested his chin on her naked shoulder. 'No priest to bleed your heart. Tell me, Alice, how would you repent?'

She refused an answer.

'Sisters of mercy down the ages. How did they pay their master? What trick did they do for him? What service did they supply to keep their God happy?'

'You want me to say self-flagellation, don't you?'

'Ha! There is somebody at home! Yes, well done, Alice. Self-flagellation. Punish yourself and I will not have to do it for you.'

The drunken mind, a haven for self-recrimination and disorderly thought. Alcohol had laid her psyche defenceless. Ghouls and phantoms could tempt, persuade and trick her without fear of recognition. They flitted, infiltrated, advised and cajoled. *'Rise above this iniquity.'*

'Show your pious defiance. Cleanse the body, drive out the chimera.'

'Penance, Hussey. True monastic reverential reparation. Scourge the flesh. Pain and humiliate the body and mind. Show God you're still his disciple.'

'Why serve? Why suffer humiliation? Unless the reward begets satisfaction.'

'A thousand cuts will not absolve your sins, Hussey.'

'*Look at him.*'

'*Look at Hughes.*

'*See how he thirsts. See his weakness. He hangs on your sexual manoeuvres. There is your power over him.*'

The thump of implement striking the table stirred Alice from that babble of obsession. Two hefty fifteen-inch tails attached to a nine-inch plaited handle lay before her. The pliable time-worn leather tapered from an inch in diameter to three eighths. Something stirred, through the haze of inebriation an idea rippled and aroused.

'Well, Alice, what's it to be?' Hughes pressed.

'What terms?' she mumbled.

Hughes laid a hand to the strap. 'You keep me entertained, or I will take over with this.'

'Entertained? You want a show?'

'I want to be educated, Alice. I want to know what true God-fearing penance is.'

'You'll have to free my hands.'

Freed, Alice held the quirt, leather handle squeezed in a fist. Bleary-eyed she studied the tails, stout and identical in every aspect: weight, thickness and *cutting power*.

Hughes settled. Legs crossed he idled in an armchair, happy to let Alice take her time and looking forward to her inevitable pain and humiliation.

Thoughts, suggestions ebbed and flowed. Crude images flashed and departed. Lurid notions spilled and multiplied. Her exposed skin seethed, flesh cool, prickling with expectation. Her breathing slowed, her focus concentrated. Her pulse hammered, heart thumping ponderously.

Sex gate-crashed a questionable equation. Intense green eyes settled on Hughes' mighty shaft, the man flagrantly coaxing his cock to full strength. He winked, unmoved by her moral discomfort.

Sheila bent double, supported by a bar stool. Her wrists were taped to a crossbar, her ankles to the legs. A rope passed around her lower back and the seat, biting into the flesh, pinning her, pushing her backside up.

Words remembered from the not-so-distant past bolstered her confidence. *'You, Ali, are all woman. To be perfectly honest, too much woman. You inspire a passion that places me on the edge of insanity. Fucking you will never be enough.'*

Alice reached behind, fingers locating the short zip above her buttocks. *'You have it in you to crush the pathetic creature. You have the tools and the power. Play your game well, and 'it' will be putty in your hands.'*

She lowered the cups from those consummate breasts, inched the dress over her hips, body bending, breasts tantalising. She kept her eyes fixed on Hughes, the look noncommittal, questioning. In return his fingers squeezed the head of his penis.

She straightened, posed almost naked in the pool of her dress, the adopted stance from another time. Clarity expelled the fog of intoxication, an insatiable urge to reap sweet revenge dominating. She blanked him, ignored his existence. She could never wreak the effect she had in mind while conscious of his all-consuming gaze. Modesty would contaminate the fragile conviction she rode. Her mask would slip, and another catastrophe would follow.

She ground a decade and a half of doing the right thing into an uneasy limbo, thereby sanctioning the emergence of the promiscuous Alice. She allowed those nagging spectres a free rein. Hughes would have his performance, and she? Sexual independence.

Alice turned her back on him, her left arm lifted, hand

settled on her head. She utilised every shred of potential with her right, tails lashing around her hip, slapping both buttocks, thongs stinging flesh.

She switched hands, right arm raised, left powering the quirt. Again those dense tails bit, the smart positive but tolerable. She persevered, the lash drawing marks, her buttocks slowly warmed. Hughes crept into her thoughts alongside doubt. How long would he permit her pathetic attempts?

Hughes savoured the game. Amused by her frustrated attempts at self-flagellation he permitted her longer than he normally would. The numerous brandies and the satisfaction supplied by the girl's quivering bottom kept him happy for some while. Her buttock flesh succumbed to the continued whipping, that elusive glow triggered, the ecstatic heat penetrating ever deeper.

When Hughes finally seized her wrist she had descended into a dream world, pleasure the sole commodity. Snatched from that trance she faced the ugly monster of uncertain reality. Hughes smiled. 'Expecting the crack of strap on arse, were we?'

'Sorry,' she mumbled, unable to look him in the face. 'I got carried away.'

He took the quirt from her grasp. 'Those reverend sisters knew penance could not be attained by whipping their own hides. That's why they had another do it for them. Humility, they called it. Humbling themselves before another, suffering the humiliation and pain laid on by another's hand.'

He chuckled. 'Of course that was bollocks. That was all subterfuge. And none ever challenged them, because it was communal subterfuge.'

He draped the tails on Alice's back. 'Now those humble sisters had other parts of the anatomy to abuse. Parts that would indeed offer excruciating pain.' He ran the whip the length of her back, twitched it alongside a breast. 'Try it, Alice. See if that sexual euphoria is as forthcoming with your back and tits fired.'

Alice blushed. Hughes stabbed a finger at her. 'Spoilt your game, have I? I guess I was supposed to be mesmerised by your beauty and sexuality. I wasn't supposed to notice, was I? Fucking nuisance, aren't I?'

Scrubbs sighed at the cock-jerking apparition; Sheila Doodney in white blouse, tie, and navy pleated skirt halfway up her thighs. Dark brown stockings cloaked her legs, black tops encircling her thighs.

She posed before Dennis, head bowed, hands behind her back. 'What am I to expect?' she asked demurely, attempting a lead.

Scrubbs eyed the cane on the table. In his mind's eye rattan met with yielding bottom flesh. He imagined the shriek of speeding missile and the thump of striking cane. No pretending. No wet dream. Reality.

The swelling in Scrubbs' trousers occupied Sheila, a prominence that defied probability, a glans that pushed aside the waistband. Her imagination conjured the finality of their assignation, Sheila weak with anticipation.

'What do you want?' she asked, tired. 'If you want me,' Alice paused, 'then let's do it. You were right back in the shower, therefore I surrender. Fuck me if you must.'

Hughes held his face an inch from Alice's, studying her, reading her eyes. 'Windows to the soul,' he remarked. 'White soul? Black soul? I think a grey soul. I don't want your cunt, yet. I will take that when your soul is as black as Satan's heart. We will understand one another fully by then. Then there will be no inhibitions. Then you will commit any act, no matter how filthy and degrading it might seem now.'

He straightened. 'Right now, I will be your right and

left arms. You tell me where to lay the lash and I will do it. But remember, Alice, I might prefer blitzing your lovely arse with the strap. Once I make that decision there will be no change of heart. Eighteen straight from your worst nightmare...

'Well,' he asked, whip held in front of her face, 'might I suggest we finish off the rump?'

Alice bent forward, hands resting on the table.

'You call it. And don't be shy, Alice. You tell me if it's not hard enough.'

She knew he wouldn't hold back, and no matter how much it stung she would have to demand a more stringent cut. She filled her lungs and hissed, 'One.'

Those thongs seemed to rent the air, the pair having bitten and passed in a fraction of a brutal second. The *thunk* of leather blasting naked flesh was lost in a heartbeat. The sickening detonation and ensuing inferno lasted a whole lot longer. Mind and body, lost in that sea of hurt, could offer no immediate response.

'Sorry?' Hughes said. 'I didn't catch that. Did you call two, Alice?' She shook her head. 'I didn't realise you wanted a coffee break in between.'

Defeating the man was a dream. Getting the better of him a delusion. Alice laid her front on the table, her legs parted. 'For God's sake do it. Get it over with. Fuck me.'

Quirt tails slashed her left buttock in reply, her right heaving to a hefty swipe seconds later. Alice gripped the table edge, face screwed in pain. With no respite her left cheek lurched again, followed by the right. Alice shrieked, Hughes laying a seemingly endless fusillade of lashes, her buttocks quivering with double stripe after stripe after stripe.

At eighteen he tossed the whip onto the table, the girl's buttocks torched, the flesh raging. Alice sank to her knees, face buried in her hands, her bottom smothered in flame-red welts.

'You had something in mind tonight, Alice. What was it?'

'To seduce you,' she answered, honestly and without hesitation.

'And?'

'To deny you.'

'Your seduction was working. A more experienced woman might have succeeded. Still, give it a few more months and you'll have that experience.'

Alice ran a hand over a buttock, gauging the extent of those raw stripes. 'You know something?'

'I know you.'

'When one lives in a madhouse it's almost impossible to remain sane.'

'Is that what you think? Perhaps it's hereditary madness. Like mother like daughter, eh?'

'I assume Sheila told you.'

'Does it matter?'

'I suppose not.'

Hughes took a fistful of Alice's hair and lifted her to her feet. 'New game.'

Jaded, Alice sighed, 'What now?'

Sheila folded to the stool. Ankles secured to the legs, wrists tied to a crossbar. Dennis took time to enjoy her alluring stance; the climb of sloping legs, the float of skirt hem, inviting, provocative. An inch above that periphery lay the tight bands of stocking tops, and then the white of her thighs.

Crisp starched cotton clung to her back, the pink of her flesh expressive, the band of bra strap absent. Bondage suited her, pleading eyes, the wet of fresh tears marking her cheeks. Lips parted in dread, the white of teeth catching the light.

Dennis ran the cane over her back, her body

trembling. He passed it over the waiting rump, the tip then slipped beneath the hem. Slowly he lifted, drinking of the gradual revelation. Sheer black panties edged in lace emerged, the woman's buttocks clearly visible.

Scrubbs pressed the rod into that supple flesh. Sheila took a deep breath. She longed for the best he could deliver. Dennis, unknown quantity, could choose any option, and there the excitement blew its fanfare.

Realisation lit Hughes' expression. 'She was here, wasn't she?'

'Who?'

'Rose. She was a patient of the old Hope Sanatorium. That's what brought you here.'

'What do you think you know?' Alice demanded, her guard up.

'Let me say, Alice, that I came here before rebuilding. I oversaw the prison project and conversion. Shameful what the medical profession left behind.'

Alice's heart missed a beat. 'If you know something, anything at all about my mother, then you have to tell me.'

'Your surname. It drove me to distraction. Hussey, I kept saying to myself. It rang such a tantalising bell. Then the penny dropped. It *has* been eight years. You'd easily recognise your mother, Alice. She is you.'

'You're being cruel.'

'Am I?'

'You're making it up.'

'Was she blown to pieces in forty-two, that is the question?'

Alice paled. 'If you know the answer, and there's one bit of decency left in you, then you have to tell me.'

'Decency? In me? I think not. Tell you what, Hussey. Amuse me. Whip yourself where it really hurts. Toss that holier-than-thou halo in the gutter and whore for me. Play with yourself. Crawl on your hands and knees…

'Tell you what. You can be my pet bitch tomorrow. I can stroke and pet you and smack you when you disobey.' He smirked. 'Which will be often, if you want to know about your mother.'

'And if I do all that, you'll tell me what?'

'I will tell you if your dear sweet mother is dead or alive.'

'And after tomorrow?'

'Another piece of information. Maybe.'

'If she's dead there won't be any more.'

'No? Case notes. I was up half of last night genning myself up. I mean, you'd like to know where she might be buried, wouldn't you?'

'Where does that leave me regards the offer you made?'

'It's still there. But for that you'll serve the Hope. For your mother, you'll serve me.'

Bum approaching a shade of cherry, flesh hot and wonderfully stung, Sheila chased that insatiable hunger. Sexual energy pulsated, her body aching for the cut and slash of rod, and the penetration of his huge cock.

Dennis flogged her with an unparalleled enthusiasm. Bottom bared, panties around her thighs, he struck a rapturous tune on those captive cheeks. Orgasm hovered close, every hearty thwack edging it nearer. His cock haunted: just how big? His cock would follow the flagellation, would bring about the consummation of a highly satisfying association. Only the speed of their union bothered her. Recrimination settled, guilt rubbing shoulders with aspiration.

Alice poured another vodka, which she downed in several gulps. She cut and lit a cigar, the smoke held in a corner of her mouth. Without a word she donned Hughes' trilby, tipping the hat forward, the brim masking her eyes.

Puffing smoke she gripped the whip, wrapping the thongs around a fist. Steps slow and deliberate, high heels tapping, she sashayed toward him. Tails loosed, she held the whip at arm's length, then without so much as a facial twitch she lashed a breast.

Hughes watched, the stroke stirring his penis, advancing his belief that he had her where he wanted her.

The redhead followed it with another, her breast lurching, painfully stung. She switched hands and lashed the other with two savage strokes. Hughes considered the coloration and stinging welts, the continuation beyond that delectable breast flesh, leather having drawn hoops on her upper arm.

Determined, undaunted, Alice lowered her aim, thongs biting her groin and upper thigh. Only four feet separated them. Hughes slouched, nonchalantly playing with his erection while Alice endeavoured to please. Heavy tails slashed her belly, thighs and groin, her body quickly ravaged by those dispassionate strokes.

She expected a change of tune, a directive. She thought Hughes would take control. She hovered close to her limit of endurance, but Hughes frustratingly refrained from interference. He cared little about her suffering or marks, so long as they were impermanent. He played the long-term game, his sway slowly prevailing, Alice's grip on reality slipping.

Legs parted with purpose Alice swung those thongs, leather stinging vagina and buttocks beyond. Several she applied before catching the tails behind. Her mask of indifference yielded to one of sexual heat. Her eyes smouldered. Her lips pouted. He watched her blatant sexual manoeuvres, the slide of whip's tails between her legs stiffening his cock inconceivably. She increased the pressure, leather biting into her pubic mound, sinking between vaginal lips.

Hot ash fell from the cigar, scorching a breast. Smoke drifted, her eyes reacting, filling with tears. Alice coughed, the plot lost.

Busy wiping away the tears she failed to see Hughes rise. Within a heartbeat he turned her, pushed her over the table and knocked her legs apart. His hands held her down, breasts flattened to the polished wood. Barely daring to breathe Alice hung on tenterhooks.

'Fucking useless,' he derided, then moved forward, trousers brushing the backs of her legs, his erection sliding the length of her vaginal slit. 'I thought the booze might loosen you up. Knock a few of those inhibitions for six.' He flexed his crotch muscles, his shaft jerking. 'Now I'm thinking you're no good to me.'

'I did what you asked of me,' she gasped.

'I'm thinking about what happens next.'

'If sex is the price for knowing where my mother is, then yes, I'll pay.'

'You'll pay,' he scoffed. 'You'll fucking pay.' He pressed the head of his cock against her wet lips, parting them, stretching that portal. 'I take what I want here. No one pays. Who the fuck do you think you are, Hussey? You're a pretty face. You're a shapely bit of shag. But to me you're still only arse, tits and a hole or three.'

'You're not going to tell me, are you? You're going to use what you've got to keep on blackmailing me into doing disgusting things.'

Hughes pulled her arms behind her back, tying her hands together with the whip tails; one loop about each wrist with each tail, and then pulled tight. The ends he knotted several times.

'I have no intention of blackmailing you, Alice.' He pulled her head back by her hair, forced his tie between

103

her lips and knotted it at the back of her head.

'I want you to be like Sheila. I don't have to cajole or threaten her. She does whatever, without prompt or persuasion. Want to know what she's doing now?' he whispered.

Released from her bonds, panties around her knees, Sheila readily embraced enterprising Scrubbs.

Alice shrugged.

'She'll be talking to Dennis.'

Body rubbed vigorously against body, Sheila taking the initiative. Lips pressured lips, mouths working zealously.

'She'll be getting to know him better.'

Blouse buttons loosed, flies broached, unfamiliar hands manoeuvred and titillated.

Hughes settled his hands about her waist. 'Sheila is dedicated.'

Passion elevated, enthusiasm kicked down the doors of restraint. Cock tugged from Dennis's pants, Sheila fell to her knees.

Hughes leant forward, sliding his hands over her hips and down the warm soft valley to her sex mound. 'I can trust her to meet the call of duty, regardless of personal hardship.'

Scalp grasped by Scrubbs' fingers, hair tousled and untidy, Sheila drew back the foreskin, red painted lips poised, waiting.

Hughes massaged her pubis. He flexed his cock. 'Could I trust you?'

Her wet tongue glided its length, balls flipped from their nest hung ready for devouring.

Hands retreated, his length pulled free. 'By the end of the week Dennis will be eating out of her hand.'

Sheila's world turned upside-down. Mouth filled with penis she eyed those hirsute balls still moist with her saliva. Strong arms supported her, held her close to his

104

body. Her legs divided about his head, black mesh-clad limbs wavering skyward. Dennis's face was wedged between them, damp thighs against his cheeks, mouth suckling her fanny, his tongue raked the soft pink inner.

Alice bit, the tie offering little substance. She grimaced as Hughes' bulging dome forced open her anus, and sank rapidly within. He stroked her bottom cheeks, scrutinising the welts. 'You know what I'm going to do?' he asked.

Alice laid her flushed cheek to the table, the pain in her rear finally subsiding.

He withdrew slowly. 'After I've fucked your arse, I mean. I'm going to take you back to the dorms, just as you are.'

He thrust. Alice whimpered.

'Naked except for your suspender belt and stockings.' A rapid withdrawal executed, he sank again. 'Except I'll add a collar and chain. I'll chain you to a locker at the end of Ruth's dorm. A lesson to all those girls.' He sped up, his cock ploughing in and out, the tight circle of anus about his shaft entrancing. 'The humiliation will do you good, Alice. It will teach you your place in the structure of things.'

Her whipped buttocks shivered to his exertions. The crude image of Hughes' swinging balls flashed through her mind.

'Subjugated, Alice. Dominated. I think that's your vice. Having your arse or mouth fucked is precisely your cup of tea. A *normal* fuck would be too run of the mill for you.'

Cock plummeting, his features tensed. 'I'll lay a wager on one matter, Alice. I bet there's a wet oasis between your legs right now.'

Her lips and chin covered in sperm, Dennis dropped Sheila onto the bed. She hoisted her skirt above her hips and parted her legs. Scrubbs fell between, her calves draped over his shoulders. Nine inches of erection slid into her cunt, the woman's back arching with the ecstasy of it.

A tear welled and fell. The pain had gone; it was his words – his vindictive words. He knew her like no one had ever known her before. She was wet – very wet. Minor orgasms had crept insidiously, surprising her again and again.

A tide rose, swamping her loins. Sheila cried with the pleasure, explosive energy blasting her insides.

Worse was his threat. Or promise. Collar and leash, and left in Ruth's dormitory, the laughing stock of the Hope. They would all see her whipped body. They would probably think Hughes did it. They would probably think…

Hughes ejaculated. His cock lurching in spasm, the man grunted. 'Are you there yet? Have you worked out the deception?'

Alice nodded.

'See, everyone's happy, aren't they? You've had a good night, and I'll let you know about mummy in the morning. The girls will believe I whipped you for cavorting with Ruth, ergo, justice done. And Miss O'Leary will take her twenty strokes at breakfast tomorrow.'

He buttoned his penis away. 'But more to the point, you are beginning to comprehend your bias. You are beginning to see that the lower you sink, the more satisfying our excesses become. Have no fear about loss of face. Dennis will be taking the dorms over as from tomorrow. You, Alice; I have plans for you. Learn a valuable lesson tonight. Think on tomorrow. And plan your proud exodus.'

Chapter 6

Breakfast saw the full complement unusually quiet, no one daring to act or say a word out of place. Ruth braved the porridge, hoping to give that important air of nonchalance. Alice leaned against the wall clutching her stomach, desperate to keep the meagre contents down.

'Ruth O'Leary,' Hughes abruptly hailed. 'Ten minutes of your time, if you please.'

Every eye followed the unenviable girl as she stepped forward, ramrod straight, head held high. Every sympathetic, anxious and roused inmate watched disquieted as she slipped her panties from beneath the pinafore, their inauspicious slide to polished shoes focussing every mind.

Hughes lifted an eyebrow in contemptuous response to Ruth's quizzical expression. She bent, doubled, fingertips reaching for toecaps. All remained riveted on that cloth-covered bottom, the rounded feminine lines and depression of cleft suggestive of what lay beneath.

Hem lifted, Hughes unveiled the pale flesh of her buttocks. He scrutinised the stance, her legs perfectly straight. With a firm hand he pushed her down further, tightening the taut, flexing cheeks soon to be slaughtered. Silence oppressive, Hughes, circled the girl, weapon slung from a fist.

All watched, enthralled. Hughes wallowed in the limelight, relished the power; waxed on her agony like a vampire suckling the blood of an unfortunate. A gasp heralded the strap's downward arc, a blur of limb and leather. None saw the implement strike. All heard the pronounced crack of weapon on tender flesh. Empathy flowed, many having suffered similar.

Assertive and in no hurry the principal levied a second. The opposite cheek gave before the force, the smack prolific. Some winced instinctively, but Ruth uttered no sound.

Alice experienced a torturous twist of envy, the detonations lighting Ruth's backside, effecting an interesting sensation in her own.

The sixth pushed O'Leary forward, her buttocks reddened, flesh stung. Ruth stepped back, resumed the pose, Hughes taking immediate advantage.

By ten Ruth's bottom had surpassed crimson, beaten to a mauvish hue. A thumb surreptitiously scratched, comforted an irrational itch. Hand pressed to a thigh, Alice met the tease, through her dress, against her clitoris. She visualised herself there, in Ruth's place, the prospect further vitalising her sex.

The principal glanced her way. Alice shrank before his sardonic gaze. Shame and self-contempt welled. Head dipped she chanced a look, large green eyes credulous. Hughes had resumed the slaughter.

Ruth showed her mettle, the attendance uncomprehending. Those buttocks took savage stroke after stroke. Alice tried to distract herself from the insatiable craving.

Another set of eyes wandered the assembly, assessing and undressing. He had set his cap the night before, gorged himself, realising a dream, fulfilling a fantasy. Enthusiasm fired, aspirations set loose, he searched for his next lamb…

'Alice.' The girl jumped. 'Sorry, I didn't mean to startle you.'

'I didn't notice you behind me, Mr Scrubbs.'

'Dennis, please.'

Leather slammed into lambasted bottom for the last time. Ruth slowly straightened, unable to mask her discomfort. The slide of her skirt gradually eclipsed that massacred rump.

'Savage, isn't it?' Alice said, unsettled.

Dennis thought for a moment. 'I suppose the powers to be would say corporal punishment, for the reason it is administered, must prove insufferable if only to serve its purpose.'

'To beat a girl's backside black and blue?'

'It's correction,' Scrubbs countered. 'And it's discouragement.'

'That won't deter Ruth. As soon as her bottom's returned to normal she'll be at it again.'

'At what again?'

Alice gazed at the man suspiciously. He probably knew Ruth was beaten for sleeping with her. 'Ruth is incorrigible. She's been caned more times than anyone else. She seems immune to physical punishment.'

'So what do you suggest?'

Alice shrugged. 'She needs to learn a trade, not be subjugated.'

'Prison is supposed to be harsh. It puts them off coming back.'

'By that, I assume you don't countenance change?'

'I think your dictionary is bigger than mine.'

Hughes interrupted the conversation. He slipped an arm around Alice's waist, and smiling at Dennis, guided her away.

'Who released you?' he asked, the question a camouflaged demand.

Alice shrugged. 'So it happened then?'

He squeezed her, fingers delving her flesh. 'Why, have you doubts?'

'I was drunk. I'm not sure what was dreams and what wasn't.'

'Okay, who did you dream set you free?'

Alice smiled. 'You, of course. You led her out of there, the bridled bitch, nearly as naked as the day she was born, her bum smothered in whip welts.'

'Not only her bum, I seem to recall.'

'No, her tits and fanny too.'

'Was there any more to this dream?'

'Only the sex.'

Hughes' smile evaporated. 'When you say sex, I assume you mean anal?'

Alice shook her head. 'No. Normal sex.'

'By me?'

'Not sure. That's a bit hazy. You were there... oh, I can't remember. No, Mr Preesal was on the floor.'

'Mr Preesal had you on the floor?'

'No. He was there, I said, in residence. This is weird. Sheila turned up, too. I do believe it was Mr Scrubbs. Mad, mad dream.'

Disconcerted, Hughes agreed. 'Dreams usually are.'

'My mother?'

'What about her?'

'Dead or alive?'

'You haven't earned that information yet.'

'Tell me if my mother's alive, please.'

Hughes smirked, unsympathetic.

'Tell me or I'll stir up one hell of a hornet's nest.'

'Threats?'

'How about if I run out of here stark naked and down Flint High Street, screaming all the way?'

Hughes thought for a moment, then his smile gave to a grin. 'She's alive. Or at least she was when she left here.'

'Thank you. That's all I needed to know.'

'And the poor residents of Flint?'

Alice shrugged. 'They're reprieved.'

'Last night, I might have acted a little over-enthusiastically.'

'And?' Alice waited on the punch-line.

Hughes seemed uncomfortable. 'For that I apologise. I have no excuse.' He settled his gaze back on Alice. 'But it will no doubt happen again. Mixed, our chemistries seem explosive. Move your possessions to my house. Dennis will take over the dormitories as from today.'

'I don't think that's a good idea,' Alice mooted, as much to see his reaction as to inform him how she felt.

'You don't trust me?'

'It's your plans I don't trust.'

'Okay, so what would you suggest?'

'Mr Scrubbs takes over Pierce's old room and I keep mine.'

'But I don't trust you, Alice. I can't count on you to stay out of those girls' beds.'

'But Mr Scrubbs will be overseeing. Won't that be enough?'

Hughes thought for a moment. 'Fair enough. But you're not in charge. Scrubbs is. Stay away from the dormitories, and keep away from O'Leary. Is that clear?'

Alice allowed a smile to flicker, mischief twinkling. 'Or what, Mr Hughes?'

'I catch you in bed with that girl again…' he wagged a finger at the redhead, '…and I'll flay you alive.'

Chapter 7

The passing days neither scurried nor dawdled, autumn steadfastly ripping the life from nature. Mists crept eerily from mountain and sea, muting the world, intensifying the dark. Drizzle and damp took up a seemingly permanent residence, fences, lampposts and trees eternally dripping. Grey lead dominated the sky, eclipsing light and the sun's warmth, while winter marked its coming with the first northerly gale.

'Shut the door, Alice, I want a chat,' Hughes abruptly announced the following Friday evening.

'That sounds ominous,' she whispered, rising.

'I won't beat about the bush. Contract. Will you accept my word?'

Alice shook her head. 'Anyway, I've changed my mind. I don't want any part of your filthy trade in pornography.'

Hughes' eyes narrowed. 'Capricious, aren't we?'

'I see it as coming to my senses. I mean, it's not my welfare you're thinking of, is it?'

'Whatever became of that timorous mouse that waltzed in here only a few weeks ago?'

'You shouldn't answer with a question. You said that.'

'I want to make love to you with my tongue.'

Alice felt the floor move. 'I beg your pardon?'

'I want to tie you down, immobilise you, and drive you mad with my tongue, and *things*.'

'Things?'

'Mm, things,' Hughes confirmed.

'You know how to chat a girl up, don't you? What happened to the courting? The "I wonder if you might like to…"?'

'I can court you. I can wine and dine you.' Hughes grimaced. 'Perhaps we should miss the wine bit. Strange things happen when we're incapacitated.'

'Courting doesn't automatically lead to sex you know,' Alice pointed out. 'A girl can still say no.'

'Why would she say no? The pleasure would be immeasurable. A night of kinky passion, not knowing what will happen next. How could you resist?'

'Is that it? Is this the extent of the chat? Can I go now?'

'I hear things.'

'See the doctor. She can sort you out.'

'I hear whispers. I know this building well. Intimately, one might say. There's not a nook or cranny, crook or

112

fanny I don't know. I know you, Alice Rose Hussey. I know what stirs you, what lays suppressed deep inside that mind. You see it as a man trying to take advantage. I see us as a forging of kindred spirits, a natural union and progression to greater experimentation.'

Alice stood her ground. 'We loose our morals, drop all restraints, ignore those inhibitions and become animals.'

'We are animals, Alice. Not so many years ago I was nonchalantly killing my fellow human being. Soldiers took sordid advantage. German, Italian, Yank and English, we all did. We hung up the rulebook for five years. We did just what we pleased, and no one questioned our actions or condemned them.'

'And that's how quickly man can fall.' Alice opened the door. 'You can't always buy what you want. However, you'll find I will respond to the right approach.'

'Mother?'

Alice nodded.

'Soft or coarse rope?' Hughes probed.

'I have a preference for coarse.' She didn't look back.

Saturday delivered a freezing deluge. Heavy rain drove in from the northwest, stinging pellets lashing all before it. Alice watched the hurry and scurry of Flint's inhabitants, half-drowned through the onslaught. Her mind far off, she chewed endlessly on Hughes' words the night before.

A punishment meted out after breakfast aided and abetted those deliberations. One hapless inmate was despatched to walk the quad for a half-hour, before meeting with Scrubbs' demon rod. Soaked to the skin, with only a tight pair of white shorts between her chilled backside and his cane, she writhed before the overly aggressive assault.

Twelve wicked strokes pulverised those susceptible buttocks, provoking a dozen puffed and extremely tender tramlines. Dennis Scrubbs demonstrated a vindictive streak that morning, one that cooled the unpredictable temperament of those who witnessed his reaction to what he saw as impertinence.

As the twenty-year-old gripped and rubbed at that ignited rump, Alice fought an inner turmoil. The irrepressible and irrational urge to stand in those shoes, experience the indignity and scorch of twelve harsh strokes to her intimate flanks proved to be irresistible. Whatever madness consumed her at times, she could do little to ignore it. Hughes had inferred, almost promised her, another dip into that ecstatic world, and her bent demanded satiation. The girl's only problem was how to trigger such and still be able to hold her head up.

Having watched how Scrubbs levied that cane also set her to considering how to manipulate the man into punishing her. A direct request would most likely prompt a rapid and painful reply, but that was not in Alice's make-up. She could only allow herself to be punished for good reason, and pride rejected a contrived result.

The self-inflicted marks had faded to obscurity; Hughes' lashes mere ghosts of what was. Her bottom ached for the cut and dance of implement, her soul for the adrenaline rush of the uncertain.

A knock on the door dragged her from those mental gyrations. She opened it to find a smiling Hughes.

'Morning,' he snapped, stepping passed her.

'Morning,' she replied, wondering what prompted his visit.

'How is Alice on this miserable wet day?'

'Fine,' she answered, trying to read his intent.

'Not a lot one can do at the moment, is there? Bored, are we?'

114

That ardent passion she had been experiencing dwindled. Apprehension sneaked between the folds of scheming. 'No, not particularly,' she fended.

'I am.' He rammed hands in pockets. 'Bloody bored. Guess what I feel like doing.'

'No thanks.'

He pulled a face. 'Oh, go on, play the game. Guess.'

'It will either be shagging or whipping,' Alice ventured.

'Oh,' Hughes straightened, 'is that what you think of me?'

'To be honest, yes.'

'Actually I'm here to offer a bit more info on your dear old mum.'

Stunned, Alice swallowed. 'Really? What?' she asked eagerly.

'Payment first.'

'I was right, wasn't I?'

Hughes laughed. 'What if I was to tell you anyway? Could you find it in yourself to show some gratitude?'

'What if I said yes and then went back on my word?'

Hughes shrugged. 'We'll go there anyway, sooner or later. And I might just lose the file.'

'I told you I'd do just about anything for information, didn't I?'

'You did.'

'So tell me.'

'Your mother was transferred to a sanatorium in Yorkshire.'

'Is that it?'

'The shorter the piece of news, the more chances I get to play with you, Alice.' He grinned. 'Let's face it, as soon as you have enough you'll be off. That is not in my interest.'

'Tell me where and you can do what you like.'

Hughes rubbed his chin. He studied her carefully.

115

'The Wakefield, near Harrow.'

Alice experienced a ripple of exhilaration. 'Really?'

'Oh yes, Alice. Really.'

'Do you think she'll still be there?'

He shook his head. 'Doubtful.'

'Why?'

'The place was closed down two years later.'

Her heart sank. 'What now? How am I going to trace her?'

Hughes smirked. 'Well, I can help you there.'

'You can?'

'In time…'

Seductive polished wood met her explorative touch. Hard, not hostile. Cool, not cold. Stomach stirring, dark oak unsettled. Worn slats invited the press of soft warm tummy. Cedar-red leather restraints begged to wrap closely about jerking limbs, driven into the pale flesh of parted thighs. Pressuring the small of the back, compelling naked buttocks to stand proud and *so* vulnerable.

The clammy grip of anxious excitement wrapped its sensual coat about her body. Need fenced with purity. Scruples wilted, ethics collapsed before the irresistible onslaught of impetuous passion.

Memories that should have shocked and sickened with their return, conjured instead breathless possibilities. 'Oh God,' she whispered, knowing she *would* succumb, that she couldn't wait to surrender.

Hands drifted beneath her skirt, settled on slender thighs. Fingers intimidated, coaxed the flow of pussy juices. Her breath deserted gasping lungs as his touch ascended, glided expertly over roused upper thighs.

Lids veiled green eyes. Lips parted, pouted sexual. Her groin buzzed, his fingers there, playing through her panties.

116

'You smell of *come fuck me*,' he whispered close to her ear. 'Your body cries for lust, it begs for interference.' His lips nuzzled her neck. 'Tell me, Alice; tell me you don't want my erection snug inside your tight hole.'

'You talk of tongue and bring me cock.' Her hands settled on his, to guide them inside her panties. She pressed his finger to her vaginal slit. 'This demands oral satisfaction, not the tiresome thrust and grind of a lusting primate.'

Hughes chuckled. 'Lusting primate, eh? What of when I have you at my mercy? Tied so tight you can't move a muscle? Legs parted, nothing between your pussy and my primitive cock? What then?'

'You will act the gentleman, that's what. You'll honour my wishes.'

Hughes turned her, ripping her panties away as he did so. Arrogance met her disbelieving expression, fingers brazenly feeling between her legs. 'I will take what I want, Alice. And if that happens to be your cunt, then so be it.'

'Then the deal's off.'

'What about mamma?'

'I'll see proof first.'

Hughes pulled a face of resignation. 'Rose Hussey. Committed July twenty-eighth, nineteen-thirty-eight. Gave birth to Alice Rose, October twenty-eighth, nineteen-thirty-eight, at four-twenty a.m. You weighed in at seven pounds and six ounces. Father...' His feel moved to her bottom. 'Father? Bastard that you are, you must have one. Some primate must have thrust and ground dear mommy Rose, eh?'

'Don't pretend you know. Rose refused to tell anyone.'

'Do you know why she was here, Alice? Have you any inkling?'

117

'Some.'

'Her records make interesting reading. A very emancipated lady for her time. Tell you what, Alice. You keep me sweet until Christmas and I'll give you the lot. Everything I know.'

Alice pushed his hands from her hips. 'No.' She opened the implement cupboard and removed several lengths of coarse rope, which she tossed one by one to Hughes. 'Come Christmas you'll defer things. You'll say you weren't happy with my performance somewhere along the line.'

Hughes caught the coils. 'What do you propose then?'

He waited on her answer, the girl removing her shirt. 'How many pages in this file?'

Hughes shrugged. 'I haven't counted them.'

Alice discarded the blouse and reached behind to release the bra catch. 'How many?'

'About thirty,' he surmised, watching her breasts spring from the lace cups with youthful vibrancy. He slowly shook his head. 'They have to be the finest example of tits ever bestowed on a female.'

Alice ignored the crude praise. 'I will do a turn for each valid piece of information. Give me something I can verify, prove you're telling me the truth. Then I'll turn another trick for you. You call it, I'll do it. You can rope me, chain me, whip me, cane me, flog me with anything you choose, on any part of my body. I will suck your primate shaft. I will lick your balls. You can stuff my arse. But… but, you will keep your dick out of my vagina. Those are my terms.' Her skirt slid to the floor, presenting the consummate female.

He eyed her for some time, openly perusing her body, then snapped a length of rope between his fists. 'I'll tender my apology now, Miss Hussey. I know nothing other than uncouth and rough.'

Alice forced a smile. 'And that's how I suppose I

would prefer it.'

The whipping bench she found so irresistible supported Alice in another, perhaps more inspiring if arduous fashion. Her rump pressed to those distinctly uncomfortable slats, the individual bars embedding their lengths, etching her bottom flesh. Parted legs stretched, angled downwards, ankles pulled back and tied to the supporting framework. Worse, backbreaking, her torso hung from the other side, her wrists secured close to her ankles.

Hughes wore the mask of devout sadist, his intensity fevered. Lust controlled and stole all decency. Her crude position disturbed and provoked. Her vaginal fissure dominated. It seized and held his eye, bewitching, enticing, egging him on to commit the ultimate profligacy.

Hughes fondled his cock's dome, fingers probing cloth. Imagination invoked feeling, the sublime slide of hard shaft into that welcoming slit beckoned obsessively. Hughes ran a hand through lank hair. He liked to hear her cry, beg, plead for her honour. To relish her whimper as he fucked her, took what would consummate her defilement.

His hand settled on her mound, thumb draped decisive, dipping those vaginal petals, probing her sex. Buttons unfastened he eased his aching cock free.

'You know how I'd have my revenge?' Alice voiced, as if she read his mind. 'You take that without consent and I will separate your balls from your cock. Sooner or later,' she added.

Hughes knelt, her sex lips just before his face. 'You're a very sensual young woman,' he whispered, more to himself than Alice. 'You ooze sex from every pore. You're built to excite. You're made for fucking.'

Sinking his teeth into her pubic heights he added, garbled, 'You're made for hurting, too.'

The back strap pinned her by the belly. Hughes had drawn it ever tighter. Her buttocks were forced against the slats, corpulence pushed between, her backside corrugated. A coarse rope looped about the tarnished leather. Knotted directly beneath, it traversed the pubic mound then plummeted between her legs.

Alice stared mistily at her upturned world. Extraordinary sensations seized her, breaching all mental barriers. Her body felt alive, thrumming with sensual energy.

Hughes changed his mind, gagged her, stuffed her mouth with a rubber phallus, cords wound about that and her jaw, silencing her. Another he used below. The immensity of the thing filled her with trepidation. Its insertion, a screwing, thrusting motion, brought tears to her eyes... but the monstrosity satisfied with its stretching bulk.

She ached to witness the crude penetration of rope, the vulgar manner in which it sank between her sex lips. A prearranged knot provoked a pyrotechnical fanfare, her clitoris alternately bleating then careening toward rapturous heights.

Fingertips trundled across her belly, enlivening the flesh. The girl's libido approached screaming-pitch as they wandered over her flexed abdomen to stroke down toward her ribs. Expectation soared, anticipation roared, Alice's flesh erupting in goose bumps. Hughes teased; the hand departed before the expected grope of breasts.

He crouched. He smiled down on Alice's flushed countenance. 'Dilemma. I want to whip the fuck out of you, just as you are. I want to see that pure hide of yours crisscrossed with welts.'

Fear quivered through her body. That dark, twisted world beckoned.

Hughes settled a hand to one of her breasts. Gentle, the fingers toyed. 'But I have a mind to do far worse, to

120

torment you beyond your wildest dreams.'

Alice couldn't begin to conceive what he might have in mind.

'Back hurting yet?' he enquired sarcastically, and Alice nodded.

'How about we secure the parcel with sealing wax?' Alice frowned. 'Red sealing wax,' Hughes iterated. 'Then of course there's the soles of the feet.' His face brightened. 'And the palms of your hands.'

Horror mixed with confusion, the girl unsure.

'You look so inviting with a cock rammed in your mouth, Alice. How does it feel, miss-prim-and-proper-catholic-girl, to have your cunt filled with hard rubber? How did it feel to have it screwed into your hole?'

Alice detected the smell of savagery, the scent of unpredictability, Hughes approaching dangerous, the bonds of reason beginning to escape him, Alice frightened of his capability.

'How did it feel to be put on a collar and leash and chained up for the night, virtuous catholic girl? Was God there? Did he offer consolation? Did he spank the bad boy that done it?'

Hughes rose and unfastened his trousers. 'I fear not. There's you the religious believer, and me the unbeliever. There's you strapped to that bench with your back near busted, and me undoing my flies. Makes you wonder whose world it is. God's servant about to be miserably abused, or the anti-Christ about to sexually exploit the Almighty's disciple. Bolt of lightning?' Hughes gazed up. 'Can't see one coming.' His trousers fell to the floor, underpants following.

Alice gazed up at the man's stiff, horizontal cock, its seed sacks monuments to manhood. The warlock knew his witch. 'You see it,' he said, not caring to look her way. 'Deny it thrills you.' His shirt fell to the floor, the man naked except for his shoes and socks. 'You can't, can you? It's Catholicism that betrays, shackles willpower, throttles freedom of expression. Admit it, Alice, all you want, all you yearn for, lust for, is my cock, thrust deep between your legs.'

Hughes knelt. He held that impressive phallus against her cheek. 'It's in there.' He jabbed her forehead. 'Isn't it? You can see your cunt lips stretched tight around my cock, and it excites you.'

Hughes rubbed the head of his erection across her face. 'That mental picture stimulates you more than anything else, and yet you can't admit it. Not even to yourself. Why not, for fuck's sake?'

Alice could only stare back, eyes trying to tell him how much she loathed him, how much he turned her on.

'What's the worst I could do?' he goaded, Alice holding his stare. 'You've no idea what I'm thinking. What I'm planning.'

Then to Alice's surprise Hughes dressed, replacing trousers and shirt, his underwear discarded. 'Call it a benevolent arrangement; me being thoughtful. And, something I'm sure you'll appreciate wearing.'

Hughes opened the door, beckoning with a finger, and Alice struggled to witness who he summoned, her own body blocking the view. Hughes pushed the arrival forward, Alice's quixotic mood abruptly and cruelly shattered. Toppled from those enraptured heights and brutally aware of her outrageous exposure, the mortified girl cringed with shame. At that dreadful moment dying seemed like a good idea to Alice.

Sweet stopped and gazed stupidly at the redhead, the odd angle, the phallus rammed in the girl's mouth caused her to doubt who for a moment. Then disbelieving, shocked by the gross excess of Alice's predicament, she gazed at Hughes, expecting some form of explanation, failing to fully comprehend the one provided.

'I said I wanted two backsides, didn't I, Alice? Ruth has shown her mettle. Now it's Sweet's opportunity. It would seem the Hope has been infected. A cancer that I intend to eradicate before it spreads any further.'

Hughes seized Hazel by the back of her neck. Fingers dug painfully into the flesh, he steered the hapless girl to between Alice's parted legs. 'Do you deny, Sweet, that you performed an act of perversion with Ruth O'Leary?'

Alice expected a denial at the very least, a barrage of excuses and lies, perhaps. But Hazel spitting in Hughes' face she deemed an act of madness, a desire to commit suicide.

He wiped the saliva from his face. 'That I will assume to be a confession.'

Hazel smiled, then whispered, 'Fuck you.' Then she flinched to Hughes' raised arm, expecting a slap to her face, but his hand slowed, touched her cheek, the forefinger stroking downwards.

Quietly he taunted. 'You saw what twenty with the prison strap did to O'Leary's backside...' Hazel paled. 'Imagine what forty will do to yours.'

'I'll lodge a complaint,' she countered.

Hughes wore the guise of surprise. 'Complain? I suppose that's your right. Tell you what, Sweet.' He dropped his hand to her front, fingers delving the gap in her blouse. 'I'll thrash you, and then you can complain.' He wrenched, the girl's shirt ripped apart. 'Because then you *will* wear the marks of injustice.'

Stunned, she stared stupidly as Hughes tore her bra from her breasts, those exquisite orbs shuddering with the jolt. He levelled a pointing finger. 'Take the shirt off.'

That and her bra fell to the floor, Hazel attempting to conceal her shapely bust. Hughes gripped a ten-inch strap as he told her, 'Hold out your right hand.'

'What are you going to do?' Hazel demanded.

'Help you to remember.'

The girl frowned. 'Remember what?'

'To keep your hands out of another female's pants. Now level that arm.'

Slowly, cautiously, her limb rose, hand flat, fingers stretched. Hughes struck with venom. Even Alice flinched to the dreadful crack of leather on traumatised palm. Hazel squealed. She grabbed the wrist with her left, an intense burn drawing tears.

'Left,' Hughes demanded.

Slowly, grudgingly, that hand lifted. Nervous, her arm trembling, she fought to keep it there.

A blur of quarter-inch thick leather struck, igniting the meagre flesh. Biting her lower lip Hazel shook the appendage, attempting to assuage the hurt before ramming it between her thighs.

Hughes gave her time. He savoured the moment, relishing the next hour or so. Sweet would rue the day she opted for the Hope. She would mourn that lack of respect, her insulting manner. And later, maybe in a day or two, Sweet would be elected.

'When you are quite ready, Miss Sweet,' Hughes mocked, quite taken by the dance and quiver of those delightful breasts.

'What do you want me to do?' the girl asked, before quickly adding, 'sir.'

'Hold up your right hand,' he answered with cruel intent.

The hand in a state of numbed pain, she held it up. Hughes struck with unrestrained savagery. Hazel screamed and fell to her knees, sobbing.

Alice grunted; she could do no more. Hughes cast a look that spelt volumes. Alice understood. He antagonised her. He dangled the suffering Hazel, the possibilities, the perhaps and maybes. He would abuse

124

her as a continued taunt. Hughes would vex her unnatural appetite. He would whip Sweet's naked backside, in the certain knowledge that that desperate need would vanquish propriety. There was the man's torture; Alice had been strung to watch, to endure the pangs of envy, and to suffer humiliation.

Sweet squealed her pained song to six on each hand. They hung useless and throbbing. Hughes circled her. He derided, eyed, plotted and schemed. The provocation of the concealed. The push of skirt. The lure of pale, rounded buttocks beckoned, enchanted, beguiled.

Hughes let the suspense mount, to take its toll, weaken his victim, heckle the witness and charge his libido. He held the tip of a cane to Sweet's bottom and gently pressed. The reluctant give of juvenile flesh excited. The spring and return of those packed cheeks, and the sexual implications thrilled him more than any drug ever could.

He stood close to her back, so close she could feel his breath on her shoulder. 'I am going to whip you, Sweet,' he promised. 'Make no mistake about that.'

He circled, pausing before her. He brazenly scrutinised her face, her breasts, her flat tummy. 'And then,' he said, 'we'll test your mettle.'

'And I will make an official complaint,' she returned stupidly.

'Yes, you said.' He nudged Hazel forward until her body touched against Alice. 'You might take a leaf out of Miss Hussey's book,' he suggested. 'Learn the game, and play it to your advantage.'

Fingers flicked the buttons of her skirt undone. 'Even Alice has seen the wisdom of whoring, and she's a good catholic girl.' He wrenched the young woman's skirt down, Hazel reduced to her panties. 'But you have the edge there, Sweet. You've already whored a lot.'

'I don't see why I have to,' the girl objected. 'I'm a

125

prisoner, not a slave.'

Hughes drank of Hazel's voluptuous bottom snug in French knickers a size too small. He tapped her rump with the cane. 'Where did these come from?'

Hazel shrugged. 'They were all I could find in my locker this morning. Everything else has disappeared. They're not even mine.'

The *fwip* of cane offered little warning. Eight inches of highly flexible rattan followed the natural curve, stinging compact buttocks. 'Sir,' Hughes reminded.

Face screwed, Hazel pressed a hand to the sickening smart.

Hughes revelled in the exhilaration of inventive outrage. Despotic and manipulative, he gained as much pleasure in inducing fear as he did in inflicting pain. To witness his victim dangling on the gallows of anticipation aroused and provoked the predatory beast. He studied the girl, the scrutiny further jangling her nerves, then indicating her knickers, he said, 'Leave those on.'

Dark green hugged and enhanced tantalising hips. Laced silk announced enticing buttocks. Lustrous fabric clung, delved, flaunted the sexual prominence of her mound and enhanced the fissure of her sex.

Hazel's anxious disposition aggravated Hughes' sadistic bent. The self-conscious attempt to cover her breasts with uncertain hands screwed his ill-suppressed desire. 'How friendly are you with Miss Hussey?' he enquired.

Alice frowned a warning.

'I've already told you, sir.'

'So you did. Were you close, though?'

'Not exactly,' she replied.

'I see.' Hughes pressed the cane to Hazel's back, urging her forward, but upper legs hard against Alice's thighs and crotch, the girl resisted. 'Time to get better

126

acquainted, I think.' The rattan sliced skyward and then descended with sickening speed. It wrapped the topmost sweep of buttocks, the ensuing smart gut-wrenching.

Sweet bucked, back arched, hips thrust forward, she flung hands to cosset the pain. Face a picture of intense suffering she forgot all except that mind-consuming fire in her bum.

A second lashed short of her fingertips, sensitive flesh agonised. A squeal followed Hazel's rapid descent, the young woman acknowledging her antagonist's demand.

Naked flesh met naked flesh. Breasts engaged, squeezed and flattened. Hazel stared down at Alice. 'Sorry,' she whispered.

Hughes contemplated the pair. 'How do you feel, Hussey? Bound tight. Vulnerable. I suspect you realise what I'm about. The slash of leather on flesh. But not your flesh. Justice, perhaps.' He stared down at her. 'Divine justice, maybe.'

His hand took Hazel by surprise. Fingers sank inside the elastic of her French knickers. 'Sweet, you are a prisoner. You are locked in the Hope of your own volition, because, I assume, you thought it an easy choice. Six months instead of twelve. Whatever.' He shrugged. 'You opted for a brief, arduous term. Or perhaps you believed the stick was reserved for dastardly crimes only. Whichever.'

His fingers stroked her bottom. 'The however, I'm afraid, is I don't give a fuck about you, your miserable life, or your so-called rights. To me you're just another social outcast and misfit. While you're penned here you will yield to my every whim. Or, Hazel Sweet, I will make your stay exceedingly uncomfortable and your life as miserable as possible.'

She winced as he pinched a welt. 'Whatever I want, you will provide. Whichever way I want it, you will dance my tune. And however I may desire, you will satiate that.'

He abruptly moved away, hand snatched from her knickers, and removed Alice's gag, the girl greedily sucking air. 'Do you have an opinion to voice, Miss Hussey?'

'What... what would be the point?' she asked sullenly.

'Note, Sweet. Miss Alice Rose Hussey bound naked, and extremely uncomfortable to boot. Miss Hussey, employee, with a shaft rammed in her cunny and another just out of her gob. If I can do this to her, it follows I can do far worse to you.'

'Just nod, Haze,' Alice suggested. 'He's going to do whatever's in his twisted mind anyway.'

'Pearls of wisdom. Listen to the oracle. Try "may I suck your cock sir?" and see if that makes matters worse.'

'The act of pleasing his cock will only guarantee an unpleasant extension to his entertainment, Hazel. He'll still whip your bum and whatever else he decides on.'

'Why do you let him do this to you?' Hazel blurted without thought.

Alice smiled, a sardonic turn of the lips. 'Because, I suppose, I'm just as twisted as he is.'

'Opposites, Haze,' Hughes scoffed. 'Or,' he added, 'she's seeking penance.'

'No,' Alice whispered, 'I'm pitted with the devil. There will be no absolution, and hence no need for penance. Hell is where I'm bound.'

'Catholic girl through and through,' Hughes mocked. 'Cut her in half and we'd read Vatican throughout, just like a stick of Blackpool rock. To you pleasure can only be provided by sin. Every fucking rapturous avenue has to be ignored, denied, seen as temptation. You and your holy lot are the sinners.

'Made in *his* image. Therefore made with his wants,

his needs. The need to eat, to drink. The need to learn, to discover and to explore. The need for comfort, for attention, for love. But for some reason coition is taboo. Reproduction is not to be enjoyed, although homo-sapiens are provided with the euphoric blast of climax. In fact man cannot avoid that zenith of sexual consummation. But it is the bait of temptation. Don't fuck for the fun of it, only for reproduction.'

Alice bit. 'For a supposedly educated man, you can talk some biased crap.'

'Merely offering a view not castrated by a catholic or religious doctrine. Some would call it free thinking, as in freedom of expression, of thought and of being.'

Hughes leant close. 'The point is, Alice, we are mortal flesh and blood. We are not built for higher immortal conjecture. We are animals, and as such respond to our natural urges.'

'You're an animal.'

'And we've been there before.' Cords hung coiled and unused from the bench. Coarse jute he'd previously knotted to steel rings in preparation. A length he passed over Hazel's lower back. 'So what's your urge, Alice? What at this very moment do you want most?' Threaded through an eye on the opposite side he added tension, Sweet yielding to the rope's pressure.

'To stick a knife into your heart, except you don't have one.'

Hughes tugged, the rope burning Sweet's skin. 'Oh I do, Hussey, black as the darkest, deepest pit imaginable.'

He smirked. 'Groin to groin, breast to breast.' Hazel's wrists he anchored to Alice's, the girls brought uncomfortably and intimately close, the illicitness of contact throwing minds and bodies into turmoil. Resistance against the flood of sensations proved futile. Alice's mind teetered on the brink of devil-made excess.

Bolts of devious sexual ingenuity lashed her thoughts and resolve. Suddenly her body yearned for the worst Hughes could offer, and the best Hazel could provide. Alice craved the filthy, sordid enterprise of the beast.

Fear numbed the jet-haired Sweet. Alice could feel the girl's shakes, and although perturbed by the sin of it, she bathed in a sordid gratification, speeding her intoxication.

Sweet's legs crudely parted and secured to Alice's limbs, Hughes took time to admire the package. 'A delightful sandwich,' he mused. 'But you need a filling,' he added, picking up a thick red candle in one hand and a twin-tailed quirt in the other.

'Listen to this, Alice. Listen and be envious.' Hughes swung the quirt, sixteen inches of plaited, tapering handle launching two lethal eighteen-inch thongs. The whistle of heavy cords triggered a desperate pang, Alice jerking with its intensity. The explicit slap of hide on knicker-squeezed rump drove a hot needle of sensual energy deep within the redhead's sex, and Hazel's wretched shriek only served to heighten Alice's approaching climax.

Whip ends draped on Hazel's back, Hughes asked, 'Who would you like to make your complaint to, Sweet?'

The muscles in her back twitched in anticipation. 'No c-complaint,' she quickly stammered.

He drew the lash the length of her back. 'What's changed?'

Alice intervened. 'You were mistaken, weren't you?'

'Yes.'

'Mistaken…' Hughes lit the candle. 'In what way?'

'She thought you were going to beat her for something she hadn't done.'

'Thank you, Alice.' Flame lowered to within an inch of those billowed breasts, he tipped, Hazel's flesh taking

130

the first drops of the scorching, viscid substance. The girl jerked and writhed, the effect on their bodies stirring him further.

Alice took the next scattering, the delicious burn accentuating a sexual madness. The ingredients of her situation conspired to push her toward total bodily submission.

Hughes noted the difference, Sweet succumbing to terror and Alice to ecstasy. He showered Hazel with random drops, the girl not knowing where he would strike next. Her breasts, shoulders and flanks suffered, Alice twitching, eyes closed to the few remnants that missed Sweet.

The raven-haired girl's body extensively decorated, red spots and streaks having transferred their discomfiting load, Hughes paused. He stood beside the pairs, gazing down at Sweet's rump and Alice's stuffed sexual beneath. He lifted a short knife and slashed open Hazel's knickers, exposing the girl's buttock division, opened, the squeeze of her compressed buttocks forcing it apart.

Hazel held her breath, expectant, while Alice gasped, surprised. Hughes' fingers rested on her vaginal lips, his forefinger probing above the insert. His other hand rested the inch thick candle at the lower end of that bared buttock valley, hot wax dribbling into the fissure. Hazel gasped and shrieked as Hughes drew it slowly the length of that lascivious divide. She twisted and tugged, an unbearable fire lighting her arse.

Alice drifted silently, privately, in a sexual haze, Hughes' digit working her clitoris. The writhing tormented Hazel, her warm body energising Alice's, and further encouraged needs despatched from the vaults of depravity.

The extinguished candle rolled abandoned across the floor, a band of congealed sebaceous crimson rising from Hazel's satin-covered pussy. Hughes crouched on one knee, mind and eye on the vulnerable, Alice's sex anchored, disposed to any indignity.

He eased the phallus clear, the suck of her fanny telling a sordid story. The gap between he and she closed, his tongue readied, Alice's slit unawares. The touch of that wet organ ignited a climatic explosion Alice could only have dreamt of. The most intoxicating detonation engulfed, overwhelmed, flooding body and mind.

The redhead's gasps and sighs of delight puzzled Hazel. She knew not where Alice visited, nor that Hughes had three fingers trust into the girl's sex, his tongue raking the inner pink of her vagina.

Sexual intrigue closed on Hazel, Hughes' other hand delving the split in her knickers, lengthening the damage. Uncertainty and exhilaration mixed and churned, invoked an irresistible high. Sweet twigged, realised where Alice lingered. A complete understanding spread its tentacles, Hazel recognising the provocative blend of Hughes' manipulative and immoral institution.

The brush of his hand fired an interest. Months of abstinence demanded satiation. Six phallic inches of thick rubber pressured the gates of her sex. Her eyes widened, a screwing insertion triggering a curious abdominal tingle. She expected only pain and suffering, and the shift in direction confused, Sweet realising as Alice had, Hughes could not be relied upon. He was about as predictable as a drunken carrier pigeon, none sure which way he would fly.

Hughes launched them both on a sexual tsunami. He teased them through enervating climax after climax. Rag dolls hung breathless and fatigued, their minds swamped in delirium.

Hughes wiped the juices from his face. He rose, jaw

132

aching from nigh on twenty minutes of cunnilingus. He observed the near-unconscious pair. They lay unsuspecting and relaxed, neither having thought about what he might do next.

Quirt lifted, he brought the brute down, the hiss of parted air too late a warning. Twin cords struck with devastating speed, Hazel's back torched. She screamed with the shock and pain, writhing with the sheer intensity.

Hughes whispered close to her ear. 'Just wanted your attention. Thought you might be nodding off.' The burn lingered, a continuous reminder, but he had something else on his mind. 'Sweet,' he voiced with exuberance, 'you could have a future.'

Suspicious she scowled.

'You're an attractive girl with a pleasing shape. And you don't bear the hardened looks of a whore.'

Hazel tweaked a weak smile.

'I *could* elevate you from the dorms. You *could* have your own very healthy bank balance. You *could* live like a queen within the Hope boundaries.'

'Why?' Alice demanded.

'Not talking to you, strumpet. I'm chatting with Sweet. Have the decency to show some manners.'

'Take the striping, Haze,' Alice urged weakly. 'It'll be less painful in the long run.'

Hazel risked a suggestion. 'Release me, and we can talk.'

'You can talk where you are. That position has its advantages.'

'What he means is don't disagree,' Alice warned.

'Miss Hussey is merely jealous. Self-righteousness prevents her from making *her* fortune.'

'We won't see *you* degrading yourself for thousands to ogle,' Alice riposted.

'Tell me what you're doing at this precise moment,

133

Hussey.'

'This is in privacy.'

'There's a difference? Is that hypocrisy I smell? Explain to me, Alice. Is it not the debauched act that commits one to sin? Are you trying to tell me it's okay as long as no one is watching?'

'It's not that and you know it. Money changes everything.'

'Another misconception. You are gaining satisfaction from this debauchery. Even Alice Hussey has finally admitted to herself she has to indulge, if only for sanity's sake. If I were to lob you fifty quid at the end, would it change your enjoyment? It think not. It would merely make you fifty pounds the richer.'

'Degeneracy is not an immediate thing. It is slow and insidious.'

'Fine. I'll have you photographed as you are this moment, and pay you fuck all for the privilege.'

'There's no point arguing with you.'

'That's because you don't have a valid point.'

Puzzled, Hazel asked, 'Are you doing this because you want to?'

Alice felt her face burn.

'Oh yes,' Hughes answered for her. 'Alice is bending over backwards to please me.'

'It's not what it seems,' Alice corrected. 'It's not what you think.'

'It's quite simple,' Hughes continued. 'If the word whore was pronounced innocent, and voluntary as victimised, Alice would be happy to sink beyond redemption. But alas she is blinded by sanctimonious crap.'

'I'm wrong because I disagree with you.'

Hughes changed the subject, attention back on Hazel. 'You've been imprisoned for theft and prostitution. You have no experience. What will you do when you leave the Hope?'

'I haven't thought about it, sir.'

'Then think. Who will provide a reference for what one might term a decent job?'

'I've only Carters.'

'You did well at school. Prefect. That should help. But what of the missing years? How will you explain them?'

'Lie,' she admitted.

'You'll be found out. You'll be sacked and further discredited. You'll end up either in the gutter, a whorehouse or drudging. But you could be in furs by the time you leave here.'

'How, sir?'

'I can arrange a career in modelling.'

'Huh!' Alice barked. 'He can arrange your descent into a hellhole you will never be able to climb out of. Not until you've lost your looks and figure, and they throw you out like some piece of rubbish.'

'By then you'll have made your fortune,' Hughes countered.

'By then you'll be ruined mentally and physically. You'll be alone, used and abused, and probably an alcoholic.'

'What an imagination! Why, Alice? Why would Sweet be used and abused and an alcoholic? What in that narrow mind makes you think that?'

'That's what that sort of life does to a woman.'

Hughes smiled cruelly. 'I can show you a woman that has *survived* this so-called *diabolic* trade. A beautiful green-eyed, auburn-haired lady, who has peddled in *her* flesh for nigh on twelve years. And I tell you now, Alice, she is still one of the most alluring, radiant females I have ever had the privilege of meeting. She has a temperament like yours, naïve in some ways, bountiful, giving and forgiving. But unlike you she has

135

come to terms with what she is. She utilises her God-
given gift for the better of all. She has seen the light.
She knows and understands that life is for living. It's
her personal choice, one that is not affected by
mediaeval practices and cultures.'

'You bastard!' Alice exploded. 'You've known all
along, haven't you?'

Hughes gazed impassively. 'Known what, exactly?'

'Where Rose is.'

'Ah! You make assumptions. Typical Hussey. The
world revolves about her and her wants. I'm surprised
God himself hasn't been to visit, summonsed to sort out
your tiresome tribulations.'

'Then who is this woman?'

Chapter 8

Every part of her body shook. Gillian Morris had lost
control of her limbs, her muscles, her bladder and her
bowel. She watched in horror as her mistress lashed her
wrists to the handlebars. Spittle wet her jaw, the girl's
voice still hoarse from begging.

Grey eyes misted with tears still pleaded, Gillian's
expression shocked, appalled, disbelieving. Her tingling
face displayed the raised marks roused by Amanda's
hand, crimson cheeks moistened by tears.

Summary justice. Summary execution. Gillian had
witnessed the bottoms and backs lashed by Miss
Jenkins' horsewhip. She had heard the screams of other
servants drifting distant from the garages. She had seen
them sobbing uncontrollably, then wincing for hours,
their poor bodies crisscrossed with vicious welts.

Gillian had believed she could avoid the psychopathic
side of Miss Amanda. She had believed that hard work

and loyalty would place her apart from the rank and file as well as, most importantly, Amanda's implement cupboard.

Gillian survived six months. And in that time Amanda Jenkins mooted no reason to whip her, until that very morning.

Gillian had already suffered the pain and humiliation of the verbal accusations and initial assault. Spilling the truth gained no quarter. The more Gillian had protested, the worse her ultimate punishment became.

The maid's adolescent, slightly chubby body had never before suffered the cut and slash of any implement. Gillian was a virgin to corporal punishment. Where the other working girls had felt the wrath of Jenkins' slipper, belt or cane, she had escaped. But she had seen. Amanda instilled fear. She ruled with an iron fist. She whipped a backside on a regular basis, the boys and girls labouring in her house and workshop liable to a striping for the slightest infringement.

Morris watched Amanda tie her ankles to the footrests. Dread played on her nerves, the horsewhip where she could plainly see it.

The walk to the garage, knowing they all watched, had worsened the whole nightmare. They always tracked the hundred or so strides from the security of various hiding places, every girl and boy ghoulishly curious, so glad it wasn't them. They scrutinised the naked body struggling forward in sunshine, rain or snow, legs often incapable of support. They coolly estimated that severely lashed individual's return, even laying wagers on their state and condition.

Until then no one had seen Gillian without her uniform, ergo clothes. No one could have guessed how she looked without. But stripped of every stitch and paraded out in the yard, every occupant of Drakes House and the adjacent workshop knew precisely how she looked. Those boys could see everything. Her bouncing breasts, her jostled bottom, and even – Morris blushed with the shame of it – those boys would have relished the coil of pubic hair. Mortified, Gillian laid her face on the petrol tank.

To have argued with Amanda's demand would have meant committing herself to almost double the hurt. One boy did, and his torso and thighs suffered what must have been the worst whipping Gillian had ever seen. Even his penis and testicles bore the marks of the six-inch tip, the flexile length that seemed to locate the most sensitive places.

Guilt also descended on Gillian's shoulders. She recalled the sordid pleasure she had derived from seeing those teenage lads marched naked across the yard, hands on their heads. That solemn march there, and the return, their flesh slashed and marked, their buttocks a mass of ugly red welts, had motivated the finger-dipping she also abhorred in retrospect.

Gillian Morris, seventeen-year-old maid to Amanda Jenkins, and a bastard child to an influential noble, had been raised away from suspicious noses and prying journalists to avoid a scandal. Gillian believed her mother dead and her father unknown. She had been raised by a charity, and then lodged for employment with Amanda. Hence she would remain, even after Amanda had mercilessly whipped her, because she lacked experience, knowledge and courage. Better the whip than destitution.

Alice massaged her lower back, the ache dulled but still very much evident. Shame had arrived with the cold light of day. Her participation annoyed and embarrassed. The length of time she had held out against Hughes' pressure rankled too. Why did she let Hazel take so much punishment? She might have guessed Hughes wouldn't give, and it would only be a matter of time before she capitulated, agreed to his terms. But the promise, the actuality of those cords whipping her own flesh coerced her to wait.

Alice inspected her own marks; short welts to the sides of her boobs and an occasional stripe about her ribs. She had received only the lashes that overreached their target. Hughes refused to appease her. He stubbornly kept those tails short of her pussy, laying them hard to Hazel's, determined to get his own way.

Eventually Alice yielded. Knowing Hazel could take no more she agreed to some of his terms – and he to some of hers. She dressed, her choice deliberate, her psyche scheming for satisfaction.

Amanda wiped the sweat from her palms, her pitiless eyes checking her handiwork. Morris's posture met with her approval. A packet of biscuits left for temptation had ensnared Gillian. A packet of garibaldi scoffed by a starving servant, the wrapper discarded beneath Gillian's bed, had proved sufficient evidence. That and the fact Morris had the time, and was seen close to the kitchen.

Her denial increased the levy. Her admittance because she could see no other avenue, increased it further. Amanda browbeat and slapped her until she blurted what the shrew wanted to hear. Injustice, another's transgression, Morris had no alternative but to endure.

Six inches of stiffened leather and six of swingeing attachment slashed Gillian's naked buttocks, a bottom stretched and tensed to increase the sickening smart. Hands tied to the handlebars, her torso pressed to the seat, rump positioned over the taillight. Her legs stretched at an angle, ankles secured to the driver's footrests. A rope passed over the girl's lower back, forcing her down and her bottom up and out. Large

139

breasts cushioned and billowed about the angle at the front of the seat, prime targets for Amanda's brutality.

Alice descended the stairs more at ease with herself than she had been for months. Doubts still niggled, but her reasoning provided excuse. Hughes held the key, of that she was sure, and she felt justified in taking action necessary to gain that information.

The principal, governor, devil, bastard, whatever, used Hazel to get what he really wanted. Alice finally agreed to pose along with Sweet. She acceded to stills of a soft nature, what many would term as ineffectual.

She had no doubt which road Sweet would follow; the girl seemed hell-bent on self-destruction. Alice even doubted the story leading to her supposed demise. For Alice, Hazel Sweet leapt too quickly. She grabbed Hughes' offer with overt enthusiasm.

Scrubbs bugged her. Or more to the point, her introduction by Hughes rankled. Alice had not found the opportunity to explain her predicament. Explain? How could she provide a rational account for being topless? How could she face the man knowing he had seen her boobs?

Dennis tried to orchestrate an accidental meeting that morning, but Alice spotted him and took a detour. The fog of inebriation clouded the scene in Hughes' spare bedroom. She couldn't be sure whether Scrubbs acted the gent or the cad. She couldn't recall whether he had his hand between her legs, or if it was a dream.

Crossing to Hughes' abode she noticed Hazel behind the glass and bars of her dorm. The girl waved, then offered the thumbs up. Alice looked away, refusing to be drawn.

Hughes let Alice in. 'How's your mate's bot this fine sunny morning?'

'Hazel Sweet is an inmate. Inmates and staff are not

140

permitted fraternisation. You know that.'

'Glad you're finally taking note.

'Sweet has signed—'

'It's meaningless.' Alice cut him short.

He studied the redhead. 'You're going to renege, aren't you?'

Resigned, she shook her head. 'But you can't draw up a contract under coercion. In fact the very thought of a contract between a governor of a prison and an inmate is frankly laughable.'

He folded his arms. 'Okay. I haven't. Sweet hasn't signed anything. But you can.'

'No.'

'What do you mean, no?'

'I'll swim with the tide, and provided I don't get swept away I will keep swimming. I'll do precisely what I feel comfortable with…'

'Or uncomfortable, I hope,' Hughes added.

'It's simple. You stick to your promises and I will stick to mine.'

Pipe in hand, the man turning it over and over, he stunned Alice with an admission. 'I've known your mother for a number of years.'

Alice felt her legs weaken. She backed quickly to a chair and sat. Ashen, she begged, 'No bullshit? Please, this is too important.'

'I didn't make the connection at first, even though you are so alike. Rose only stayed in the old Hope Sanatorium until it was bombed. She wasn't transferred, she was released.'

Alice held a hand to her mouth, her heart pounding.

'Her fine upstanding family gave her money to disappear and bought you in the bargain.'

Tears ran down Alice's cheeks.

'She was here in Flint when I took over the Hope. She worked here for a while. She changed her name. She's

141

not Rose Hussey any more. That's probably why I didn't make the connection straight off.'

'Have you seen her recently?' Alice ventured, choked.

He shook his head. 'Not for a couple of years. She moved away from Flint. She started afresh in Manchester.'

'So she doesn't know I'm here.'

'No, I haven't spoken to her in six months.'

'You know where she is?'

The man nodded gravely. 'And I know who she's with. If you turn up on her doorstep you could wreck her new life.'

'You actually care about someone else, other than yourself?' Alice asked, incredulous.

'I care about Rose.' He let the statement hang.

'Do you know who my father is?'

He nodded.

'I won't ask. I'm not even certain I want to know. But please tell me it isn't Richard.'

Hughes threw back his head and roared.

'What? Don't you dare laugh! Have you been winding me up?'

'Barker?' Hughes giggled maniacally. 'Barker!' he bellowed. 'Why the hell do you think it might be that piece of shit?'

'Nightmares. I've dreaded finding out in case it was him.'

'If you knew Rose you would also know that she would not stay in the same room as that weasel, let alone sleep with him.'

'No?'

'No. Your mother is more likely to be found courting an archduke or a rear admiral. She has that *je ne sais quoi* that attracts the rich and famous.'

'My father, then…'

'That's for her to tell you, not me.'

142

'Then you will make an arrangement?'

'I'll go and see her. And that is the only promise I'll make.'

'All that about psychiatric reports?'

'Total bullshit. You don't really think the medical profession would leave that behind, do you?'

'I guess I'm gullible.'

Hughes placed his hands on her shoulders. 'You need me, Alice. It's as simple as that.'

'Was she mad?'

'Are you mad? Is it hereditary?'

'I guess I'm confused.'

'I guess you have been.'

Alice looked him in the eyes. 'If I find out this has all been a ruse to win me over, I will chop you into a thousand pieces with a blunt axe.'

'And talking of pieces, I have a new piece of apparatus. Care to try it out? Give me your honest opinion?'

Gillian still sobbed although her backside had been beaten numb. Welts smothered that ample rump, livid stripes lifted from scarlet dunes. That had been nothing compared to the whipping of her loins, lower back and shoulders. The slash of that six-inch tip around her sides took her well beyond what her imagination could have conjured.

Amanda released her, the girl unsure about movement. She still lay, her flesh tender and sore. 'I wouldn't have thought you a thief and liar, Gillian,' the woman nagged. 'But I shall keep an eye on you from now on.'

Morris prised her body from the motorcycle, the act of rising painful. 'I'm sorry, madam. I don't know what came over me.'

'I know of a place where they lock thieves away. A

143

harsh regime, where the inmates would eat a girl like you. Any more of your hanky-panky and I might see if they'll take you.'

Gillian wriggled from the motorcycle. 'As I said, madam, I'm sorry. It won't happen again.'

'You can stand in the yard for half an hour with your hands on your head. Let the others see what happens to a thief.'

'Yes, miss.'

The door thrown open revealed rain lashing the cobblestones outside. 'That should cool your hide somewhat,' the mistress sneered, pushing Gillian out. 'And remember what I said; any more thieving and I'll see you locked away.'

Heels clicked on stone, Amanda striding back to the house. She scanned the windows, outhouse and toilet, seeking a face. Any one of the dozen she could accuse of time wasting. Another snivelling wretch she could discipline. Morris had proved insufficient for her needs.

Hughes kept the contraption in a small disused chapel, the prostitution of the house of God amusing his twisted sense of humour. The building, once part of the sanatorium, had long been stripped of all its furnishings. Only the oak doors and arched stained-glass windows remained to speak of its one-time sanctity.

Chill damp air met their entrance, Alice shivering. A low vaulted ceiling imitated a church, the room it protected the size of a large lounge. Flagstones chilled the space further, split into two levels, the floor raised where the altar once stood.

Hughes' furniture stood before the altar space, a reasonably simple piece which immediately set Alice's pulse racing. She had not seen the like before. Hughes tapped the structure. 'Well, what do you think?'

'Explain it to me,' Alice suggested cautiously,

although she had already guessed.

'I see it being used for lengthy periods of contemplation,' Hughes replied.

Alice ran a finger the length of the apex. 'One sits there, I suppose?'

'Legs either side.' Hughes surreptitiously rubbed his cock. 'There will be something above. Depends where it ends up. The wrists will be shackled and chained and held aloft.'

'How long would a girl be expected to stay on it?'

'Until she can take no more, and then some.'

Alice studied the piece, a form of horse, for want of a better description. An apex formed by slanting sides, both three and a half feet by one, capped it. Stout thirty-inch high legs attached to a supporting framework, raised the top edge to just under three and a half feet from the floor. Cross braces between the legs, six inches from the floor, reinforced the whole.

'Well, Alice? What's your opinion?'

'They just sit there until you release them? Is that the idea?'

He grinned. 'Not completely.'

'Can I make a suggestion?'

'Please do.'

Alice blushed. 'I thought…'

'Intrigued, are we?'

She swallowed. 'Somewhat.'

'Want to be the first?'

'Depends.'

'On what?'

'Whether you're in tease mode or not.'

Hughes spread an arm toward the equipment. 'Feel free. Drop your knickers and climb aboard. What was the suggestion, anyway?'

'Weights or a pull on the ankles.'

'You've got it bad.'

'What?'

'And you call me sadistic. Having rid yourself of pointless indoctrination and restrictive inhibitions, you can now enjoy that hereditary trait.'

'We'll see. You could also… you said hereditary.'

'Did I?'

'What are you telling me? My mother's the same?'

'Pity you chose to wear those trousers,' Hughes teased, ignoring her question. 'Now you'll have to remove them as well as your knickers.'

'Answer me. Is my mother a masochist?'

'Masochist?' He pulled a face. 'And I thought you were a perverted deviant.'

'You're not going to tell me, are you?'

Hughes deliberated. 'I like your concept. The weights. You were going to suggest something else?'

'A pillory, that was all. Set on top. Adjustable in height, perhaps.'

'Excellent! I shall have the thing altered, and you shall be the first to try it out. We'll leave it at that for the time being.'

'I thought…'

'No, better to wait.'

Frustrated, Alice nodded her agreement.

'I have a couple of things for you. They're back in the office. Something to say thank you for joining the Hope Enterprise Board.'

Interest tickled her heart. Intuition urged caution while her libido demanded action.

'Nothing especially grand, but a token all the same.'

Back in his study, Hughes offered her a gift-wrapped box, which Alice tore open.

'You're not excited?' Hughes asked, teasing her.

'Not especially,' she replied, trying to appear calm.

'Good. Hope it's not a disappointment.'

Inside, the item was wrapped in tissue paper, Alice

146

pulling it aside, gazed speechless before lifting an expensive sheer white dress. 'I don't know what to say.' Alice ran a hand beneath the cloth, noting its transparency. Hughes remained enigmatic, offering no readable sign. She made no comment.

'There's more. Underneath.'

Alice rummaged, unearthing a camisole, French knickers, a suspender, and a half-cup laced bra; all crafted from an expensive looking white diaphanous material. Opaque white silk stockings completed the lingerie.

'How can I...? Why? You can't buy me, you know.'

'Just try them for size. Take a shower first if you have a mind to.' She eyed him warily. 'I won't intrude. Scouts' honour.' He read her thoughts, adding, 'Yes, I did say a couple. That's one. The other will be waiting for you.'

The young woman held the dress against her body. 'It's very short.'

'You have the legs.'

'The front is cut low.'

'You have the boobs.'

'It might be a little bit tight by the look of it. And a little bit see-through.'

'You have the body. Don't concern yourself. You'll look delectable.'

Picking the box up, Alice asked, 'What shall I wear, the underwear or the dress?'

'Either? Or?' Hughes said, aroused. 'You decide. Surprise me. Maybe even shock me, if you've a mind to.'

Pictures spilled to the polished surface. Misery ensnared in black and white slid across the glassy top. Hijacked, moments of agony. Captured, contorted faces and whipped bodies.

Suede gripped her flesh, clung to her rakish body. Velvet hide hugged the intimate and private. Thin kidskin embraced, moulded to her slight curves, her arms, breasts, bottom, hips and legs. Tight about her; delving, probing, working her cunt when she moved. How Amanda loved that sensation; leather rubbing, fondling her sex. How she cherished the squeeze to her bottom, tight leather pressing.

Alice kept a wary eye on the door, dreading he might, hoping he would. Naked she showered, memories of Hughes' spanking returning. He had held her, thinking her to be someone else. He spanked her wet bottom with venom, her buttocks pounded and reddened.

Suds daubed her naked flesh. Hot needles deluged her back. Expectancy and opportunity merged to light her imagination. She expected *him* to renege on his word, and she had done nothing to prevent that. The door remained unlocked and ajar. She longed for him to burst in, manhandle and chastise her with the flat of his hand, all against her will, of course.

Time passed. She could remain no longer. Disappointed, Alice towelled herself.

The dress moulded to her curves like the black one. The sheer cloth clung to her, emphasising bust, waist and hips, and displaying her flesh. Without underwear Hughes would be able to discern it all. He'd perceive the misty thrust of breasts, the rose jut of aroused nipples. He'd see quite clearly the shadow of pubic hair. Fevered blood coursed her veins, adrenaline levels rising close to overdose.

Towel-dried hair hung tousled and damp. Uncertain, decided, Alice ventured back into his office.

Hughes looked up, studying her in silence. 'My God,' he eventually whispered. 'Helen of Troy's looks launched a thousand ships. You, Alice, could launch a

148

million ejaculations. I know you intimately, and yet you leave me in awe. I have an erection just looking at you. I believe I could climax without even touching you. You are a fortune incarnate. You, Alice, have the most incredible future waiting. All you have to do is say yes.'

'I want to meet my mother first,' she bartered.

'I'll do a deal. Portfolio first, then I'll sort something out with Rose.'

'What's she like?'

'You. Look in the mirror. There you will find Rose.' Hughes reached out, signalling. 'A twirl.' Alice pirouetted. 'Too fast. Let me feast on that delectable rear.'

Alice complied. Arms across her breasts, hands on shoulders, she posed, hips kicked to one side. 'Why no underwear?' Hughes asked.

'The dress is not made for anything other than…' she held her arms apart, indicating her body.

'And I haven't had any breakfast.'

Alice knew. Alice understood his innuendo.

'Your other present.' Hughes pushed it from beneath his desk with a foot, and another much smaller box lay gift-wrapped on the floor. 'Look at it as a birthday present. I see from your records it's not far off.' Alice hesitated. 'Go on. Open it.'

She tore at the paper, the prospect of more finery egging her on. A layer of brightly coloured paper removed, she tried to open a cardboard box. She tore at the tape and reached inside. She felt first, intrigued.

'Want the scissors?' Hughes asked.

She shook her head, frowning, settled on her haunches, perplexed.

'What? Don't you like it?'

Alice stared at the contents, hackles rising. 'Your idea of a joke, is it?'

'I'm not leading you on, honestly,' he replied,

chuckling.

'This is just so typical of you,' she accused.

'Never look a gift horse in the mouth, so it's said.'

'Jekyll lavishes gifts, understanding and kindness. Hyde tosses in the cruelty. One negates the other. And that's the way you are. You can't stand the thought of anyone seeing you as philanthropic.'

'No one here would comprehend the word, or the act. I run a tough environment with savage hombres…'

'That's men, not women. Hombres are men.'

'Thank you, professor Alice Hussey. I'll try and remember that valid point. Sorry, should that be professoress?'

Alice held up the dog collar and lead in one hand, and a bit and curb in the other. 'What had you in mind?'

'I've told you. Put it on. Try it for size.'

'You really know how to take the shine off an occasion. Alice tossed it to one side.'

Amused, Hughes pointed at the horse furniture. 'That's more to *curb* your tongue, every *bit* as good as a gag, eh?' The man laughed.

Alice dropped the pieces back in the box. 'You've wasted your money.'

'Alice, put the leash on.'

'No!'

'What was it I said? For your mother, you'll serve me.'

The bitter taste of hurt pride in her mouth, Alice reached for the leash. Grudgingly she put the leather around her throat, and then locked the small padlock attached.

'Notice there's no key,' Hughes pointed out.

'I'll cut it off.'

He shook his head. 'You'll wear it until I tell you not to.'

Alice reared. 'I'm not wearing this all the time! I'll be

150

the laughing stock of the Hope.'

'Call it humility.'

Unpremeditated, instinctively, Alice picked up a mug of tea he'd left too long before drinking, and threw it in his face. The man reared, his shirt and trousers soaked. Chest so tight she could barely breathe, she hissed, 'You pig's shit!'

Hughes shook his head. 'You don't realise how stupid that was. It's not my clothes. They'll wash. It's the paperwork.' He picked up a number of sheets. 'A week's work fucked. Home office forms, fucked. Reports fucked.'

'So punish me,' she stormed. 'That's your usual answer, isn't it?'

Hughes closed the gap, and ignoring her sexuality he told her, 'The punishment room, in two hours.'

'What would you like me to wear? Clothes, knickers or the usual nothing?'

'A suit of armour if you have any sense,' he replied sardonically. His genuine concern for the damage she'd caused worried her. She made an attempt to help, Hughes brushing her off, telling her to go. Alice reached the door, fingers about the knob. 'And leave the collar on.' He glanced at his watch. 'Twelve, Alice. Not a minute later.'

Chapter 9

Woodbine smouldering, Alice stared and pondered. She felt embarrassed for her stupidity. Why, of all the courses open to her, did she throw tea in his face?

She drew on the cigarette. *'An hour.'*

Smoke blown toward the ceiling, Alice looked out across Flint. *'What will he do? Cane? Strap?'*

151

She paced, nervous. *'How many? Six? A dozen? More?'*

She had switched the dress for trousers, though still seeming exceedingly thin. She felt naked. The girl scanned her reflection, noting how tight the cloth was to her bottom. She bent slightly, the material moulding to her buttocks. Unsure, she drew deeply on the cigarette.

A knock disturbed her thoughts, her nerves. 'It's open,' she called.

Scrubbs edged in. 'Not disturbing anything, am I?' he asked, somewhat reserved.

Alice shook her head. 'No. I'm dressed today, as you can see.'

'Ouch!' the man offered. 'Can I tender my apologies for everything I have ever done, thought of doing, and might do in the future?'

An image flashed. Recollection stung her. 'Oh, you mean like trying to take my clothes off?'

'Yes, that sort of thing.' He puzzled over her odd neck decoration, but chose to say nothing.

Alice eyed him icily. 'And pushing your hand between my legs?'

Scrubbs bit his lip. 'Ah, didn't mean to do that. Biggest apologies for that one.'

'You admit it then?'

'Trying to ascertain the extent of the assignment, that was all. I needed to know.'

'Go on. This is beginning to sound like a case for the judge.'

'I, well, I…' He pulled a face, lips tight. 'Oh, fucking hell, you are the most gorgeous girl I've ever laid eyes on. I would crawl a mile over broken glass for a glimpse of your naked body. I would burn in oil for the chance to feel me against you. I would die for a bloody shag.'

'And that's it?' Alice asked, astounded. 'That's your excuse?'

152

'No good at them. I did it. I hold my hand up. But I didn't mean to. That's the truth. How about that shag?'

'Close the door behind you please, Dennis.'

The man left a little chastened, his opinion of Alice altered. Instead of the expected tart, he found a strong and proud young woman, one he vowed he would try and bed before the year was out.

Nervous, stomach knotted, Alice locked her bedroom door. The upper halls empty and silent the girl descended to the next floor, and her appointment with Geoffrey Hughes.

Apprehension gripped as she rounded the corner. Several inmates waited in a line outside the punishment room. Alice slowed and checked her watch. *'Two minutes to. What's he playing at? What's his game?'*

The three faces weren't from O'Leary's dorm. They were all from the youngest section, none being more than eighteen. Alice folded her arms and leaned against the wall on the opposite side of the corridor.

Mary O'Conlan took courage. 'Are you up for a striping too?' she asked.

'I'm here to see Mr Hughes. That's all you need to know.'

'He striped Jessie Tanby not twenty minutes since. Twelve strokes. On the bare, too. Poor bitch looked like she'd been bitten by a nest of scorpions. Ran down the alley rubbing her arse like there was no tomorrow.'

'Who's in with him now?' Alice asked quietly.

'He's back in his office seeing that new guy, Mr Scrubbs.'

Mary, head of the queue, massaged her bottom. 'Fifteen.' She forced a smile. 'Fifteen strokes of the cane. That's what I'm down for. And if it wasn't for Mr Scrubbs it would all be done with.'

'What did you do?' Alice asked.

'Beat the shite out of Jessie Tanby. That girl's got an

evil mouth.'

Alice looked at the other two. 'And you? What are you here for?'

'Talking when I shouldn't,' replied a cute blonde.

'Answering her, when I shouldn't,' added the other.

'And?'

'Six,' the blonde revealed.

'Same,' said the other.

'And you?' Mary asked.

'Best you know nothing.'

Time barely moved, each long minute counted by a clock on the wall. All four squirmed. All four could only speculate on the agony that awaited them.

Eleven minutes past twelve the door opened, Hughes beckoning to Mary, the weapon of her torment clutched in his other hand.

One long minute later the dreadful slap of cane whipping bare flesh reached their ears, the two girls visibly paling. Ten seconds later the second slashed bared behind, the girl squealing like a stuck piglet.

The blonde shook. 'I can't take that. No way can I take that.' Panic set in, Debra turning to flee.

Alice grabbed her wrist. 'You run and you'll get twelve. Better to suffer six now than twelve later.'

Barely able to speak, Debra replied, 'Yeah, you're right.'

Three minutes later a red-eyed Mary O'Conlan staggered out. Lip trembling she chose not to engage any of the other three. She sniffed as she passed, her hands beneath her skirt, a pair of panties hanging from the finger of one.

Debra took her place. Legs barely able to support her, the girl stepped into the fray. Alice remained, fear licked at her belly, adrenaline trifling with nerve.

Debra shrieked to six explosive slaps with a strap, forewarning Jackie of precisely what to expect. The blonde exited like a startled grouse, Alice believing she would have flown the corridor had she been able. A few minutes later a pained Jackie left, knickers screwed in a fist, her face distorted with pain.

Hughes levelled his attention on Alice. 'You.'

Alice straightened and strode past him without a word. Inside she stopped dead. Dennis Scrubbs parked his behind on the whipping bench. 'We meet again,' he remarked, somewhat conceited. 'And unfortunately it would seem to your disadvantage, yet again.'

Alice glared at Hughes. 'What's he doing here?'

Solemn, detached, the governor stated, 'An additional six.'

Alice pointed at Scrubbs. 'Not in front of him!'

'I warn you. Any more and I'll increase the penalty.'

'He's not stopping, and that's it.' Stubborn, Alice folded her arms.

'I intend a regulation corporal punishment. By law I have to have a witness. Mr Scrubbs is available and has offered his services.'

'Since when has doing it right bothered you? Tell him to leave.'

Hughes shrugged. 'Leave, Dennis…

'Don't think you're off the hook,' Hughes warned as the door closed behind Scrubbs. 'You're lucky I wasn't scalded.'

'I wouldn't have thrown it at you if it had been that hot.'

Hughes' mood chilled. 'I am going to cane you, Alice.'

Green shards of ice levelled on the whip grasped by his fists. He bent the beast, the creak of leather worrying. 'What's that for then?'

'After I cane you it will be time for repentance.'

She looked into the man's eyes, her blood running cold. 'What exactly am I repenting?'

155

'Your sins?'

'I haven't as far as you're concerned.'

'You've sinned,' he assured.

'In what way?' Alice wasn't sure which way he would blow. She didn't know whether she sparred with Jekyll or Hyde.

His eyes seemed to bore to her soul. 'Where did the money come from?'

Her heart missed a beat. 'Money?' she questioned.

'Stashed in your room.'

'That was stolen,' she announced.

'Precisely. Is that not a sin?'

'For whoever took it, yes.'

'So who gave it to you?' The pair continued at crossed purposes.

'No one,' Alice replied, confused.

'So it was pinched then?'

Alice scowled. '*I* took it from Jonathan. Someone here in the Hope stole it from me.'

'No, Alice. It's still in your room.'

Alice frowned.

'Bottom draw, under your panties.'

She sighed her relief.

'Been bothering you?' Hughes asked, and Alice nodded. 'That would have been fitting. Stolen money nicked.'

Puzzled, Alice asked, 'Who said it was stolen?'

'You.'

'When?' Alice managed a half-turn as leather sliced air. She took the lash fully on the bottom, the smart worse than sickening.

'Stop the fucking double talk. A straight answer if you please. Where did the forty pounds come from?'

Alice rubbed her behind. 'You really want to know?' The teenager eyed the raised whip. 'I stole it,' she admitted.

'At last. So it was a sin?'

'No more so than what you keep proposing,' she argued. Alice decided in a split second to take the second swingeing stroke on the bum again. 'Fuck!' she mouthed, the sting beyond her.

'Just answer the question.'

'Yes, it was a sin. It was a rotten thing to do to a very nice bloke. But there again, I borrowed it. I have always meant to return it. And one day I will.'

'He knew you took it?'

'No.'

'Then you stole it.'

'Yes.'

'Case proved. I dare say we could determine a number of other sins, if we took the time to lift a few rocks, eh?'

'I dare say you could.'

'Once you wanted to pay,' he reminded. 'Not so long ago you would have subjected yourself to a severe flogging to pay your God and discharge your sins.'

'Yes, I would have.'

'What changed?'

'I guess I did.'

'And now?'

Alice shrugged. 'How can I discharge my sins with a penance, which I, in my sick mind, actually enjoy?'

'We'll see if you do.' He pointed. Alice glanced in the general direction. 'Lay it on the floor and fill the requisite holes with your limbs, please.'

Alice stared at the contraption. 'Is this for throwing the coffee in your face?'

Hughes nodded. 'I should flog you before the whole establishment, if only to dissuade any other fools. If word of what you did gets to the ranks of the flotsam then bear in mind I will have no other option. Is that understood?'

Alice nodded her acceptance as she dragged the piece

into place. 'And just how many have I earned for damaging your pride?' she asked.

'So many for the insult, some for the lack of respect, a few for the shirt, a salvo for the trousers, and some more for your attitude.'

'Oh,' Alice remarked, placing her ankles in the slots. She bent, doubled, then rested her wrists in the other apertures.

Hughes perused the offering as he kicked the gates shut, locking Alice in the box stocks. 'Keep your legs straight now. A dip will equate to two extra stripes. And don't forget the extra six I promised.'

Hughes pushed the whip handle between the girl's thighs. He pressed it against her vagina, then eased it back and forth. 'I will promise one thing, Alice. You won't care for any contact between your delightful arse and anything else for a day or two.'

Her heart pounded, lodged in her windpipe. Doubt twisted anticipation. The trap amplified her posture and vulnerability. It captured her bottom; thrust it up for the flogging. She thirsted for more; the rough grasp of sweat-burnished leather, the heavy restraints of manacles and chains. She wanted – but remained unsure of the consequences.

She observed his choice. Hughes tried several rattans. Her chest tightened with the man's advance, a six-millimetre rod flexed between his hands. That flexible wand rested against her buttocks. Muscles tensed, teeth clenched, she ceased breathing.

The rod lifted, rose above Hughes' right shoulder. The void of question cast its suspense, Alice's world hung in limbo. Slashing cane upon fragile bottom would soon eradicate the uncertainty.

A second's flight. A moment's sickening apprehension. The flash of rod, its shriek terrifying. The thump, a blast of punitive energy discharged in a heartbeat, agony lingering, buttocks devastated with the appalling impact. The withering scorch seemed endless, red-hot pincers squeezing crippled flesh.

Long before those fires calmed Hughes inflicted a second. Buttocks pulverised by the impact, the girl's lower cheeks etched with a welt that would remain for days.

Still she refused a verbal utterance, preferring to stand on dignity. Her rump burned with a nauseous intensity. Pride is a sorry master, one that demands the surrender of reason. Injured vanity propels vengeance and hostility and irrational reprisal. Alice refused the man satisfaction with her silence, Hughes more and more determined to extricate a squeal. He had been seriously offended, more than Alice could have imagined, and was determined to derive compensation from her pain and humiliation.

Alice thought a harder stroke impossible. Hughes proved her wrong. The third whipped her upper bottom with a force beyond her. Alice couldn't prevent a spontaneous cry, a muted screech that proved music to her tormentor's ears...

Those upper limits of brutalised flanks still stung as Hughes lashed her behind for the twelfth time. He ripped his shirt apart, buttons wrenched from their holes. Cane still in hand he wiped at the sweat on his chest. Alice bent her knees, tortured backside dipped. She could feel every one of those dozen strokes, the welts sore and throbbing.

'Are you absolved?'

'From what?' Alice asked, her buttocks burning.

Hughes focussed on those trouser-covered buttocks, hand tight about that flexible cane. 'Has the guilt eased?'

Pride continued its merciless rampage. 'Is your ego satisfied?'

Coffee in the face was a difficult scenario for Hughes to handle, let alone accept. Her lack of regret irritated him further. 'Apologise.'

'Sorry.'

'Apologise and mean it.'

'Okay.'

Hughes smiled.

'I'm ever so sorry, Mr Hughes, that the coffee wasn't hotter. In fact I'm sorry it wasn't boiling oil. How's that, sir?'

Rattan whipped backside with brute savagery, Alice not even attempting to contain the yelp. The man reached down, seizing a fistful of her hair. He pulled, her head painfully lifted. 'It starts here, now,' Hughes promised. 'And it finishes when you show some contrition. I mean genuine regret.'

'I thought it started thirteen strokes ago,' Alice gasped.

'No, Alice, I am going to have a photographic, blow by blow account of your snivelling submission.'

'Don't you dare!'

'Simon,' the man bawled, 'come in and set your stuff up.'

Alice struggled to see the door, expecting Hughes' personal photographic friend to enter. Instead a fresh-faced young man of about twenty-five strode past him and proceeded to set his cameras up. 'This isn't on,' she moaned. 'I haven't given my permission—' A particularly strenuous execution of her bottom silenced her.

Simon screwed a Roleicord, two and a quarter square on to a tripod. 'Bloody good looking bird for a con.'

Hughes smirked, sadistic. 'She is indeed. Like the apparatus, Simon?'

'I'm no con,' Alice protested.

Puzzled, Simon looked to Hughes. The governor

shrugged. 'Does it matter?'

'I guess not.' The young man assembled a second unit. 'What's the format?' he enquired.

'Yeah,' added a disgruntled Alice, 'what's the format? Perhaps you'd like to give *me* a clue.'

Hughes moved with intent to the girl. 'She already has fourteen...' the rattan whipped taut buttock flesh, '...fifteen, stripes on her backside.'

Alice's knees gave, her stricken bottom slowly dipping before rising again.

'The plan,' Hughes said quietly. 'No plan, just pain.' He ran a hand over the girl's scorched buttocks. 'Maybe some pleasure.' Fingers sank beneath her waistband. Trousers eased down to expose the upper few inches of naked buttock, Hughes lifted the cane and delivered a forceful stroke, the sound of rattan smacking naked flesh explicit.

'Twenty-four stripes with this cane.' He whipped her covered lower seat. 'A lengthy strapping.' He pulled her trousers to halfway, her discoloured and squeezed cheeks heavily etched. Alice suffered a savage eighteenth, her bottom severely jolted. 'You photograph what you want, Simon, but keep my face out of your shots. Hers? Feel free. Oh, we'll settle your hash today, you capricious bitch!'

'And what if I do say sorry? What then?'

'You won't.' He laughed. 'I know you, Alice Hussey, and I know you won't.' The nineteenth slammed into the crease between thighs and bottom, and lights and reflective umbrellas in position, the first click of camera announced the commencement of a pictorial record.

'And why won't you?' The twentieth seriously stung the naked upper portion, Hughes shrugging. 'You tell me, Hussey.'

Teeth still gritted with the raw hurt, she answered, 'You know it all. You tell me.'

161

'Because you want me to discipline you. You crave the sensual fire. Your soul is torched by abuse, by degradation, by degeneracy and depravity. You are truly alive for the short time I whip, tie and sexually use you.'

Alice said nothing. The twenty-first cut to her behind momentarily silenced her.

'All that is wrong is right for you. Your ego boasts religious conviction. Adhesion to the scriptures. Respect for modesty. But your dark side demands the opposite. It demands extremes.'

Number twenty-two struck, her bottom shuddering.

'But the dark side is the strong side, the dominant side. You have a dominant submissive side, Alice. Without the obscenities of the flesh your life would be destitute.' Hughes laid the last two in quick succession, extricating a yelp from the suffering girl.

'Apologise, Alice. Make me believe you are sorry. You won't because you are too curious, too intrigued by what I have in store. A stranger winds and clicks the shutter, but are you bothered? Are you the least bit concerned that this unknown man will be privileged to witness the undoing of Alice? The baring...' he wrenched her trousers to her knees, '...of this divine arse. See how well she sports her trophies? No hideous mauve stripes with this backside.' Hughes took a buttock in his palm and squeezed. 'Firm, Mr Wells. Able to endure my worst.'

Her mind demanded acute shame. Her breeding dictated anger and revulsion. But her core screamed for more, for worse, for degrading suffering.

'Just remember, Mr Wells; keep that damned lens off my face.'

The young man nodded.

Hughes knelt, unlocked the confining boards, Alice rising stiffly, her trousers falling about her ankles. 'Deny it,' he urged.

162

Alice gently shook her head. 'No point. You're such a self-opinionated bully you wouldn't listen. I've told you before, Mr Hughes, you don't know me. You never will know me. And whatever may transpire, here, later, a week down the line, I don't ever want your cock in me. Remember that.'

Hughes grinned. 'Bend over the bench, Alice. Part those lovely legs as wide as they'll go. Fill Mr Wells' eyes with sin.'

Reminded of her naked lower half, Alice tugged on the hem of her shirt. 'That would be an admission. I've been more than aptly punished for throwing…' his warning came back, '…for what happened.'

'But not for this and that,' he reminded.

'Why not include perhaps and maybe? Same vagary.'

'Let me put it this way, Alice: voluntarily equates to about a so many. Forced, I should not feel appeased until I'd strapped you say, a lot more than that.'

Standing on tiptoe, leant forward, Alice whispered close to his ear. 'Over my dead body.'

'Immobilised, not dead,' Hughes replied humourlessly.

Alice thumped down on the cold slats, the speed and outcome of her skirmish with Hughes dumbfounding. Her shirt twisted and held by a fist, he fastened the broad belt across her naked lower back, wrenching it until the leather pinned and squeezed her torso. The belt gripped her skin like sandpaper, her body hot and damp with the effort of defence. It forced her belly against the slats, flesh squeezed between.

Determined to fight to the end she reached back, fingers grappling with the buckle. In reply Hughes hit those fumbling hands with a two-inch wide strap. Her hands still stinging he tied them to the bench, stretching her arms, ropes tight around her wrists. He parted her legs, pinned them, anchored those shapely limbs as far

163

apart as his strength would permit.

'Feel vulnerable?' he asked, vindictive.

'You've no right,' she whispered.

'No?' He knelt, nuzzled to her side, lips an inch from her ear. His hand touched, roamed, fingers examining the welts navigating her flank.

'Do you want this on film?' the photographer asked.

'Why not? A portfolio for our Miss Hussey.'

He lowered his voice. 'A reminder, eh, Alice? You can lie to me, girl, you can lie to every son of a bitch that gets his dick between your thighs, but you can't lie to yourself. And you can't lie to your God, either.'

'What's your point?' Alice demanded.

'I wasn't joking about the portfolio. Simon will have it ready in a week or so.' Hughes stretched his arm, reaching between her thighs. Fingers touched and played, toyed with her sex. 'You can look. You can outwardly remonstrate, feign disgust and hostility, but Alice, you can't escape yourself. You can't pretend to yourself. You can't ignore the thrill, the excitement, the sexual arousal. Like you can't deny this…'

He thrust a finger between her sex lips, then withdrew and held it before her face. 'Dew? Piss? Or maybe come?'

'I've not denied it, but it should be my choice, not down to some arrogant bully who throws a tantrum if he can't get his own way.'

'But it can't be your choice, can it? How can you decide to be stripped and whipped when it's just as much the act of suppression as it is the act of abuse that turns you on? Where the hell can consent come into that?'

Alice stared him in the eyes. 'You think you know me.'

'I know you're sexually lubricated. Deny that.'

'I can't, can I?'

164

'Is it Simon? Does he have this effect on you?'

'I'm not beholden to you. I don't have to excuse or explain myself to you, pig.'

'Arrogant bully, pig, any other insult before I take a belt to your backside?'

'Why see them as insults? If the cap fits?'

'Dwell on this, mouth almighty. Simon will be photographing your cunt, prissy missy. Pictures to adorn thousands of porn mags. To be pawed and wanked over for years to come.'

'And can I do anything about that?'

'Maybe it's better this way.' Hughes took off his belt and folded it in half.

Alice set her jaw, prepared herself for a lengthy flogging. The prospect thrilled, it frightened, it stirred the dizzy lather of euphoria.

Hughes struck with force as she knew he would. He wanted reason. She gave him excuse. Justified flagellation worked better than contrived. He felt justified in flogging her with enthusiasm, which aided his sexual thirst. And Alice shied from complicity, her need to be subjugated, her choice thus removed.

The slaps of leather loud, her cheeks burned with his furious assault. The click click of camera sounded in the background, that aspect furthering the intensity of her involvement. To be punished in front of another, a man she didn't know. And to be photographed. Her stomach knotted with enthusiasm.

Minutes later her backside blazed, gave to a fired crimson. The burn penetrated deeper, touched and torched her nub, climax gathering force. The belt cracked and licked close to her sex, Alice longing to feel the stinging slap between her legs.

Instead Hughes laid it to a thigh, working his way down to the knee, then up the other to the scorched cheek.

Desire gave to frenzy, both Hughes and Alice dipping Pandora's box, playing with sexual mayhem. Living with the aftermath deserted commonsense, Alice yearning for worse and worse, Hughes incapable of giving less.

Dennis Scrubbs tossed a newspaper to one side. He rose, paced to the window and stared out toward the hills. Bored, hands thrust deep into trouser pockets, his fingers touched a reminder. He withdrew a folded piece of paper and unravelled it. 'Alice Hussey. The Hope. Flint,' he read in a whisper.

He screwed the paper up and dropped it in a bin. 'I think pretty is an understatement; a very modest description.'

A sound took him from his thoughts. Scrubbs turned, staring at a single wardrobe propped in the corner of his room. Bemused, he approached and opened the door, frowned and then grinned. Inside cowered a highly embarrassed Hazel Sweet, with only Dennis's hat and scarf between her and total nudity. 'And to what do I owe the pleasure?' Scrubbs enquired, taking in the scene and Hazel's curves.

'A gentleman wouldn't stare. A gentleman would get me a blanket,' Hazel scolded.

'There you have it, Sweet. I'm sorry, but I'm no gent.'

Silk scarf tied about her breasts, hat held against her groin, Hazel sidled past him, naked bottom kept from his sight.

'Where are you going?' Scrubbs asked.

'Back to my dorm,' Sweet offered, nervous.

Dennis shook his head. 'No, I don't think so. You give me an explanation, a satisfactory one, and then you can return to your dorm.'

'It was a prank, that's all. Like a jack-in-the-box, or like one of those girls that leap out of a box at a party and shout surprise.'

'It's a surprise all right. When did you intend to leap out?'

'Soon.'

'With my scarf hiding your tits and my hat your bush?'

'I didn't want to break any rules,' Hazel submitted.

'Rules?' Scrubbs held up a finger. 'I have a book on rules. Let's see what's said.'

'I really would like to put some clothes on.'

'And I would rather you didn't. After all, that wouldn't make sense. In fact it would make me think you're something of a liar.'

Scrubbs flicked through the Hope rulebook. 'Out of prison uniform. Out of bounds. Lack of respect to a duty officer. That's three whackings there, I think, Sweet?'

'Truth is, sir,' Hazel looked away, 'I was forced to do it.'

Dennis picked a cane up from beside the wardrobe. He flexed the length. 'I had never actually caned a girl before coming here,' he admitted. 'It seems rather savage whipping a naked bottom with one of these.' The cane slashed air, Hazel wincing.

'It wasn't my fault!' she pleaded.

Dennis examined the rattan. 'It's when this actually lashes the bare flesh. That sound. The bounce and twitch of rod and bottom, rather mesmerising in a way. Names.'

'You know I can't.'

'Then the mark. Pale at first, then it colours. Then the flesh lifts, and depending on whose bottom the stripe can go all sorts of shades. How does your bottom handle the cane, Sweet?'

Dread sparked an angry response, the seeming unfairness of the situation fostering an unwise reaction. 'Don't threaten me. I've had enough of you sadistic

167

perverts. I expected just discipline, but not outrageous lechery.'

Scrubbs eased off his jacket. He rolled up his shirtsleeves. 'By outrageous lechery, you mean to imply I have sexual reasons for my proposed course of action?'

Hazel squirmed. The lack of clothes undermined her stance. She felt vulnerable. Her backside already smothered as a result of Hughes' whipping the night before, she dreaded another. She'd seen Scrubbs use that rattan and had no wish to feel his wrath. 'You seem to relish caning my bare bottom,' she offered as defence.

'Not relish. No, that's the wrong term. It's a simple matter of punishment, suffering and deterrent. The more it hurts the less inclined you'll be to re-offend. Simple psychology, Hazel.'

Unable to take her eyes from the twist, flex and turn of dense rod, she suffered a lapse of conviction. 'Drake. She put me in the wardrobe.'

Dennis strolled past her, Hazel turning, keeping her exposure from his eyes. 'Drake? That's the lumbering ox, isn't it?'

'You could call her that.'

'Why did she do it?'

'A prank, that's all.'

'You went along with it?'

'No. I told you, I didn't.'

'You are aware that the minimum punishment is six strokes. You have just earned yourself the minimum. Don't lie to me again, Sweet.'

The girl's flesh crawled. Her buttocks twitched with anticipation. The position he demanded would reveal all. 'I didn't.'

'Nine.'

'No! Why?'

168

'Why stay in the wardrobe if you didn't have to? The truth please, Hazel.'

'You're going to give me nine strokes?' she asked, stunned.

'Yes, I am. And if you don't tell me the truth very quickly I'll make that twelve.'

'Would it make any difference if I told you Mr Hughes flogged me last night?'

'Troublesome creature, aren't you?'

'It was sexual.' She levelled her dark eyes on the man, and let the hat fall from her groin. 'I fucked him, after. I could fuck you, Mr Scrubbs.'

He met her sexual gaze. 'And I suppose I could forget the nine strokes…'

Chapter 10

Hughes tossed Alice a long maroon skirt. 'Put that on.'

Backside feeling razor cut, thighs fairing no better, the teenager slipped the garment on, hem about her ankles.

'We should have done a super eight,' Hughes remarked. 'Seems a waste, all this for a few pictures.'

Alice folded her arms, mind and body keen to persevere. 'And I thought you were being your usual self. You know; artful, cunning, slimy. Disingenuous, really.'

'You really admire me, don't you, Alice?'

'Ah, you do know something about me after all.' She glared at the man. 'I have *some* taste.'

'You have a weakness.'

Alice perused the whip he held. 'I have a madness.'

'You have a weakness for me. I do for you what no other man has ever done. I fill a void no other human can. Deny it.'

'I admit I have a madness for you. There is no rhyme or reason to it. You are the most obnoxious vermin I have ever had the misfortune to meet.' A slight smile played on her lips. 'But, I can't ignore the affect you have on me.'

Hughes closed the gap. Whip stock in fist he curled fingers inside her shirt opening, Alice knowing, ready for his next move. 'Without satisfaction your libido will keep up its demands. The lust will just keep on insisting.'

'And you have the remedy.'

'Me.'

'I'd sooner do it with a cucumber.'

'Do that. I'll watch.'

'You're sick.'

Hughes ripped her blouse apart, her breasts bared.

Scrubbs broke the embrace. Mouths parted, he flattered the girl. 'Beautiful lips, Hazel. Soft, welcoming, sensual. Stir the loins, they do.'

'Stirred enough are you, sir?' she asked, guiding his hand to her groin.

His free hand flat on her head, he pushed the young woman down. 'Check for yourself. And while you're down there see what you can do with that sexy mouth, there's a good girl.'

Cane still gripped by a fist he pored over her previously marked posterior, the girl knelt before him, bottom pushed out, fingers undoing his flies.

'You're looser today than I've ever seen you. Acceptance?'

'To a degree, maybe. But wanting and having are two different entities.'

Hughes sighed. 'God, you're an uphill fight. What fucking moral issue are you going to raise now?'

170

'Just that. I want your hands on my tits. I want you to squeeze them, kiss, lick and bite them.' Mouth turned down, she added, 'Immoral, isn't it?'

Hughes filled his paws, exquisite breasts settled in his hands, nipples delving his palms. 'An interlude, that's all.' He slipped an arm around her side, ran his hand down her back. 'I've still got work to do.'

Alice exhaled, the breath ragged. 'I want a lot more, but some things are just not possible.'

Hughes lifted his face from her throat. 'Such as?'

'Your cock sunk deep between my legs, for one.'

'Another?'

'I want to be chained naked and spread-eagle to the Hope main gates.'

'That would be some tourist attraction, but I don't think the Home Office would go a bundle on the advert. Now the cock between your legs; that I can do for you.'

'Sadly not.'

'Why?'

'Because I think it would be wrong, that's why. I mean, why let a man you loathe into your bed, especially when there's one available you don't loathe?'

Hughes sunk his teeth into her nipple. Alice gasped and threw back her head, face screwed in pain, in ecstasy. His tongue followed, licking avidly at the hurt. 'Who?' he asked. 'Scrubbs?'

'Maybe. Maybe I'll let him. Maybe I'll let you watch.'

Hughes straightened to his full height. 'And maybe I'll just knock the cunt senseless.'

Scrubbs' swaying monster beggared belief. 'It... it...' Hazel stammered, 'it's enormous.'

'No woman has managed it all. Not yet.' Dennis leant over her, lifted the cane and smacked a bottom cheek, the half moon marginally stung. 'Please me, please.'

Circumcised, the mighty mauve plum swung gently before her face. Glistening with expectation the portion seemed impossible. Hazel hesitated, Dennis promptly striping her arse, the cane stroke persuasive.

Lips parted, kissed the pulsing tip. Her tongue darted, caressed, Dennis showing his appreciation, his hand on her head, cane held at bay.

Hughes held the redhead down. A knee on her back, he pressed the girl to the whipping bench. Her tresses he held in a fist. His free hand replaced the collar, fingers attempting to buckle and tighten the heavy studded leather about her neck. Her refusal to just accept, her struggles, increased Hughes' enjoyment, stimulating him further.

Simon held the camera freehand, closing in for a shot of the girl's contortions, her expressions, her pressed and distorted breasts.

Hughes seized a wrist, the other soon caught and both cuffed behind her head to the collar. He connected a lead and then let Alice rise.

She stood upright, face a mask of anger. She offered no words, just the glare.

The lead hung from her throat, four foot of leather and chain, the other end around Hughes' curled fingers. 'I think you make a good bitch, Hussey.' He wrenched open his flies and released his erection. 'Lick it.'

Alice tried to lift a foot, her intention to kick him where it hurt, but the skirt prevented the necessary angle. Hughes met her attempt with a cut of the whip, the leather slapping her side and lashing about her back. Fire ripped through her, the hurt lingering.

Six vertical stripes adorned Hazel's bottom. One struck amid the cheeks, the rattan having sunk between those cross-marked flanks with gut-churning results. So

Scrubbs had to coax, the girl's petite mouth insufficient for the job. Stretched, her lips encompassed his plum, the head wedged in her mouth, her tongue pressed. The act, the submission, the fact he held dominion proved enough. Scrubbs let her hang there, impaled by his cock, her mouth crammed with his excess. He satisfied time by groping and mauling her flawless breasts.

'Can't hear no more,' Smith revealed. 'There was them half dozen, and then nothing.'

Ruth glanced at Drake. 'Seems like she's made an offer he can't refuse.'

'Like what?' the big woman asked.

'Probably her fanny. That's the trouble wiv a bird like Sweet, and a bloke like Scrubbs. She'll do anyfing to avoid it, and yer can't rely on him to stay professional. He's fucking her. Mark my words, he's fucking her.'

Erection slung from his pants, Hughes laid another three lashes about the girl's back, Alice twisting and squirming. She understood. It was more homage he sought. But to surrender lay beyond her pride.

Alice's wilfulness slowly eroded Hughes' patience. His scheme to steal her dignity seemed doomed to failure. Her back whipped and smarting he dragged her down and forward by the lead, her face pressed to his crotch, her lips to his erection. There he tried to force her capitulation...

Seconds later Simon reached, grabbed for his equipment. The very atmosphere seemed to erupt. A laughing Alice, free of Hughes' grip, mocked a doubled, roaring, cursing monster.

Irrational fear seized the photographer as a red-faced Hughes launched his weight and rage at a ducking, evasive Alice. A hand still grasped his bitten penis, the man trying to corner the girl, the whip tight in his fist.

Her eyes mocked. Adrenaline set her heart racing. Alice avoided, Hughes lashing out in anger and frustration, the tail hitting the bench between them, the crack awesome.

'When I get,' he growled, 'my fucking hands on you, I'm going to skin you alive!'

'You're lucky I didn't bite the damn thing right off,' Alice warned.

He leapt towards the bench, whip thong cutting air. Alice dodged back, the tip just catching a breast, the pain sickening. 'Bastard!' she spat. 'That hurt!'

Hughes jumped the bench, landing feet in front of her. 'Like this?' he asked, laying the lash across her back, the tail cutting around her side and biting her soft belly.

Alice reacted. Spontaneous combustion. She straightened and lashed out with a foot. The skirt reached full stretch and split, her limb ripping through, her foot catching a disbelieving Hughes in the privates. He staggered back, his hands clasped to his groin. 'Bitch! You'll regret this!'

She shook her head. 'No, it's you that's in mourning. For your balls.'

Simon wound and fired repeatedly to catch the unexpected action.

Hughes exhaled, grimaced and straightened. 'Remind me next time to chain those feet together. Must be getting slow. You wouldn't have got away with that a few years ago.'

Alice knew he tried to distract her, that he'd try and take her by surprise, and when he did she would pay dearly for her defence. Her head spun with an overdose of adrenaline. She thrilled at every second, her senses alive. She backed to the wall, vulnerability magnified by her stance. Her cuffed hands prevented protection of her imperilled breasts, which swayed and trembled, proving an enticing target, one Hughes would not ignore.

That inch long welt still stinging, the skin puffed, Hughes launched another, making certain he was clear of her feet. Alice tried to turn, to avoid its snaking path, the tail slashing the same breast, a two-inch mark etch into that soft tissue.

'Ooh, you pig!' she screamed, turning to face the wall, guarding her breasts, pressing them anxiously to the surface.

Wells closed in, snapping and winding, taking shot after shot. Then Hughes was directly behind her, pushing his body against hers, forcing her hard against the wall. 'Just a taster,' he threatened. 'The gloves are off now, girlie. Anything goes.'

Her fingers curled, sharp talons seized his face, sunk into his cheeks. Hughes cursed, grabbed her wrists. 'You bitch!' he yelled, pulling away, scarlet smeared across his face.

Alice spun to face him. 'Gloves off. Your choice, not mine.'

'Seems she's a match for you, even fettered,' Wells remarked.

'Think it funny do you, cameraman?'

'Not funny. Just an observation, that's all.'

'You just keep on snapping, boy. I'll give you something to stun your clientele.'

He slashed the whip in an arc, Alice seeing too late his intention. Leather kissed her face, smacked her cheek with enough force to bring tears to her eyes. In that second of disbelief he was upon her. Alice turned, Hughes slapping her tensed belly with the flat of his hand, the force enough to double her. He propelled the girl forward, Alice falling heavily against the whipping bench.

She tried to retaliate, kicking and twisting, but her incapacity and his strength proved too much. The belt was over her back in half a second, pinning her to the slats.

Wiping his face with a handkerchief Hughes circled the unfortunate, the whip-stock wet in his sweating fist. He eyed a portion of flesh exposed and unmarked above her bottom. The struggle had bared an inch of buttocks.

The thong struck with the violence of a tornado. Flesh briefly lurched. Fire erupted, the mark a strip of volcanic lava. Alice cried out, the hurt crucifixion.

Hughes continued his circuit, Alice watching, waiting. She saw his arm rise. She writhed, the hurt too much.

He bent, gripped her skirt and yanked it high, the girl's bottom partially bared. He perused her mottled and bruised thighs. He stroked between, a finger riding the valley. Fingertip against her vagina he pushed, Alice gasping.

'Masochism can be so rewarding,' he mused. 'Provided, that is, you have a sadist you can trust.'

The man stepped back, Alice expecting. The whip slashed her upper thighs, Alice writhing with the insufferable smart.

'Kicking him in the nuts and clawing his face are not conducive to the respect and close relations necessary for such an intimate and random rapport.'

Flesh above her knees exploded in agony. There she hung in transient hell, legs balanced on curled toes, the limbs ramrod straight, the muscles tight and strained.

'Ours should be a special conjunction. A union of empathy.' Her fired legs proved too tempting. Hughes lashed them again, the tail navigating both, curling about the furthest and biting the fore. The girl lurched, her vocal gurgle unintelligible. He watched her antics, her obvious suffering pleasing him. 'Chain her ankles, Simon.'

The man looked up from his viewfinder. 'Sorry?'

'I said, chain her fucking ankles together. I want to see this bitch fettered. I want to see her in chains.'

Wells flinched to the almighty crack of whip on beaten rump. 'When you've had enough, Alice, just let me know,' Hughes taunted. 'Then you can crawl, prostrate yourself, beg me to…

'There lies an interesting scenario,' he pondered. 'I think we might go there.'

The girl squirmed, struggled to cope. She deserved the flogging; the Almighty was justified in the contrivance. Misty-eyed, tears wetting her face, she determined to endure. She would do nothing further to deter or terminate the punishment.

She felt the cold bite of steel. Simon fitted the manacles, heavy cylinders connected by two feet of thick chain.

'They suit, Alice,' Hughes remarked. 'Maybe we'll leave them on. Maybe I'll parade you later.'

Leather striped thighs again, Alice bucking, yelping aloud. He tossed a key to the photographer. 'Free her hands, Simon. Let's see if she's calmed down…

'Well?' the governor enquired as Alice rubbed her wrists and arms.

'Why don't you try shoving your cock in my mouth again?' she goaded. 'You know, trust me.'

The door flew open without warning, a hand seizing Smith and dragging her inside. Ruth backed away as the door slammed in her face. 'What the fuck?' she exclaimed to Drake.

Scrubbs held Rachel by an ear. 'Was this something to do with your being in my wardrobe, Sweet?'

Biting her lower lip, hauled onto tiptoe, Smith took in the scene. Hazel lay in Scrubbs' bed, blankets pulled to cover her nipples. Hands behind her head, the raven-haired beauty appeared nonchalant.

'What will you do to her if I say yes, Dennis?'

'When I was a lad in the children's home, and I

misbehaved, they used to make me stand with my back to the open fire. Naked like. And while I heated up, roasted like a chicken, they had their dinner. Bloody cruel that was.'

Smith noted the blazing logs in the hearth. 'I'm fucked if I'd just stand there and pissing roast. No one would.'

'If your hands are tied to your privates, and your ankles are bound together, and there is a sprinkling of sharp objects should you try to hop or kneel, there isn't a lot you can do except burn.'

Rachel glared at Hazel. 'You open your gob, Sweet. You say anyfing and God help me you'll fucking pay dear.'

Hazel lit a cigarette. She blew smoke and then a ring. 'Is that so, Smith? Best do it, Dennis. Let's watch the cow roast.'

'You fucking grass! We'll get you for this.'

'Fucking grass? Guess I must be. O'Leary says, so it is. Best play the part I've been branded with, eh? It was Smith's idea to shut me in your locker, Dennis.'

'You fucking liar!'

Hazel drew on her cigarette. 'Whatever, Rachel. Are you going to cane her like you said, Den? What was it now? Fifty, bent double with her legs wide?'

'Maybe. Strip, Rachel.' He let her ear go.

Rachel backed away, rubbing at the hurt. 'Go fuck yourself. You ain't Hughes. You're just that tart's flunkey. You ain't doin' nuffin' to me.'

Scrubbs grinned. 'Oh, I do like a bit of a challenge.'

Another set of fetters landed in front of Alice with a thump. 'Put those on your wrists,' Hughes ordered, wiping his hands with a cloth.

'Shove them up your arse.' Alice smiled.

'I thought we were getting somewhere.'

'You expect. That's your problem.'

'Put the shackles on her, Simon.' Hughes wandered, studying her body, thinking on the next course of action. Alice offered no protest. She merely watched as the man ratcheted the thick metal about her wrists.

Simon rose, Hughes stopping him. 'Have a feel, Mr photographer.'

The man hesitated. 'What, precisely?' he asked.

'As precise as you like. She's a tramp, a whore. She's been paid for whatever I want to do.' He leant towards the man. 'Squeeze her tits some, eh?'

Her breasts, perfectly shaped, firm, had tempted from the outset. Simon didn't need persuading to cup his hands about them.

Alice closed her eyes. She drifted in a sick, surreal and sexual world of anything goes for gratification. Morals, inhibitions, do's, don'ts, acceptable, unacceptable, tumbled about her mind. Confusion reigned supreme. She liked his touch, sensitive hands exploring, not paws groping. She enjoyed the stimulant, a man she barely knew feeling her in such an intimate way. Morally wrong? She didn't much care.

Dennis held Rachel in a shoulder lock, her arms pinned horizontal, his hands flat against her neck. Hazel, wearing one of his shirts, unfastened Smith's pinafore and then her blouse. Smith seethed. She said nothing. Instead she plotted an apt and terrible revenge.

'You want her completely naked?' Hazel asked.

'Every last stitch.'

The pinafore lay heaped around the blonde's ankles, her petticoat on top. Hazel looked up at Smith, a smirk on her face. Eyes laughing, she hauled the girl's knickers down. 'Just her shirt and bra left, Mr Scrubbs,' Hazel informed him.

'Undo her bra.'

Sweet released the clip. Dennis let the blonde go, deftly gripping the cuffs of her shirt as he did. A twist and turn and Rachel stood almost naked, a hand holding the bra cups against her breasts, the other pushed to her groin.

'I'm gonna complain about you and her,' Smith threatened, nodding at Hazel.

'Do that,' Scrubbs replied, unfazed. 'Have the governor ask you why. I'd like to see you explain without provoking violence to your arse.'

Five minutes later, after a brief struggle, Rachel Smith stood before a roaring fire, her wrists tied to wrought iron mantle supports, her feet apart, ankles bound to the brass hearth fender.

Hazel calmly bent over the bed, her shapely legs apart. Smith watched, peeved and envious, Scrubbs take the jet-haired bitch. Back to her, he unfastened his flies and released his cock. She noted Sweet's gasp as the length thrust into her.

The blonde warmed, her thighs and backside growing hotter by the minute. The heat penetrated and punished her flesh, her thighs, buttocks and back shrinking from the flames, her discomfort bordering on the unbearable. Scrubbs lunged, the suck of wet pussy undeniable, angering Rachel further.

The pair twisted in their sexual contortions, Smith able to see the slide of rigid penis, the enviable stretch of vagina. The blonde winced, hips thrust forward she pushed her rump as far from the flames as possible.

Orgasm retreating, Hazel watched her. 'Perhaps *she* wants it, Dennis. Perhaps Smith would like to feel the benefit of your massive cock.' She levelled smirking eyes on Smith. 'Is that it, Rachel? A bit envious, are you?'

Expression pained, Rachel ignored her, trying to move her rear from the heat of the fire. Body sweating she forced herself to speak. 'She ain't gonna last ten seconds, you know. You can't protect her all the time. And when you ain't looking someone is going to make her fucking sorry.'

Half a dozen energetic and prolonged thrusts and Dennis sighed. He pulled his stem free, and wiping it on a towel, faced Rachel. 'You seem to think Hazel's a favourite.'

Smith wrestled with the bonds and her burning arse. 'It's fucking obvious!'

Dennis shook his head. 'No, not at all. Just accepting what's been offered, that's all.'

Hazel stared, aghast. 'Dennis, you said...'

The man approached Smith, placing a hand on a tensed bottom cheek. 'Phew!' He whistled. 'That's hot, Smith. That must be really hurting by now. I know, I've been there.'

'If I said please?' Pleading blue pools on him.

'I know,' Dennis said enthusiastically, 'why don't you two switch places.'

'What?' Hazel squealed.

'You heard Smith. She thinks you're a favourite. Be best in the long run, if I prove you're not.'

Hughes stood over the pair, Alice choosing not to look up, Simon preoccupied. 'Seems she likes you, Mr Wells.' He rubbed his jaw. 'Perhaps you should fuck her.'

'Ignore him,' Alice advised. 'He's deluded.'

Strap eased, buckle pin clear, Hughes expected Alice to rise, but she remained, staring at Simon. The photographer climbed to his feet.

'Enough for today, Simon,' Hughes said. 'Thank you kindly. Please do your processing bit and send me the proofs.'

Alice lifted her torso from the bench, the slats pulling

from her flesh with a slurp. 'That's it then?' she asked.

'For Simon, yes. Not for you though, sweetheart. I haven't finished with you, not by a long chalk.'

Wells packed his cameras, the tripods and umbrellas. Alice sat on the bench, folded arms concealing her breasts. 'What do you think you're going to do, Adolf?' she asked Hughes.

'Forewarned is forearmed,' he replied. The chains impeding her assault Alice took a swing at him, but the man ducked in time as heavy links whistled over his head. 'Jesus!' he snorted, grabbing the girl around her waist. 'Five years fighting the Jerries, and they never came close to taking my head off. Seems I can't trust you. Seems I will have to disable your arms. Seems my pet poodle will have to suffer further restraint.'

'Why? You've had what you wanted. You've got your photos. What is it with you?'

Hughes turned her, held her against him with one arm, the other hand lifting her chin. He forced his lips to hers, the kiss insanely passionate. Alice resisted, then gave ground, meeting his foraging tongue with hers. The girl roused and confused, Hughes admitted, 'If I can't have what I love, then I hurt it.'

'Love?' Alice mocked. 'You don't even understand the word.'

He embraced her harder, their bodies pressured. 'I thought I was immune, but I guess there must be a streak of human being in me somewhere.'

Alice stared, incredulous. 'I doubt it. It's lust. Pure, unadulterated lust. You want me to offer me unequivocally. Love doesn't come into it.'

'You hard-nosed bitch. Marry me.'

Alice pushed him away. 'A union made in hell, hm? Me wondering who you're seducing next?'

'I'd be faithful to *you*.'

'You have no real inkling of what that means. It's a

word to you. It's a way of getting what you want.'

'Okay, have it your way. Get dressed. I'm just about finished here.'

Alice offered her wrists. 'Keys?'

'Probably. Somewhere. No idea at the moment.'

'How can I get dressed with these things on?'

'Try a hairpin.'

'Oh, funny!'

'Come to my office in about an hour's time. I'll see what I can do.'

'And in the meantime?'

'An apron. Go see cook, and ask him for an apron. At least that'll cover your boobs, if not your whipped back.' Hughes smiled. 'But who's going to see you? Cook? A few cons, maybe. Preesal. I think he's on duty downstairs. I'm sure you'll come up with something. You're so smart, after all.' He left the girl simmering, wondering what he was up to.

Hazel wrenched on her bonds. 'I thought we had a deal?' she stated, teeth clenched.

'Jailers don't generally negotiate with convicted criminals, Haze. Sorry if I gave the impression they did.'

'You double-dealing snake! I thought you liked me. I hoped we might…' Face red with humiliation, tears wetting her cheeks, she pushed her hips away from the fire.

Dennis forced a hot-arsed Smith over the back of a chair. 'I do like you. You're a fine looking girl. But as for anything else, well.' He scratched his head. 'I believe non-fraternisation is a rule here.'

He slapped Rachel's butt with gusto, the girl jerking so forcefully the chair legs screeched on the floor. 'Once I'm done with this,' his hand stung the other cheek, 'I'll deal with you.'

183

Sweet whimpered. 'But I'm burning here!'

'Serves you right,' Smith snorted, her hot backside shuddering to a steady rhapsody of vigorous spanks.

'You exaggerate,' Dennis added, Rachel squirming, face screwed in pain.

'What did you mean, deal with me?' Sweet demanded.

Smith rose to tiptoe, her buttocks tight, thighs pressed together. She whimpered with every slap.

'I mean, Sweet, you and Smith must share the responsibility of invading my privacy. Ergo, you suffer the same.'

Smith squirmed. She stuffed the corner of a bed blanket in her mouth, biting hard. Still Scrubbs' hand pounded, still his tough palm slapped her raging behind.

'You've played me for an idiot, haven't you? You're worse than Hughes.' Sweet screwed her face in pain. 'For God's sake, I'm roasting here!'

The man stopped, hand gently rubbing the fired bum. 'You fooled yourself.'

Alice heard the thrum, the blat, the roar. It meant nothing at the time, just another noisy motorcycle passing the Hope. She tied the shirtsleeves around her neck, the garment covering her back. 'Pig!' she spat, searching the room for something to cover her front. 'What's he up to?'

She picked up her trousers and held them to her breasts. 'What next? Why an apron? Why these chains? Why this mauve skirt?'

Alice swept by his office, the door wide open, Hughes sat working. 'Pig!' she hissed, Hughes glancing up, Alice gone.

She took the steps one at a time, her tether allowing no more. Cook worked in the kitchens on the ground floor. Alice didn't want to ask, but she knew Hughes.

Turning up on time wearing just an apron would probably be the only way of removing the shackles.

One flight down she detected the unmistakable tap of shoes. She leaned over the rail, trying to see, Mavis' voice drifting up.

Alice turned to go back. Five steps and she stopped, realising the door on the next landing was locked, and her keys were on the top floor in her room. She held her wrists out, staring at the chains, her trousers falling from her breasts. 'I bet you planned this, too.'

The click of heels on stone grew closer, Alice realising Mavis was not alone. She stayed where she was, facing up the stairwell, leaning against the wall. *'Please just go straight on up. Don't stop. Don't chat. And don't mention the chains, please.'*

Mavis drew alongside, glanced at Alice and smiled. Then she spotted the manacles. Blushing, she said to the woman with her, 'This way.'

Amanda Jenkins ignored the suggestion. She inspected what she assumed to be a con in chains. There in the gloom of the second floor stairwell, defiance faced the implacable. Pride challenged perfection. The immovable met the irresistible.

Amanda reminded Alice of the wicked witch of the north, except she was incongruously dressed in motorcycle leathers, with a crash helmet and goggles tucked under her arm.

Long dark-brown hair snaked about a thin, almost gaunt face, the woman's cold blue eyes large and penetrating. Her 'beak' protruded, the tip hooked above thin bloodless lips, the woman's jaw minimal. 'What's this prisoner doing on the stairs, Mavis?'

'Oh, Alice…'

'None of your business,' Alice replied, feeling aggrieved and taking a dislike to Amanda.

'Ah, the voice of the gutter. No more than I would

185

expect from a… what are you? Whore? Thief? Thug?'

'Pervert. Try pervert.'

'I think you should know…' Mavis tried again.

'That I'm a special case,' Alice continued. She held her wrists up. 'I have to be chained.' She lifted the skirt. 'Ankles, too.' She laughed. 'Houdini, I am. Out more than I'm in. Dangerous, too.'

Hand on hip Amanda suggested, the proposal meant to disconcert, 'Perhaps the chains aren't enough.'

'And what would you suggest? A good whipping, perhaps?'

'That might teach a worthless piece of rubbish a lesson in manners, if nothing else.'

Alice turned to make her way downstairs. 'I expect it should have been nice meeting you.'

Amanda scowled at her. 'As I was saying, there's one who could do with a lesson in manners. I shall have a word with Geoffrey about that one.'

'That was Alice.'

'*Alice*,' the woman repeated.

Rachel kicked wildly, arms thrashing, fingers clawing air. Tears ran down her blotchy face, the girl sobbing and pleading. 'Anyfing, please, I'll do, say, tell you anyfing. Just don't hit my arse any more. Please, Mr Scrubbs.'

Dennis laid a studded paddle on the girl's crimson and mauve behind. 'That's a different tune, isn't it? Much better. I like that.'

Smith slumped over the chair. 'What yer want to know again?' she asked, glaring at Hazel.

Dennis gently massaged the girl's beaten cheeks. 'Ruth and Alice,' he whispered close, Sweet unable to hear, 'what goes between them?'

'Bit of rubber I suppose,' the girl replied, misunderstanding the question.

Dennis hit her rump, Rachel screeching. 'Where does Sweet come into the equation, then?' His finger stroked into the crease, Rachel relaxing.

'She's an old mate of Alice's. She's slept with Ruth, and some say Alice as well. Don't know about three in a bed though. No one's said owt, and I've not seen anything.' She kept her voice hushed.

'What do you know about Ruth?'

'She's hard and she's devious. She bears a grudge and never forgets. She'll take you down in a way that suits her, probably when you least expect it.'

'Have *you* slept with her?'

'Nah. I ain't like that. Blokes is all I'm interested in.'

'How long since you slept with a bloke?' His fingers slipped between her thighs, resting against her vagina.

Rachel shivered. 'About eighteen months.'

'Think about it much?' He toyed with her sex lips.

'Yeah. Nights mostly, when I'm trying to kip.'

'How long you got to go?' His finger dipped between the folds, the girl sucking air.

'T-two years.'

'Do you know what I'd like, Rachel? What I really need at this moment in time?'

'A fuck?'

'Besides that. I could do with a pair of ears on the dorms. I could do with eyes watching Alice, watching Ruth, watching Hazel. I would like to know when they meet, what they say and what they do. Their relationships with the staff, namely Sheila and Mr Hughes, would be interesting too.'

'I dunno, Mr Scrubbs.' She nodded towards a distraught and inquisitive Hazel. 'If she hears any of this…'

'It will negate the enmity between you. In other words, Hazel will have something on you, and you on Hazel.' Dennis hit her backside with a force nine,

187

twelve being his ultimate. Studded leather crucified extremely sore buttocks. The girl squealed, her hands tending the hurt. 'Don't like your answer, Rachel.'

Panting, waiting for the initial fires to subside, she finally managed, 'Okay, I'll do what I can. But I can't follow Alice too much.'

'It's really quite simple, Rachel. You are, you see, in a privileged position. You are privy to Ruth O'Leary's thoughts, deeds and plans. And as such you are privy to much that happens in the Hope. I would like to be privy too. And if I happen to hear a titbit from somewhere else, I guess I'll have to *correct* the situation.'

'Okay,' she whispered, the man's fingers deep inside her pussy.

'Simple choice, Rachel.' Dennis lit a cigarette and placed it between her lips. He poured a short measure of whiskey and sat the glass before the blonde. 'Or...' he added, the paddle striking her rump with a force ten.

Rachel coughed, smoke going up her nose and in her eyes. She grit her teeth, eyelids squeezed tight.

Dennis leant down and kissed the fires. He ran his tongue over those bruised dunes, Rachel dragging on the fag, not wanting to miss one luxurious puff of the *Players Navy Cut*. Dennis lifted the girl's legs, Rachel placing a hand on the chair seat to steady her position. Scrubbs stood with her thighs either side of his face, the girl's reddened bum squeezed and tensed with expectancy. Still she puffed, the whiskey glass held by the same hand.

He slid between vaginal folds, his tongue licking deep. Rachel jerked, her body tensing, buttocks drawn tight. Scrubbs' hands wandered to that devastated bottom, gauging the heat, the aftermath of his persuasion. His fingers delved the fiercely stung cheeks, tips testing the juvenile quality of that erogenous corpulence. His tongue probed and poked, Rachel succumbing, coasting toward an ecstatic climax. Cigarette butt tossed past Hazel into the fire, she took to coaxing that orgasm, her hand energetically squeezing her breasts. Her sensations rapidly gathered momentum, her thighs tensing with the rapturous approach.

Rachel glanced Hazel's way, the girl glaring at her with hatred. 'Perhaps *she* wants it, Dennis. Perhaps Sweet would like to feel the benefit of your tongue. Uh, that's good!' She levelled loathing eyes on Hazel. 'Is that it, Haze? A bit envious are you?'

'Yes, Mavis,' Hughes said without looking up.

'It's Miss… ouch!'

'Miss who?'

Amanda Jenkins swept by, crop in hand. 'Geoffrey,' she barked, holding out a gloved hand.

'Amanda.' Hughes smiled. 'You're late.'

'That's a moneybags' prerogative. Now, tell me, who is the angel in chains?'

Hughes indicated for Mavis to leave with a wag of a finger. 'I'm fine, thank you. How are you, Amanda? Would you like a cup of tea?'

'A new recruit?' the woman persisted.

'Maybe a biscuit? Or am I in a position to buy you lunch?'

'Whore or tealeaf?' Amanda asked.

'Missionary,' Hughes replied, unable to resist.

Amanda laughed. 'Yes, they do usually come to a sticky end. Is she for me?'

'Don't tempt me.'

Amanda pulled a roll from her pocket. Holding the cash up, she said, 'That could be *just* the deposit on a girl like that.'

'And what would you do with such a consummate creature?'

Jenkins unzipped all but the last two inches of her

189

leather jacket, Hughes noticing the lack of clothing beneath. The unlined doeskin followed the contours of the woman's body, a figure he found quite appealing.

'I'd curb her tongue for a start.'

Hughes smiled, eyes sparkling. 'Oh, wonderful, you've met with the barbed tongue. And I was beginning to think she reserved that just for me.'

'Why do you allow it? That's not the Geoffrey Hughes I know.' She cast him a look of suspicion. 'Is it because of her looks? Her figure? Has a girl finally got her claws into you?'

Hughes opened the drinks cabinet. 'Brandy? It's nigh on evening.'

'A small one, thank you.'

'Curb her tongue. I like that. I might just do that.'

'Why is she chained? Confined to the basement, I could understand. But running freely about the building?'

'Hardly running, Amanda.'

'You're not going to enlighten me, are you? God, you can be so frustrating at times!'

'That Scottish brawn you employ. Do you think he could modify a piece for me?'

'He could make you a scold's bridle.'

'Talking of Scots. How's the brainless brawn these days?'

'Thinking about an end to her sentence, so I believe.'

'Will you keep her?'

'She still has a penchant for whoring. Young Robert pays her on a regular basis for sex. And I flog them on a regular basis when I catch them.' Amanda paused for a moment. 'I expect I shall sell her to a madam I know in Glasgow. At least the bird can talk the heathen language.'

'You'll be looking for a replacement, then?'

'I've seen her.'

'Alice is not for sale. She never will be.'

'My, my, and here stands a man who would sell his own mother for the right price.'

'It all boils down to purpose. My mother is past hers, Alice isn't.'

'So, why the chains?'

'A lesson, no more.'

'Breaking her in?'

'I don't want to break Alice. I want to help her.'

'Shall I come back when you're feeling better?'

'Alice is already what I want her to be. She simply doesn't realise it.'

'Where did she spring from? What did she do?'

'She sprang from Manchester Railway Station, I believe. And what she did was fall in love and hate. Now, she's desperately seeking a Lancashire Rose.'

'Some days – no, most days – there's no point talking to you.'

'Then talk, don't pry.'

'Lambing season soon, isn't it?'

'Twenty-five for a copy this time.'

'It had better be good.'

'It always is. This time, though,' Hughes lit his pipe, Amanda waving the smoke away, 'I'm thinking of a duet. Two for the price of one.'

'Ah, good, any chance of a preview?'

'That would spoil the surprise, would it not?'

'Twenty-five is still bloody expensive. I could rent a girl for that, and experience it in person.'

Hughes shook his head. 'No, Amanda, you couldn't.'

'I've had the room modified. I think you will find the performance uncontrived and extremely sensual.'

Smith exited, leaving Hazel to Dennis. He pulled the slip-knots free, Hazel dropping to her knees, hands tending her heated backside.

'It's dangerous to assume, Hazel. I think I've saved your bacon, but you'd best sleep with one eye open, as they say.'

Sweet untied her ankles. 'Can I take my incinerated bum and go?'

'I promised you the same as Smith. Now haven't you learned anything? If you go back to your dorm with no sign of a slapped arse they'll think connivance. Best return with a severely spanked bottom, Haze. For your own good.'

'I's too busy to fart about getting' you's aprons. Can't yer see I's makin' the tea?' Ewan McKenzie glared down at Alice, the man's bulk, some said, was the eighth blunder of the world. 'Well?' he barked when the girl didn't leave.

Mr McKenzie had a reputation. Inmates were assigned to kitchen duty on a rota. The Hope didn't care to pay for a full complement, and from Hughes' point of view dedicated, vindictive staff who loathed society's misfits were hard to find. So McKenzie acted as overseer to ensure no one put anything other than edibles into the menu.

'Mr McKenzie, I don't want to pull rank...'

The huge man roared, 'Pull rank, my dear? You's don't have any rank to pull down here. Especially in chains, you's don't.' He picked up a large metal serving slice.

'I's be just as likely to heave you's over that there trestle as anyone in this kitchen. So if you's don't mind, I's got work to do.' McKenzie turned his back on Alice.

One of the roster girls whispered as she passed, 'Best leave it, miss. He's got one on today.'

Alice glanced at the carpenter's trestle McKenzie utilised for punishments, and then at the metal slice. 'Just tell me where the aprons are then.'

The man looked over a shoulder, his face a scowl. 'What we's got ain't what you's looking for.'

'How can you know that?'

'Scat,' he growled. 'Before I's takes the slice to that pretty arse.'

Alice padded barefoot back up the stairs, climbed to the top floor and pressed the bell. Some minutes later Dennis Scrubbs unlocked the door for her. 'Forget your keys?' he asked, running his eyes over her.

Alice marched by. 'They're in my room.'

'What was it, fancy dress?' he enquired, following her.

'You know what it was. You're just upset because I wouldn't let you stay.'

'Nice chains. That your actress's wages?'

Alice threw open her room's door and tossed the trousers onto the bed. Breasts bared, she asked, 'Hughes. What did he tell you?'

'Lovely tits. Is there a message there somewhere? Am I missing a point?' Alice opened her mouth to reply, Dennis continuing. 'No, I haven't missed the point. There are two very seductive and enticing points right under my nose. Well they could be between my lips…'

'Not both at the same time, though.' Alice regretted the words as they left her lips. They suggested something she didn't feel – friendly.

'He just invited me. Never said a word about what or why.'

'Can you sew?'

'I was in the army for four bloody years.' He smiled, perplexed.

'Don't suppose you can pick locks, though?'

He gazed at her mouth-watering breasts. 'I would happily spend the next six months trying.'

'I want you to stitch a pair of knickers, a bra and a camisole for me. While I'm wearing them.'

'To fuck Hughes?'

'Oh yes.'

Alice lay on the bed bereft of every shred of clothing, watching Dennis cut the gusset in a pair of her panties. She knew the impact she had on the man; that was evident by what he could not hide. She couldn't ignore the effect he had on her either. She could have played it more subtle. She could have kept her intimacy more private. But rebellion prompted outrageous acts, Alice as keen to shock, to disturb as she was disturbed. If Dennis could have read her mind, there amidst the tangle of contradictions, the tide of change, the hurricane of rage, lay the newborn, promiscuous and naïve Alice Rose.

Dennis played for good manners. He kept his eyes diverted from temptation, his focus on the job in hand. 'I'm not going to even try to fathom this place and the crazy goings on. Some fucking madhouse, ain't it though?'

Alice lay on her side facing the man, knees drawn up, arm slung over a hip. 'What's this crazy bitch doing naked on the bed in front of me? Why's her butt been beaten black and blue? Why's she been whipped?'

'Never entered my head.' Dennis held up the modified panties.

'You're growing on me.'

Dennis held them to her feet. 'What's this all about? Why'd he do this to you?'

Alice pulled the elastic to her waist. 'Why did *I* let him?' She parted her legs, Scrubbs passing the cloth between those inviting limbs.

'Well I guess there might be some redemption for him there.' Dennis focussed on the job in hand. Mouth dry, he swallowed. The new stitches required his supporting fingers. 'Do you really want me to touch you there?' he

194

asked, sure she would say no.

Alice leant against the wall, body angled, legs parted. 'Without shaking,' she replied.

His gossamer touch of fingers took her breath. The close proximity of the man's hand to her vaginal slit, the sight of his finger inside her panties, brushing against her pubic bush, launched a tingle she found difficult to ignore.

'A bit intimate, this,' Dennis remarked. 'Bit of a torture, too.'

Alice watched, her sex lit. 'I'm not going to explain it. I don't even care about the rights and wrongs any more. I've done it. I've gone through with it.'

'This is taking friendship a little too far.'

'At times it was incredible, and at others it was utter hell. But all the time I was with him I felt so alive. And do you know what? Now, striped and bruised, my heartbeat back to normal, I feel so calm. Guilty, but calm. An inner peace I haven't experienced for years.'

Scrubbs tied the stitches off and broke the thread. 'That was more heroic than anything I did in the bloody war.'

Alice sat, Scrubbs putting her strapless bra on for her. 'This is a first. I usually take them off. Why guilty?'

'Because it's not right. I know it's my body. I know it's only me getting hurt. But no matter how I look at it, it's not right.'

'There's a lot worse going on in the world minus the recrimination bit.'

'Maybe, but this is me. This is the battle between Alice the puritan and Alice the slag.'

Dennis fed the camisole over outstretched arms and head. 'Who's going to win then?' he asked, sitting on the bed beside her.

'Every day the puritan loses a bit more ground. I'd say by Christmas the slag will be in control.'

'If you ask me, even though I don't know you very well...' Dennis lay back, gazing up at the ceiling.

'Yes?' Alice asked.

'It's the bloody puritan bit that makes you all the more attractive. I mean, you've a lovely face, don't get me wrong. You've a body worthy of worship. You've probably the best tits and arse north of Watford. But it's that little piece of angel tucked inside your heart. That's what turns us blokes to jelly.'

'Just when a girl gets to hating every bastard with a cock between his legs, you have to spoil it.'

'Oh, don't take no notice of me. I'm genuine bastard right the way through. I've got certificates, so I have. You go on believing all blokes is motherless. Don't let me spoil it.'

Alice pulled on a knee-length skirt, Dennis not missing the rise and squeeze of rump as the waistband passed. 'Like I said, best arse north of Watford.'

'And what's south of Watford?'

'Jacqueline Pontefract.'

Alice chuckled. 'Oh look at the sad bitch. Fettered like a slave.'

'You didn't say why.'

The girl sighed. 'Cos we're mad, I guess. Games, Dennis. His games. My games. His bid for dominance. My refusal to let him. My deep down inner wish to be dominated. If I didn't have any pride it would be so easy.'

'Maybe he doesn't want it easy. Maybe it's the battle that keeps him coming.'

'I'll go and see him. He'll start. I'll lose my temper. Then I'll do something I won't be sorry for. And hey presto Alice gets done unto. Trouble is, Alice wants to get done unto. Even when Alice has spent the day getting done unto.'

'Go with your heart. Ignore the head bit.'

'Temptation, Dennis. Surrendering to temptation. There is logic to the teachings and why we should resist. There must always be a point where we must say no. Either that, or slide into total and complete decadence. What makes us the supreme animal is moral standing. What makes life tolerable is morality. Satan seeks anarchy, the breakdown of law and order. Do you see my point?'

'Yes, I see your point, Alice. If you go back to him dressed in chains and an apron Satan wins and the world will come to an immediate end. The price of beer will double, tobacco will be rationed, every prostitute will disappear up their own orifice and Geoffrey Hughes will win the war of the Rose.'

'I will bend but I won't break.'

'Oh, I think the bending will suffice for the governor. Go see him. Have your game. Be bendable. Don't break. Spit on Satan. Then ask yourself, am I happy? Am I fulfilled? What more do I want out of life?'

'Sanity,' Alice replied, sighing.

Chapter 11

Wrapped in a blanket, Sweet squatted on her cot, seething. She said nothing, glowering at anyone who dared to venture close or attempted to speak. Rachel squatted on a bed chatting with Ruth, both glancing repeatedly Sweet's way.

Drake caught Dawn Summers by the arm as she came in. Smirking, eyes on Hazel, she whispered something to the girl.

Drake knew Summers. She knew the girl didn't give a damn about anyone or consequence. She leant on the doorjamb to watch.

'Is that this winter's collection?' Dawn asked, leaning on the foot-rail of Hazel's bed. 'Coarse blanket direct from 'arrods, eh? Sorry, you don't do coarse, do you? Just refined and superior.' Dawn held a hand up. 'No, sorry, I stand corrected. What was it now? Cock coming out of your big gob cos it was shoved so far up your cunt. Ingratiate? Is that the word?'

Ruth took up residence beside Hazel. 'Can't trust no one, can yer Haze?' she goaded, aiming to annoy.

'Fuck off.'

'What did yer expect?'

Hazel shrugged.

'Trouble wiv playin' favourites, ain't it?'

Sweet ignored the accusation.

'Been tellin' tales, ain't yer?'

'You're bound to believe Smith. No point in me saying anything, is there?'

'I know Scrubbs fucked you.'

'So because I got fucked I've been telling tales? Has it occurred to you I might not have wanted to be fucked?'

'Rachel reckons yer give 'im yer cunt. Makes you a fuckin' liar, don't it?'

'And what was Smith...' Hazel fell silent.

'What? What was Smith what?'

'Doesn't matter.'

'I don't know whether it's cos you fink you're a cut above. Whether you is thick as pig shit, or it's cos you're a slimy backstabbin' cow. But you bin talkin', ain't yer?'

'I've had it with all of you. Just because I come from a better family than you gutter dregs it makes me a grass.'

'You know what I think?' Ruth leant close.

'I don't care what you think.'

'I think we're gonna have to sort yer.'

'You know what I reckon you'd look good in?' Dawn

198

offered.

'Go on,' Hazel challenged. 'Let's hear this pearl of wisdom.'

'Barbed wire. That's what.'

Rachel Smith leant against Summers, her arms on the girl's back. 'Yeah, I'd go along with that. Wrap the bitch in it.'

'Especially her gob,' added Carol Wisbeck.

'That's about your level,' Hazel defended. 'About what I'd expect from a bunch of ignorant savages.'

'Fink it's a great idea,' O'Leary opined. ''Cept there ain't none.'

Hazel pulled the blanket tight about her body, long legs drawn up. Her lack of clothes added to her vulnerability. Clothes that had been stolen or hidden.

'There is,' Drake corrected.

'Like where?' Ruth asked, intrigued.

'Like here.' Joan Catterall held out a canvas bag.

Hazel paled. Her dark eyes darted back and forth, the girl trying to decipher whether they meant it or whether it was just a cruel joke.

Ruth looked inside the bag. 'Oh look, rusted to fuck, too.'

'Might give the bitch gangrene then,' Dawn goaded.

'It's tetanus, you dopey bitch,' Hazel corrected.

'Where did yer get it?' Ruth asked Catterall.

'Didn't. Drake did.'

The big woman smiled. 'When I heard what she did to Rach I thought of that. I thought how nice the stuck-up cow would look wrapped in it. And I knew Preesal had it for taking home. He nicked it from the stores, so I pinched it off him. Seemed just, that did.'

Ruth held the bag at arm's length and let it go, the sack hitting the floor with a thud. 'Be all right, Haze, as long as yer don't move.'

'Or breathe.' Summers laughed.

'Oh that would be nice.' Rachel ran a hand through Sweet's hair.

Hazel drew the blanket tight. 'And if you think I'll let you get away with it, then you're all barking mad.'

'We'll need a pair of pliers and some cutters.' Ruth wrenched the blanket from Hazel, the move unexpected. She scrutinised the state of the girl's back and hips. 'Ain't your week is it, gel?'

'And what about her?' Hazel nodded at Smith, the blonde looking anxious. 'Has she said what all the whispering was about?'

'What whispering?' Rachel demanded.

'You and Scrubbs, whispering away. That was before he gave you the fag, and his tongue as far up your cunt as he could get it.'

Alice didn't bother knocking. She waltzed directly into Hughes' office, her intent to disrupt and annoy.

Hughes looked up, that familiar pipe gripped by teeth. His expression stopped Alice in her tracks. 'I didn't hear you knock,' he said, ruffled.

'Who are you to criticise?' the girl riposted. 'When manners were dished out you weren't even present, let alone at the back of the queue.'

He threw out an arm. 'Would you believe that this only a few weeks ago wouldn't have said boo to a goose?'

Amanda levelled hard cold eyes on Alice. 'Give her to me, Geoffrey. I could teach her manners in less than a day.'

'Give her?' Alice questioned. 'Give her? Who do you think you're talking about?'

'Oh, she's got grit, Amanda. Don't you agree?'

'She's got a mouth that needs curbing.'

'We've been there before.' Hughes sank his brandy in one gulp. 'Maybe I'll order a saddle as well. What's your girth, Alice?'

'Just unlock these chains!'

'Why aren't you wearing the apron?'

Alice held out her wrists. 'Chains!'

The man rose and navigated the desk, strutting towards her. 'I said apron and nothing else.'

'And why should I?'

'Because,' he shoved her against the wall, her arms rising in defence, a forearm across her chest deliberately squashing her breasts, he lifted her skirt and thrust his free hand between her legs, 'I wouldn't be doing this.'

Alice failed to retaliate. Her stubborn pride prevented total capitulation. 'Who do you think you are?' she demanded angrily.

'The bloke who's got his hand inside your knickers. The bloke who turns you on or off like a tap, whether you like it or not.' He closed on her ear and whispered, 'The bloke you want to make unrestrained love to you, except you blank it.'

'Oh, I've offered it to you. On a plate. But you declined. Aren't you going to introduce me to the hard-faced pile of bones?'

Hughes grinned. 'I'm renting you out. Five quid an hour. Nothing barred.'

Alice studied Amanda. 'Okay.'

A slight smile played on his lips, his eyes bright. 'You don't believe me?'

'Why shouldn't I? I mean, you wouldn't lie to me, would you?'

'She already told us that. You got the poker, she got the little organ. And the whisperin' was Scrubbs trying to get more on you so he could really punish yer. But Rach refused to tell 'im owt. Hence the state of her arse.'

'Mine ain't faired too well, either, or hadn't you noticed?'

'Yer didn't get the studded paddle, did yer? Must 'ave been a bit of a shocker all in all,' Ruth suggested.

'What must have been?' Hazel huddled, trying to retain an air of indifference, even though her naked state and marked body elevated her vulnerability.

'Comin' 'ere. There yer was leadin' the idyllic life, everything yer could ever want – money, fineries, connections and, what else?' She looked about her. 'Come on, gels, 'elp us out 'ere. What did this grassin' rat have going for her?'

'Some highfalutin' geezer with a big posh motor,' Rachel offered.

'Did yer?' Ruth asked. 'Did yer 'ave some highfalutin' geezer? Did yer 'ave his posh nob on the leather back seats of his Roller? Or did dear pater keep his eyes on yer? But even he couldn't of saved yer last night, could he?'

Ruth's words triggered a barrage of emotive recollections. Some pertinent, some hurled from a remote and forgotten past, Hazel unsure which belonged to where. Arrogance had bedazzled and confused. Animal magnetism fostered seduction. Ill-founded faith devoured trust. All love had been fabricated. Self-loathing pursued surrender. Sacrifice offered only recrimination.

Images tumbled, haphazard, hazy sepia, all blurred and indistinct. Her mind struggled, rejecting the hazy, regretting the unambiguous.

Ruth placed an arm around Sweet's shoulders. 'So what turned yer to poison?'

Memories cascaded.

'Or was yer always a gutless, disloyal, filthy tramp?'

Hazel stared sightless at the bed. 'If that's what you want to believe.'

'I'm gonna make you beg.' Ruth landed a backhander to Hazel's cheek, the girl barely flinching.

Shadows intruded. Cast in granite he stood, a grey trilby hiding his face. Hazel shivered. A tear welled and spun, twinkling down that stung face.

O'Leary moved close, inspecting the teardrop. 'What's this, blubbin'?'

Hughes moved so close the hairs on the back of her neck stood on end. She could smell him; man, confident animal. His touch launched a bolt of exhilaration. There in the dark they acted out the epilogue.

'You ain't listening, are you?'

Hazel didn't look up. 'Unusually sensitive of you, but you're right, Ruth, I'm not listening. So why don't you fuck off?'

O'Leary laughed. 'You forgetting who you're talkin—'

In one rapid movement Hazel seized a handful of O'Leary's hair and launched the girl's face towards her waiting knee. Most heard the sickening crunch. No one could believe what Sweet had done.

Ruth rolled from the bed, hand clasping her nose, eyes flooding, crimson tainting her fingers.

Against the wall, still wearing those knickers. He was passion, raging intensity, a wicked manipulator. He orchestrated her feelings, emotions and body. He played carnal strings that Hazel wasn't aware existed. He thrilled her beyond possibility. Within minutes she gave herself. She found his cock and guided it to her cloth-protected fanny. The gusset yanked to one side, Hazel felt his solid dome there. She longed for its thrust. She yearned to be stretched and crudely fucked. Hughes didn't disappoint. Bra cups abruptly tugged from her breasts he sank teeth into the supple, heaving flesh. Hazel gasped to the pain, Hughes manoeuvring to engage a nipple. Sighs eclipsed the suckling, Hughes' mouth, tongue and teeth working that virgin areola. He ascended, tongue raking throat. Beneath her ear he kissed, nuzzled and bit before descending again. Sweet held his cock, fingers around the thick shaft, her pussy desperate for its plunge. Her other breast fell to his machinations, the man's face pressed to it, soft warm flesh cushioning his mouth and nose. Then he dropped, his erection torn from her grasp. Knickers snatched down, Hazel squealing with delight and surprise, he sank his teeth deep into her bush. His tongue immediately made amends, wet organ darting, teasing, pleasing her cunt. Face pressed to those dark coils he forced his lips between her legs, licking her lips, antagonising the ecstasy.

Then he lifted her. Hands on her whipped rump he pushed her to the wall, his cock stuffed into her cunt, thrusting deep inside her. Hazel's legs lifted, squeezing his waist, her sex enjoying every inch feasible. The couple fevered, animated, Hughes prolonged the coition, his lunging pole taking her to the edge of climax, then withdrawing. Hazel's feet found the floor, him turning her, forcing her flat against the wall, her breasts cushioned.

She waited, barely daring to breathe while he ogled those moonlit dunes, the blue-washed buttocks welted and provocative. Hazel winced to the slap, his hand levying a hefty penalty for their charm. Those lambasted cheeks suffered for thirty seconds or so, the flesh stung some dozen times. Bottom burning, Sweet made no protest to his second vaginal intrusion. Bent over, hands to the wall, legs apart she watched that torpedo take her. In that eerie half-light she revelled in the separation of her lips and the rapid plummet of bough-hard stem. She swam heady in the waters of delirium, his penis thrusting and ebbing, his mighty balls swinging beneath. Again he carried her almost beyond the brink, and then without a word he removed the pleasure, fist taking her by the hair and forcing her over the whipping stool. He bade her remain with the threat of a wagged finger, then those enticingly swaying breasts he lashed. He stung them and no more. The whip slashed and bit, breasts jostled and stirred but not welted. Scarlet stripe after stripe he lay to her bosom, Hazel lusting for every acid cut.

Still pinned there, Hughes tossed the whip to one side. His plum offered, Hazel accepted, her mouth barely able to cope. She sucked him, carried him close, Hughes withholding his seed, thereby heightening the sexual madness. Her backside inflamed him. The fullness, roundness, the curves and plump consistency drove him to distraction. The sound of implement thudding, slapping, whip-cracking on that naked hide furnished an exhilaration second to none.

Sheila's timely arrival saved Hazel and Hughes from their own excesses. 'Get some clothes on, Sweet,' she bid. 'And get off to your dorm.'

Hughes steered Alice out into the corridor. 'I don't lie. I don't have to lie.'

'You'd say anything to get what you want.'

'Such as?'

'You know my mother. It's not true, is it? I mean, it's a bit coincidental, a touch on the incredible side.'

'Most good-looking and sexy women I generally like to screw. Sweet, attractive as she is, in some ways even better looking than you, I just wanted to fuck. But you? What the hell is it about you, Hussey? To me you're more than a piece of shag. You're a Rembrandt. You're the finest piece of porcelain. You're a magnificent sunset.' His mouth tightened. 'What I'm saying, is you're far more than just a *screw*. You're damned easy on the eye. I like to look at you, Alice.'

'I suppose I should be impressed. The great Geoffrey Hughes likes the way I look. Now, mother. Rose

Hussey. Do… you… know… her?'

Abruptly uncomfortable, Hughes stuffed hands in trouser pockets. He looked away. 'It's not that she doesn't want to see you, Alice. It's been eighteen years. She never expected to see you again. Rose feels that sleeping dogs are best left lying.'

'You shit!'

He threw his arms apart. 'The absolute truth, Alice. What can I do? I can't make her see you. I can't give you her address, or her telephone number. I wouldn't do that to you. I won't betray a trust.'

'Go on, wriggle some more. And take these chains off. Game's over. We're over.'

'There's a family secret. Only another member of the family could possibly know. Yes?' Alice frowned.

'Rose asked me to tell you…' He whispered in the girl's ear. 'True?' he asked, moving back.

Shocked, she asked, 'She really doesn't want to know me?'

'Give it time. Let her get used to the idea. Coincidental and incredible as it seems, I know Rose well. She speaks for your welfare, not hers.'

'What did she say?'

Amanda stuck her head around the door. 'I haven't got all day, Geoffrey.'

'He's busy,' Alice snapped.

'Do you want my business or not?' she demanded.

'I *said* he's busy!'

Hughes turned, Alice grabbing his tie, dragging him back. 'An answer, if you want *my* business.'

'Now's not the time.'

'Now is the time. Ask Amanda to go.'

'No.'

Alice held out her wrists. 'Then take these off. You choose her. You chain her.'

'Your immaturity is showing.'

206

'This is how I feel! Now if you don't remove these hunks of metal I'll wrap them around Miss Amanda Jenkins' head.'

Nose swollen, Ruth doodled, pencil pressed hard to the paper. So hard it tore the government supplied toilet roll. Sweet's muffled cries, and the thump of her body against metal, drifted, ignored by all. 'Don't reckon stuck-up will be around much longer,' she confided to Rachel.

'What happens to them?' the girl asked, deliberately unspecific.

'I've only 'eard rumours.'

'And?'

'Can't say.'

'Who's been done in the past, then?'

Ruth concentrated. 'Jacky, she was the first. She used to be top of the league here. Vicious bitch weren't scared of no one. Then Caroline came next. Caroline Pawsey. Flash cow. Gorgeous arse. Hard outer, soft centre, and strictly bi. Third was Anne. Psycho Anne. Last was Claire. Not seen or heard of since. None of 'em.'

Ruth scrawled, childlike. 'I liked C. Miss her some.'

Hughes ran a hand though his hair. 'Okay, Alice, five minutes.'

Faced pinched, lips tight, Jenkins warned, 'She has you wrapped around her little finger. She calls, you jump. That's not like you, Geoffrey.'

'It's only five minutes, Amanda, not the rest of my life, or my bank balance.'

'The disrespectful wretch should be shown the error of her ways, not pandered to.'

'Okay,' Hughes held his arms apart, 'so discipline her. But after we've finished.'

'You what?' Alice demanded, to Amanda's satisfied smile.

'See it as an introduction. A bit of experience. Miss Jenkins is one of the most sadistic bitches in the North West.'

Blindfolded, gagged, wrapped in wire twist, Hazel barely dared to move. She knew not the barbs were represented by the odd tin tack pushed between the braided wires. She expected, probably deserved the acute discomfort of crucifixion, as hinted at by O'Leary. Shut in the locker, unable to stand or crouch, she chewed on the error of her ways.

'I'm not having the wicked witch of the north humiliate me.'

'Do you want to hear what I have to say?'

'As long as it's the truth.'

'It is. Abridged and filtered as it is. Rose leads the sort of life you probably wouldn't approve of. She's married the sort of man you might frown on. She parted with you on the understanding she would never see you again. That was your grandfather's demand. Rose lived with that for eighteen years. She finally accepted the term. Once a thing is done, it cannot be undone. Your mother doesn't want to give false hope, so she has declined to see you. And although she might change her mind, you are not to know that.'

'And me? Lied to and cheated. I wouldn't even know the score if my adoptive parents hadn't been killed. She gave me away. For what reasons, she gave me up. How can she say no, I don't want to see my daughter? It doesn't matter where. I won't push for anything more. I just want to see her, now I know she exists. She can keep her trade and her man a secret. In that I'm not interested.'

Alice twisted and turned the chains in her hands. 'Tell her that. Tell her I'll wait a while. And when I've waited long enough I'll turn my back on the north, and on her for good. If I go, I won't come back.'

'How long? How long has she got?'

'Christmas.'

The pillow slip over her head obscured much, Hazel unsure where she had been taken and what precisely transpired. The bitches held her down, the gag and blindfold obstructing sight and verbal protest.

They forced something into her vagina, something cold, smooth and wide. Hazel writhed and tried to kick, but too many handled her and held her thighs apart. Ruth did the deed, taking great pleasure in twisting the piece into her vagina, stretching her well beyond what nature intended.

'And after I've sorted yer, I'm gonna report yer for bustin' my nose. That, bitch, will earn you a fucking painful stripin'. That's before, of course, before they come for their lamb.'

'Did yer get the stuff?' she asked.

'Yeah, one pot as requested, care of the stores.'

'Warmed up?'

'Oh yeah,' Rachel Smith replied spitefully. 'I've had it on the stove for a half hour. Bit bloody hot, really. Daubed in the right places it could prove nasty.'

'And you've got Scrubbs' pillow, Drake?'

The big woman nodded.

'Yer realise, gels,' Ruth browsed the half-dozen loyal faces, 'if Hughes catches us here, or can prove it was us that taught this bitch a lesson, he'll give each and every one of us a whipping to surpass all whippings.'

'He already 'as,' Smith replied.

Ruth plunged a brush into the black viscous soup. 'Hot, yer said, Rachel?'

The girl smirked.

O'Leary slapped the brush between Sweet's parted legs, the girl jerking, bucking, writhing in Drake's huge arms.

'Was a bit 'ot,' O'Leary mused. 'Get 'er up on that contraption and wire her there. Then we'll give the bitch 'er new coat.'

'It's my body, not yours.'

'You can't demand money from Amanda.'

'I can and I will. It can go in my pocket instead of yours,' Alice replied adamantly. 'Now, take these things off.'

'Okay, I'll give you a quid.'

'I was going to ask for five.'

'Five? For a few taps on the arse? You're mad. Anyway, it doesn't seem so long ago you would have found such a proposal indecent.'

'People change. The way I see it is my bum is a magnet, so I might as well take what I can get for the abuse. I mean, why give it for free when there are those willing to pay?'

'That sentiment is as close to whoring as you can get, without actually doing it. You realise that?'

'I think we're all whores after a fashion. We all have a price.'

'What's yours?'

'What are you looking to buy?'

'Your fanny. Here and now. How much?'

Alice levelled her gaze, expression serious. 'Five hundred pounds.' She smiled. 'No cheques.'

'You don't think I've got that much, do you?'

She shrugged. 'Five hundred and you can stuff me.'

'I have close to a thousand in the safe.'

Alice furnished a *what are you waiting for* smile. 'So?'

'Ten if you suck me off while Amanda's thrashing your butt.'

'Aren't you frightened I might bite?'

He closed the distance, Alice's heartbeat accelerating. He passed hands and arms about her waist, fingers aimed downward, travelling over her rump to rest upon the lower buttocks. He nuzzled into her neck, lips pecking. Goose bumps pimpled her flesh. 'I've only ever paid for one woman's cunt,' he admitted. 'I didn't make that mistake again.' Hughes pulled her close, her breasts pressed to his chest. 'Can you guess who?' He sensed her heart thump. His mean streak took strength. 'She could have been a top drawer whore.'

'Don't.'

'You could achieve the same. In fact, you're well on your way.'

'Perhaps it's best I pack and go and save myself, then.'

'I'll ring her, Alice. I'll dial the number and ask for her. Then I'll hand the receiver to you.'

'You said…'

'I know what I said. I know what she said. But you'd like to hear her voice, wouldn't you? You'd like to hear how much like you she is?'

'You're winding me up, you pig.'

'I have a photo, Alice. Taken about five years ago on Blackpool prom. Rose Mac – oops, Rose Hussey – arm in arm with Geoffrey Hughes.'

'What for? What's the price?'

'You loose my cock, Alice. You feed it into your fanny… nice and deep, mind. Do that, and I'll ring her tonight.'

Tension stole the spit from her mouth. Body trembling, heart a flutter, Alice gazed down at the bulge masked by his trousers.

'Deep, Alice… all the way… slide it in until it

grinds…'

'Could I…?'

Hughes shook his head. 'The price is a fuck. A free, no strings fuck… and I come in you, and all.'

'There yer goes, Haze. Yer nice new winter coat an' grass's reward. Oh, an' I really loves yer arse.'

The group loitered, enjoying Sweet's humiliation and discomfort. They threw ribald and derogatory insults. Drake, Smith, Summers, Davenport, Wisbeck and Catterall formed the bulk of Ruth's retinue, all hardy, malicious souls.

The group had used stolen keys to access the chapel, keys taken from Pierce months before. The bunch gave Ruth access to numerous parts of the Hope, but not to the outside world.

Hazel posed naked and humbled upon the back of Hughes' new toy. Tied and wired, the girl had been daubed with a hellish mix of hot black paint and fish glue, feathers with cut grass added after. They had strung her painfully, a half-pint milk bottle forced into her vagina. Ropes went from her wrists, down her back and between her legs to be tied off on a tether around her waist. Tin tacks forced between the wires and rope braiding, stuck and pricked her intimacy. Forearms either side of her face, and pointing forward, the girls had wrenched and pulled before securing them. The slightest pull on her arms tensioned the whole, the neck of that bottle caught by the ropes.

Knots delved places and bit into others, Ruth having devised a vindictive revenge. Nails tied into those knots prodded and pricked the flesh of belly, groin and arse. A large banana stolen from Scrubbs protruded from Hazel's backside, the yellow fruit caught by looped ropes and angled up towards her back.

Electricians' crocodile clips bit deep into Sweet's

nipples, wires from them fixed to an arch in the ceiling. They pulled on her tits, heaving them up, two coils of tacked wire about her chest, sharp points pricking the fleshy mounds.

Strained ropes about her ankles descended to the cross-struts beneath, pulling taut on the girl's legs. The top edge of the wooden pony burrowed into her sex, the metal edge incessantly probing.

Pillowcase removed, they had smeared Hazel's face and hair with the mix, then tipped feathers over her head, adhering and irksome. Sweet remained mostly ignorant of the gross act, for they left her gagged and blindfolded.

The black sticky compound smothered every part, the girl's head, torso, arms and legs. It stuffed the void between those tortured breasts. It clung to her chest and back, the ropes there cloying and sticky. It filled the gap between her buttocks. Paint and glue enveloped her pubic mound, encroached upon and invaded her vagina. It splashed and decorated the pony and flagstone floor.

Ruth nosed close to Hazel. 'You say anything about us and I'll do more than just bust your nose, sweetheart. I'll mount yer on a fucking pole.'

The group left, locking the chapel door behind them. Furtively, suppressing giggles, the six made it undetected back to the main building.

Hughes ushered Alice into the punishment room, steering her until her bottom touched against the whipping bench. There he guided her hands. Unsure, certain; apprehensive, eager; frightened, excited, Alice unfastened Hughes' flies. Her fingers met with his stiff cock, the shaft cloaked by his pants.

Fingertips stroked. She loosed the waistband and peeled down his underwear, the man's substantial plum jerking into view. The significance struck. The reality of

213

her position churned the pit of her stomach. Her thoughts focused on her scantily protected V, a triangle of sensitised, hirsute flesh neatly tucked between her thighs; the white cotton-covered knoll that led to the sexual opening beneath.

Alice wanted him. She ached for his penis. She yearned to experience the thrust and fill of excited cock. She thirsted for the spectacle of Hughes' thick shaft stretching her cunt, her sex lips taut about that masculine intrusion.

Alice grasped his broad penis with both fists, her fingertips no closer than an inch from her thumbnail.

'Right in,' Hughes whispered. 'Fill your pussy. Impale yourself. Then see my hard cock protruding from your slit. Dwell on that; my cock rammed tight in that virginal hole.'

Panting, perspiring, mind approaching a sexual frenzy, the redhead reached beneath her skirt. She urged down damp panties with one hand, the other still clutching Hughes' erection. The white cotton fell to her knees, then to her ankles, to catch upon the chains.

'Well...?' Hughes growled, goading, his cock stiffening to an impossible stretch. 'Want to hear mummy's voice?'

Her skirt hid the initial intimacy. Neither witnessed the separation of sex lips, the immersion of that mighty head, nor the irresistible grind of sliding, lengthy shaft. Both felt the union, the give and grip of vaginal passage. Both buzzed to the chaff and rub of intrusive meat. Alice winced with the stretch, with the pleasure, with the sheer audacity of such a lewd act. Hughes' penis torched her, the girl unsure whether she would ever refuse him again.

'Now lift your skirt and look,' Hughes taunted sarcastically. 'See the filth of it, the crudity, the dreadful sin.'

Alice hesitated. Skewered, knowing he pierced her, filled her; she still hesitated to witness the sight. So Hughes did it for her. Skirt drawn up, over her midriff, breasts and head, the man cast it aside. He forced her to acknowledge the intrusion. 'Prepared for oblivion?' he mocked.

Nothing could have primed Alice for the monumental climax that rewarded that inspection. Hughes savoured the reactive squeeze, the girl's thighs, vagina, pressuring his erection. She fell against his chest, her hands seeking, finding, grasping his shaft and balls. She jerked against him, the man's cock probing, exciting her further. The orgasm extended, heightened, blasted her lower anatomy.

'Oh, *God*...' she sighed.

Hughes' hands cupped her naked buttocks, his fingers squeezed between slats and flesh, supporting. 'So, finally you've recognised my worth,' he mocked.

Her legs rose, thighs catching his hips, ankles crossing behind his back. Hughes unlocked, removed her wrist fetters, and then relieved her of her camisole and bra. Naked, she lay her arms around his neck, Alice resigned and wanting.

Bottom supported by the slats of the bench and Hughes' hands, she felt his first measured lunge, penetrating, stretching her vagina. Alice gasped as she took what she could, inches of preposterously thick meat nestled outside those fleshy gates.

She watched the withdrawal, her moisture wetting his length, more than six inches slipping silently out.

Sight misting, the girl witnessed his re-entry, the glide of veined shaft filling her, spreading her lips to exhilarating bounds. That wedge of cock beguiled, entranced, Alice taken by the moment; inhibitions, objections, indoctrination pushed to one side. There had been others, though none had actually gone further than

215

insertion. The first, the Italian, came the closest to full-blown sexual intercourse.

Hughes took his time, his method slow, ponderous, forceful. He was finally there, between Alice's legs. His problem was he wasn't sure he wanted to be. Not then. Not there.

The man paused.

'Oh dear God,' she breathed, gazing at the monster wedged between her cunny lips. 'What did you mean, oblivion?' she suddenly asked.

'I thought perhaps the Almighty might have sent a bolt of lightning to hasten your way to the fiery depths.'

Eyes misty, far away, she admitted, 'I feel wonderful. I had the most wonderful orgasm to start with. And I'm not far off another.'

'So? Sex out of marriage? Evil?'

'I don't know.'

'What the fuck do you mean, you don't know? You're sat here with a healthy portion stuffed between your legs, and you're not sure! It feels fucking wonderful, and you're not sure? For Christ's sake, Alice.'

'Precisely for his sake. The devil's lure would be wonderful, else it couldn't work. Don't you see?'

'Where are you headed then? Sexual summer or carnal winter?'

Fear sparked in her eyes. 'I shouldn't be doing this.' Alice wriggled to remove herself from his erection, but Hughes held her firm, still very much inside her.

He paused, watching her closely, then shunted his hips and forced that cock deeper, Alice wincing. 'No fuck, no mother.'

Crammed, sexually energised, desperate to feel the bump and thrust of hard penis, Alice wanted. 'I shouldn't... not yet.'

'What you worried about? I might have already sown the seed. One, that's all it takes. One hiding in a nook from the last time.'

She felt his cock strengthen. 'Take it out, *please*.'

'The last time, Alice. Want to know when that was?'

She shook her head.

'An hour before I stuffed your tight cunt.'

'You're disgusting…' she mumbled wearily.

Hughes forced his cock even deeper, Alice gasping. 'Amanda Jenkins. She pays for the unusual, the diverse. And I provide.'

'You were in that ugly bitch?' Alice questioned, disbelieving.

'She can take it all. Amanda can manage every fucking inch of it. Right up to the hilt, the curly base and balls. Amanda is knowledgeable. Amanda has sexual capabilities you can't even dream of.'

'Then what's your interest in me?' Alice panted, sickened.

'Possibilities,' he answered, the malice running wild. 'You're two inches short of taking it all, but practised cunt isn't everything.' Hughes eased his cock back, Alice settling. 'You're right, she's fucking ugly. And you've got her beat on tits and arse, too.'

Dark cherry tresses tight in his fists, Hughes forced her down, her face inches from that coition. She faced his shaft, glistening with her moisture. He pulled free, the bulb springing up. 'Now suck it, Alice. Taste the mix of you and Amanda.'

'No!' she spat, but he yanked her forward, her lips pressed to his plum.

'Suck!' She shook her head, mouth firmly closed. 'Compliance, Alice. I need—'

'A slave,' she snapped, before sinking her teeth into the bulbous tip.

'Bloody bitch!' the man roared, slapping her head.

Alice hoisted her panties and hobbled to the door, Hughes tending the hurt. Near naked and with no idea where she was headed she flung open the portal, Amanda Jenkins blocking her escape.

The amalgam cooled, dried, congealed. That formidable apex gouged her fanny, the bottle pushed deeper and deeper. Sweet suffered, her tears absorbed by the blindfold. That edge tortured for and aft, cutting into her clitoris and anus.

The giggles had ceased. Uncertainty tainted triumph. Six uneasy inmates waited on the inevitable explosion.

With no words whispered, no accusation or insult thrown, Sweet accepted herself alone. Whatever they covered her with had dried. Her skin felt drawn, dry, glued. The muck clung, the smell dreadful. Metallic dead fish. Her muffled scream failed to penetrate to the outside world, Hazel left to her torment, at least until evening muster.

Ruth edged her bets. She screwed for an alibi. With Dennis Scrubbs' cock stuffed between her legs she sought to persuade him of the benefits of mendacity.

That weird, unpredictable day clung to its fickle vein. Hughes had been handed his excuse, Amanda hers. With a five pound note shoved in Alice's panties Amanda felt entitled, licensed to do as she pleased. Hughes held Alice down, the girl suspicious about that complicity. Cruel intent begot savagery. Sensual tension provoked sexual violation. *She* and *he* practised mischief in perfect harmony. He batted from her score, she from his look, the slightest gesticulation, the imperceptible hint. If Hughes alone proved a trial, then the duo tormenting Alice would equate to an ordeal.

'What have you been up to?' Dennis asked in his casual manner.

'Nuffink exactly.'

'So why the sweetness and light?'

'Just trying to set us off on the right track, that's all.'

'Nice of you to take the effort, so it is. But the way I see it, is cons can suck up to their governors. Expect it in a way. But the warder of a kind, I suppose, should keep the status quo. Ergo, remain in charge. Is that sort of clear to you?'

'I never meant anyfing like undermining your power, sir. No, it was more like offering an 'elpin' 'and. Yer knows; someone who knows the rules, the idiosymetrics…'

'Syncrasies. Idiosyncrasies,' Dennis corrected.

'Yeah, them and all. I know this hole better than anyone. I know everyone in it. I know the governor. I even know the doc. So what I am saying is, I can make your stay here a lot more comfortable than you think.'

'Maybe you want to turn my head, Ruth. Maybe you want to blind me. Or perhaps it's deafness you prefer.'

'On the contrary. I can improve your eyes and ears. I could get yer all sorts of cock massages too. And if yer ever fancies anything a bit different, well Ruth O'Leary's yer gel.'

Dennis laid back, the cot creaking. 'I knew a gel, as you put it so eloquently, back in Cardiff. Nice looker. Would have been about twenty-five then. She seemed dependable. Had a bit of a thing about slap and tickle. Know what I mean? Liked the strong dominant man. She'd squirm and wriggle to a light session. Get the gist?'

'Oh yeah, if that's what sir wants.'

'Candy we called her. Short for Candice. She put a bloke in prison. Saw him down for a stretch. The candyman came a while later. Dead of night he paid a visit.'

Dennis lit a cigarette. 'Ever been strapped, Ruth?'

'Yeah,' she admitted, offhand.

'An hour. Strung by her wrists, stripped of every stitch. She was strapped for an hour, right down to the last second. I worked it out once. About ten strokes to a minute. Doesn't bare thinking about, does it?'

'I ain't into grassing,' Ruth voiced.

'But I might want you to. I was thinking on what your mob might do, if they ever found out you could be undependable.'

'Is that what you're saying? You'll do for me if I rat for you?'

'Happens I don't need a rat. Got one, see. But I could be persuaded to assist a damsel in distress, if she had enough clout to tend me a willing supply of, say, warm meat?'

'We're fucking screwed, I tell you,' Davenport moaned.

'Nah,' Summers shook her head. 'He's got to prove it first.'

'I ain't fucking scared of him anyhow.' Rachel Smith bit a fingernail. 'And I've had his whip on my back, don't forget.'

'And I've been birched, something I don't intend to happen again. I'd like to know what Ruth's doing with Scrubbs. She's been in there nigh on an hour now.' Maureen glanced furtively about, checking the faces of her cronies.

Drake leaned over, and without a word lifted Davenport by the scruff of her neck. 'Sounds like doubt to me. Ruth is beyond doubt. She's top dog.'

'Let go!' Maureen squealed. 'You're fucking hurting me.'

'Nah, this ain't hurting.' Two mugs of tea sat side by side on a bedside cupboard. Drake, particularly loyal, stupid and vicious, ripped Maureen's blouse apart, baring her chest. She forced the girl forward and over, her breasts dangled above the mugs.

Davenport slapped her hands on the cupboard, arms straining against Drake's pressure. 'Don't, you fucking psychopath! They're fucking hot!' Sweat beaded Maureen's brow.

Davenport's hair wrapped about her fist, Drake used her forearm against the girl's shoulder. Gradually, unable to resist, Maureen's bosom descended. Tears welled. Her lips trembled. Her torso shook with effort. 'Please,' the girl begged, her nipples an inch from the steaming tea.

No one offered support, watching intently, waiting to see Davenport's tits immersed in the hot beverage. 'I'm sorry!' she wailed. 'I didn't mean it!' Her nipples touched, her face contorting with the pain. 'Aaah, God, I said I'm sorry!'

Drake had made her mind up, or O'Leary had for her. Instructed to hurt the first one that cast doubts on Ruth's fidelity, Drake intended to carry the order out to the letter.

Both breasts plunged into the mugs, Davenport squealing, tea slopped and spilled. Drake held her there for several seconds before releasing her. Maureen pulled her bosom free, hands hovering, fingers stretched, unsure what to do.

'Cold water,' Summers advised callously. 'Douse 'em, you daft bitch.'

Her cronies' critical expressions drew a trace of guilt. 'It weren't that hot,' Drake defended, Davenport having run for the toilet.

'There again, you might right the wrong before you're found out,' Scrubbs suggested.

'Nah. Bitch had it coming.'

221

'Had it coming? Bitch?'

O'Leary giggled. 'Black gloss paint, that stuff for the iron bars and gates. And a pot of glue. All warmed up to just beyond sufferable. Plus a wrap of wire and rope. Some tin tacks and feathers and grass for toppin'.'

'So you've tarred and feathered some *bitch*?'

'Yep.'

'Where is she now?'

'No matter.'

'If the bitch is Hazel Sweet, and she is currently off limits, then I will presume you, and all concerned in that act of utter insanity, will probably be flayed.'

'Nah, it were only a lark. We'll get whipped, if anything. That's all.'

'No Ruth, Mr Hughes had intentions for Miss Sweet. If you are able to escape, then I should do so as quickly as possible.'

'Nah, you'll tell him I was with you.'

'What? For a few tales and a bit of hanky-spanky? No Ruthy, I think not.'

'I reckon we ought to get her back and clean her up,' Catterall advised, scared.

'I don't reckon she will clean up,' Maureen opined, dabbing at her breasts with a wet cloth.

Summers lobbed her guess, smiling. 'I reckon Hughes will have the skin off our backs. Birched and—'

'Shut up!' Wisbeck snapped. 'Fucking lunatic idea in the first place. I tell you what,' she glared at Drake, then cast a sideways glance at Maureen, 'scalded tits or not, if I get it I'll see to it O'Leary gets hers too.'

'Shall I make the tea?' Dawn enquired, laughing.

'What you after then?'

'A certain little birdie. No name yet. But when the time comes I will expect you to do precisely.'

'Precisely?'

'Exactly. And for that I'll cover your pretty little arse on this occasion.'

'It ain't my arse. I ain't concerned for my arse, Mr Scrubbs. It's leaving by the wrong door that worries me.'

Dennis stretched, fingers tucking beneath the hem of Ruth's pinafore. 'A gel should have more thought for her arse,' he ventured, pulling the blonde over his lap. Skirt hoisted, thin white panties veiling that luxurious behind, he added, 'Don't you agree?'

Chapter 12

Hughes holding Alice flat to the bench, Amanda tied her forearms behind her back. The two loosely twisted cords Jenkins channelled between the girl's legs, passing them either side of a forward leg brace and knotting the pair together.

Alice's discomfort began with two ropes twisted and looped about her waist and the bench, the one between her legs deliberately caught. Jenkins used a short stick pushed between the two below the seat frame, to twist and subsequently tighten the bond. Turn after turn screwed the length into her flesh, forcing her belly hard against the slats, and at the same time making her bottom more prominent.

'First the ropes,' Amanda taunted.

'Then a sound caning,' Hughes added.

'And after, I shall discover just how supple you are,' Amanda continued.

'Finally, Alice, I will provide a period of utter humiliation.'

The girl winced, coarse fibres stinging her skin.

Jenkins smiled, vindictive. 'Just a start, girl. Perhaps next time you'll show me some respect.' She pulled on the stick, twisting the ropes further. Content with the pressure, Amanda strapped one end of the stick to the bench, thereby retaining its tightness.

'This is just the first,' Amanda warned. '*My* fun begins.'

'And all for five pound,' Hughes teased.

Amanda took another set of ropes, two lengths of thin waxed cords passed through a two-inch long metal tube with dulled spikes on either end. Jenkins offered them to Hughes. 'To cause a significant discomfort. They're not sharp enough to penetrate.'

'Where do they go?' Hughes asked.

'They will strangle her breasts. The tube between, a cord above and below, then plait the ropes and push the ends through this.' She offered a flat piece of metal with a machined slot. 'Knot them around these rods.' Amanda held up two six-inch lengths.

Alice resisted the temptation to bite the man's forearms as he placed the rig. His hands brushing against her breasts; the constriction she expected; the pain she anticipated, all sent her libido into overdrive.

Amanda turned the rods, taking up the slack before exerting pressure. The continued twisting effectively shortened the whole, drawing the upper and lower cords together, Alice's breasts between, the dulled spikes probing the squeezed flesh. Hughes cupped those tortured tits, fingers gauging the cut of ropes, the depth to which the spikes had sunk. Breasts discoloured, Alice taking shallow breaths, Jenkins desisted.

A knock on the door took Hughes from the play. Annoyed, he opened it an inch or so. 'Sheila, not now!'

'What's this?' the doctor asked, looking over the man's shoulder. 'Am I relegated? Yesterday's news?' Before Hughes could reply Sheila added, 'You really are a loathsome shit.'

'Don't you go getting possessive on me. You know how it cuts. I've never pretended, so unless it was something important, goodbye.'

'No.' She folded her arms. 'Sweet's been tarred and feathered, that's all.'

The import failed to strike immediately. 'What?'

'Someone, or persons unknown, dragged Hazel to the chapel. There they sort of tarred and feathered her, and mounted the wretch on that abhorrence you have in there.'

'Tarred? Where the fuck did they get tar from?'

'A mix of paint and glue. That horrid black gloss paint you bought for the railings, and some fish glue left in the stores. Heated and daubed all over the poor cow.'

Hughes searched for words.

'I have her in the infirmary. I'm afraid she's not cleaning up very well.'

'Has she said who?'

'Of course not. But it will be O'Leary. Her and the hole in the head gang.'

'Any idea why?'

'Not really. It's usually revenge or a lesson. Sweet hasn't really blended in. She thinks herself a cut above, which would automatically alienate the rank and file. I had to prise a milk bottle from her vagina, a banana from her anus, and ropes from the goo. Her nipples are probably infected, and her skin stained for months to come.'

Hughes stepped into the hallway.

'Summary execution?' Sheila suggested.

'No,' Hughes replied. 'Keep it quiet. Let the scum stew. They'll expect an immediate reaction, a witch hunt. Let them sweat. See what it brings.'

'Do you want to see her? Talk to her?'

Hughes put his head around the door. 'I'll have to

225

leave you to it, Amanda. Please feel you have a free rein.'

Five minutes later he gazed down on a blackened Hazel. 'Who, Sweet?'

'I'll give you six names, Mr Hughes, if you'll let me sort the seventh.'

He crouched. He placed fingertips in the dirty bathwater. 'You'll give me six, eh?' His hand plunged, seized her clogged pubes and yanked her under. Fraught seconds passed before she managed to claw her way clear. 'Don't try to deal with me, Sweet. I'm in charge here, not you. As it is I fully intend to make an example of you.'

'For what?' the girl spluttered.

'You had no business leaving the building.'

'I was dragged, sir. Just look at me. Do you think I did it myself, for fun?'

'You *say* you were dragged.' Hughes stood, searched for his pipe. 'Maybe you went willingly. Maybe it turned sour after. The point is, girl, you know who has keys to escape this prison, and you refuse to tell me. That's an obstruction of justice. That could cost you, say, another five years with me.'

Hazel rubbed at a black-dyed breast. 'Then another five it is.'

Tobacco pressed into the bowl, Hughes lit the pipe. 'And bearing in mind what you *have* told me, I will have to ensure you don't embark on a vendetta.'

'You won't deal at all?' Hazel asked angrily.

'Yes, Hazel, *I* will deal. But you won't. I want a statement. The events leading up to, and those that took place in the disused chapel. I want names. I want the party responsible for stealing Mr Pierce's keys. I want the ringleader.'

'And?' Hazel asked, refusing to back down. 'There

will have to be an and.'

'And, Hazel Sweet, I shall release you from the Hope.'

The girl's jaw dropped. 'Free?'

'Yes, Hazel. Free to sign and stick to a contract.'

Her smile evaporated, distrust settling. 'What sort of contract?'

'One that will make you very wealthy.' He puffed happily on his pipe. 'If you thought whoring profitable, I can offer you a whole lot more, including a grand, never to be forgotten exodus.'

'I didn't whore. The whole business was a misunderstanding. I was used.'

'So say all the crims.'

'It's bloody true in my case. Yes, I was in bed with a man when the police raided the house. Yes, I had nicked his wallet. Yes, he had paid me for sex.'

'Remorse is only good for the parole board. We don't have them here.'

'I'm only sorry because I didn't see it coming. I'm only sorry because I didn't get the chance to make that evil madam regret her treachery.'

'I'm not interested in your tails of woe. I want names.'

'Ruth instigated it. She's been telling that mob that I'm a snitch. And when I near busted her nose she dreamt up her revenge.'

'You busted her nose?'

'I bloodied it. She wouldn't leave me be. I warned her.'

'I want that in your statement too. So who are the troops?'

'Drake. Rachel Smith. Dawn Summers. Maureen Davenport. Carol Wisbeck and Joan Catterall.'

Hughes nodded. 'Firstly, I'm going to arrange a little convalescence for you, Hazel. I would like you to stay

227

with a very dear friend of mine.' He smiled warmly. 'A Miss Jenkins. You will enjoy her company, I'm sure.'

'What's the time?'

''Bout seven.'

'No Hazel. No raging bull. What d'yer reckon's happened?' Maureen literally squirmed.

'Don't tell me the poor cow is still mounted on that little roof-like thing,' Summers joked. 'She must be cleaved to the belly button by now.'

Rachel lit a roll-up, the sixth that hour. 'Anyone seen Ruth?'

Unperturbed by the day's events and possible outcome, Drake conceded, 'She's still with Scrubbs. Seems a bit sus, I suppose.'

Wisbeck suggested anxiously, 'I reckon one or maybe two of us should sneak out to the chapel. See if Sweet's still there.'

'You're scared shitless, ain't yer?' Summers accused.

'It ain't that,' Wisbeck argued. 'I just don't understand why nothing's been said. Why we ain't seen a blackened Sweet. Why we ain't been interrogated. And why O'Leary's cosied up to Scrubbs.'

'She's sortin' her story. That's obvious.'

Drake lifted her huge frame, attitude menacing.

Dawn Summers gauged the girl and the moment. She pointed a warning finger at the big woman, 'I ain't Maureen, Drake. Big as you are, I'll take you down.'

Drake heeded the advice and retook her seat.

Scrubbs lay half asleep and exhausted. He'd stuffed O'Leary every which way. Limp, his cock now ignored Ruth's fondling fingers. It failed to respond to the lick of her tongue. Her teeth nibbling his testicles proved unsuccessful too. 'No good, Ruth,' he admitted. 'We've done covered it all. Best cut along.'

228

'Is that it? You bored with me already?'
'If that's how you choose to see it.'

Cold machined steel forced an entry, ring after ring ever wider opened the girl's anus. Another sank uncomfortably between her legs. Jenkins wound the rope that connected to Alice's forearms. Slowly it tightened. The redhead felt its effect as it gripped the buttock canal, driving a metal plug into her arse. She grunted and gasped with the thrust of a steel shaft penetrating her vagina, that stepped like the anal intruder, the thing forcing her opening and tunnel ever wider.

Jenkins tightened until the young woman's arms locked against the waist rope, Alice's back arched, her cord-encumbered breasts emphasised. Held by spurs, the rope forced the steel inserts ever deeper. Each abrupt jerk opened her rectum, her sex, wider and wider.

Alice caught the hag's attention, Amanda staring her in the face, cold eyes offering nothing. Giving the ropes an excessive turn, Jenkins sneered. Eyes thrown wide, Alice gasped with the subsequent volley of sensations, the hail of stinging, smarting, burning repercussions.

Her hips pinioned, plugs having been driven ruthlessly home, Alice conceded to the hag's ability. She edged toward ecstatic euphoria, the stimulation a sexual nirvana.

Ropes rigid with tension, Amanda secured the turning rod. She laid her fingers to Alice's cheek, gently stroking. 'I'd like to take you home. I have pieces there that would test you to the limit.'

The nails of her other hand closed on Alice's nipple. 'I could play tunes on your body that you would never believe. I can give you sex without ever seeing a man's cock, let alone feel it in you.' Amanda noted the telling facial twitch.

'That prospect arouses?' Amanda toyed with the girl's breasts. 'You rise to the possibility? Virgin that you are, you crave the illicitness of coition. There's a truth been spoken often, Alice: a woman knows what a woman wants.' The hag's fingers worked a soothing magic. 'And I already know you, Alice Hussey. I can read your body, your mind, your needs.'

'No more than I would expect from a witch,' Alice whispered. 'Been looking in your crystal ball?'

'The human flesh is so susceptible to manipulation. The stroking fingers equates to soothing.' Her hand left and returned, the slap sharp, uncomfortable. 'But if the touch lands a little harshly, then…' Amanda struck the girl's face harder, 'pain.'

Alice's eyes watered.

'But even pain can vary.' Jenkins gouged and raked Alice's breast with her long nails. 'In your state, not particularly unbearable?' she asked.

'But the face?' Jenkins struck Alice for the third time, the slap resounding. The smarting flesh screamed its discomfort, the skin reddened. 'Now if I was to slap you again, that would really hurt, wouldn't it?'

Not wanting to find out, Alice nodded.

'If I smack your breasts…' Alice winced to the demonstration. 'But if I caned them, or even whipped them…'

Alice tried to move, those tightened ropes offering no allowance.

Amanda crouched, her face against those tortured breasts. She licked, her tongue gliding over pressured and gouged flesh. She gazed at the girl. 'What would please you more? The love of a wet tongue? The slap of a strap? Or the hell of a rattan or whip?'

Jenkins bit a nipple, Alice squirming. 'I think the crack of a whip's tail.'

Wisbeck suffered second thoughts. 'Perhaps we should have asked Ruth.'

'You'd have to get her out of Scrubbs' bed first,' Maureen whispered. 'Anyway, we got to know what's going on.'

'If Hughes catches us with them keys he'll... Christ, I dread to think what would happen.'

The pair crept to the chapel, nightfall and the shadows covering their movements. Barely daring to breathe Wisbeck fumbled with the door key. 'If she is still in there we'll have to try and get her back to the dorm.'

'Where else is she going to be?' Maureen questioned. 'We'd know about it if she wasn't—'

A hand gripped each by the nape of the neck, fingers digging deep. Both froze. Both pissed themselves.

'Maureen Davenport and Carol Wisbeck if I'm not mistaken.' Hughes lifted both to tiptoe. 'Going somewhere, were we?'

Maureen stared at the door and thought on what may be inside. She glanced down at the keys in Wisbeck's hand. Sudden death seemed the best alternative.

'I'm going to ask you both to wait here, while I fetch the requisite shackles for escapees.'

'No sir,' Maureen wailed, 'I wasn't. We wasn't. Honest. We just wanted to get into the chapel, that's all.'

'Why? In need of prayer, were we?'

'Has no one been in there today, sir?' Wisbeck asked, terrified.

'It's disused.'

'Shit!' Davenport hissed.

'Both of you, feet apart, hands flat against the door.' Both complied. 'Remain there until I return. If you move so much as a muscle I will strap you both before I even think about the mess you're now in. Understood?'

Both nodded. Hughes strode into the dark.

'What now?' Maureen asked, after a minute's tense silence. 'What do escapees get?'

'Transferred, with any luck.'

'No chance of that,' a returned Hughes informed them. He tossed two sets of fetters to the floor beside them. 'Put those on.'

Carol Wisbeck eyed the steel. 'Ain't no need for them, sir. We know what to do.'

'No, Wisbeck, I don't think you do. Whatever you expect cannot be anywhere near as severe as what you shall inevitably receive. Now put the shackles on.'

The pair settled on their butts, fear tearing them apart. Maureen enclosed one ankle and then the other, the chink of metal inauspicious. 'I don't get it. Why chain us up like dogs?'

'Because, Maureen, you are no more.'

'It wasn't only us,' Carol blurted, the last vestige of courage departing.

'Really? What wasn't only you, Wisbeck?'

'The keys,' Maureen intervened. 'We didn't nick them, sir. We just came by them.'

'Is that so? See what you have to say after.'

Davenport hugged her trembling body. Tears ran down her face. 'After what, sir?'

Hughes crouched. 'After the prison strap has pulverised your backsides. Often a different tune sung then. Imagine, Davenport; twelve for attempted escape, and then twelve for stealing the keys. What will you tell me in between? To avoid the second dozen? Hm?'

He took a pair of handcuffs from a jacket pocket and snapped them around Davenport's wrists. 'What will you want to trade, Maureen?'

'Okay.' Wisbeck found her courage. 'We nicked them off Eddie, waited for weeks and then decided to break out through the chapel roof. A lot easier than taking the right keys and walking out of the fucking front door.'

Hughes locked Carol's wrists. 'Grit, Wisbeck. I appreciate grit. That's something to be proud of.' Carol eyed him warily. 'See how well your grit can serve you later.'

Alice's knees fell to Amanda's persuasion. The woman spread the girl's legs, forced them apart, then looped her bristly rope about and above the joints. Again the lengths met at the fore, beneath the captive's strangled breasts. A twelve-inch rod directly behind the knot acted as the pivot. Within a couple of minutes, the pressure slow and progressive, Amanda had the girl's thighs pinned, the gap between extensive.

Jenkins circled her victim, drinking of the girl's nakedness, her stressed posture and the ropes sunk into her soft flesh. 'How do you feel?' she asked. 'The truth, please. Forget our difference for the moment.'

'Vulnerable,' Alice answered without hesitation.

'Would you... no, not would you.' Amanda concentrated. 'You are tied and spread for a good reason.'

She leant, placed her hands on the girl's naked bottom cheeks. She noted the flinch and twitch of thigh and buttock muscles. She regarded the flex of fingers, the pull on ropes.

'A man could take you like this, and there wouldn't be a thing you could do. Moreover, it wouldn't be your fault. You wouldn't have to seek forgiveness.'

A foot lifted, Amanda roped the ankle. Three turns around the joint and she forced it against the thigh. There she bound it, tied it firm. She repeated the exercise, Alice's legs doubled, her feet tucked to her lower bottom.

'And there we must dally,' Jenkins advised. 'Soles of the feet I find irresistible.' Alice watched with dismay as the woman picked up a thin rattan. 'I suppose it's

233

because I know just how painful bastinado is.'

Cane rested against an upturned foot, Amanda stroked the wrinkled skin. 'Not the erogenous bottom. Nor the sexual tits. Not even the sensual padded thighs, or the naked back.' She lifted the cane and struck, Alice sucking air. 'More a sickening hurt. Yes?'

Alice nodded.

'Not particularly talkative, are you, Hussey?' She whipped the foot harder, the girl jerking, swallowing the scream.

'I don't mind you begging, or squealing in agony. Feel free to cry for mercy.'

Chained and cuffed, Hughes led the pair to the rear of the building on the ground floor. He nudged open a door, a uniformed woman leaping from her seat, the book she'd been reading falling to the floor.

'Sorry to interrupt,' Hughes apologised with sarcasm. 'You know these two, Officer Roberts?'

'Of course, sir. I know every crim in this establishment.'

Erin Roberts, a local Flint girl had worked at the Hope since leaving school. Tall, steely-eyed with a fit and almost muscular frame, most had the sense to avoid Erin. At twenty-three she had built a reputation as a hard taskmaster, merciless in the execution of her duty and any backside she felt the need to punish.

'Attempted escape,' Hughes divulged. 'For that I will strap them both tomorrow in the breakfast hall.'

Maureen felt her knees weaken.

'By then I would like to know who else was involved in the tarring and feathering of Hazel Sweet. I would also like to know who acquired Eddie Pierce's keys. Use whatever means you deem necessary, Officer Roberts.' Hughes grabbed the girls by the ears and lifted. 'Now, you damned whores, I shall know the truth when I hear it. And I'd better hear it. Tomorrow at eight-fifteen sharp I shall slaughter your backsides. You will each receive eighteen on the bare with the prison strap. I will not give a damn if those butts are already whipped, bruised and swollen. Is that understood?'

The man twisted their ears. Both lifted their fettered hands, squealing their replies.

'After your execution you will both be placed in solitary for six weeks. You will say nothing to your cohorts. Not a bloody word!'

He released Maureen and lifted Wisbeck by her hair. 'If you try and tip off anybody, Wisbeck, I will whip you every morning in front of the whole establishment, stark naked, for the entire duration of your confinement.'

'I'll tell you who if you let me off the flogging,' Davenport offered, but before Hughes could answer Carol had wrapped her chains around her neck and was trying to throttle her.

'You fucking dirty cowardly weasel!' the blonde screamed, both crashing to the floor.

Roberts and Hughes fought to part the two, Wisbeck punching, scratching and clawing Maureen to the last possible second. Dragged apart, she pointed a finger. 'One fucking word you yellow bitch, and I swear I'll stick yer like a fucking pig!'

The women locked in separate cells, Hughes remarked, 'Might be a long night.'

'It's a shame you can't stop,' Erin replied, recalling the many times he had.

'By the way,' Hughes added. 'Whatever you get out of those tramps tonight, Ruth O'Leary's name will not come into the frame.'

'There might be a price for my silence,' Erin suggested, her meaning indecent.

'If I had the time I'd pay in advance, be assured of that. But yes, whatever you, or your body, desires.'

A dozen slashes to each foot and that hell ended, but instead Amanda lashed the tender flesh of Alice's inner thighs. Moderation not a word Jenkins used, Alice suffered. Sickening incendiary after incendiary fired her limbs, that quarter-inch cane striping a grievous legacy.

Heels clicking, Jenkins circled the girl. 'You think me cruel perhaps?'

'I don't think of you at all,' Alice provoked.

'One week,' Amanda promised, her cane whipping Alice's left buttock. 'One week and I would have you trained.'

Chapter 13

Ruth moved stealthily to her bed. There she slipped off her clothes and slid between the sheets. Summers had waited long enough. 'Where you been, O'Leary?'

'Getting screwed. Jealous?'

'Sweet never surfaced.'

'I know.'

'So what's happening?'

'Nothing by the look of it.'

'Davenport and Wisbeck have disappeared too.'

'How can they have disappeared?'

'They've gone and the keys have gone.'

'That don't make no...' Ruth climbed from the bed. 'Stupid fucking cows! They've gone back to the chapel!'

'In that case they'd be back by now.'

'Unless they got caught.'

'And if they have?' Summers smirked. 'Hughes

would have been working his way through every arse in the place by now. Our tarred and feathered bird will no doubt be singing her head off.'

Stirred beyond reason, Alice relaxed. Steaming hot water topped with a carpet of suds surrounded her naked body. Beneath, fingers gently played, thumb gauging the swelling of her clitoris.

Hughes could tease and play her like no one else. He knew precisely how to moisten her well, and how to make her yearn for *that* too. Sexual intercourse claimed her thoughts. Alice closed her eyes and delved deeper, four fingers sliding in, almost satisfying the need. Erotic position after position provided the mental imagery.

Wet hair lay tousled and tight to her scalp. Rope marks etched her body, the skin red, sore and burned by friction. Strangely Hughes had saved the day. The man returned with a certain notion. Alice's naked and tightly bound form served only to inflame him further.

Amanda offered little defence, her leather suit peeled from her body in seconds. Alice watched that lean frame stripped, the woman's bosom surprisingly full and well shaped. Panties torn from her hips. The frantic embrace. The dance of arousal. The glimpses of a woman more erotically designed than Alice could have imagined precluded a rough and passionate sex.

Her room lit by the pale yellow glare of street lighting, Alice lay on her bed, her skin damp, still tingling from the joy of hot water. Sex still danced in the moonlight. Lust still hovered, its tentacles wrapped about her loins. Fingers remained captivated, her vagina wanton, frustrated. As fast as orgasm wiped the horny slate clean, so the spiral rewound.

His cock rammed into *her*, stretching, pumping. The manner in which he took her beguiled, beckoned for Alice's own deformed temperament. Spun, Jenkins was

237

pitched forward, Alice stunned by her femininity, her figure quite shapely.

There Amanda tried in vain to resist. A half-dozen hefty slaps to her bottom seemed to lend the desired effect. Hughes took her. His stiff cock rammed between Jenkins' thighs, opening her vagina, sinking rapidly. The woman made half-hearted attempts to protest, all met with the unforgiving palm.

The memory played and replayed, she endured a lust that could only be satisfied by a means beyond her call. Amanda's frantic sexual throes had carried Alice to a pinnacle dangerous in its intensity and implications. But worse, she hungered for Hughes and the gratification she knew only he could serve.

The man's cold savagery and unpredictability combined to make him irresistible. Alice sought solace in every excuse she could think of, but in every instance she came back to the same answer. Hughes did something for her that no other man had ever come close to.

The vivid picture floated. Amanda horizontal, her back resting on Alice's, her legs wrapped about Hughes' hips. That was the second fuck. He supported Jenkins' buttocks, Alice wishing they could trade places.

Another life, one not so long ago, and Alice would have shied from the debauchery. Yet within the blink of a month she watched unabashed the plunge of stiff wet cock. She eyed with envy the thrust and poke of hard meat. She begrudged Amanda the pleasure, the feel, the explicit lewdness of the third act.

Amanda bent over Alice. She lay with her breasts draped on the girl's shoulders, her hips tucked tight to the girl's bottom. Arms around Alice's torso, Jenkins took her breasts in her hands. Persuasion ensued, temptation slopped against Alice's capricious gates.

Hughes shafted her there, from behind. Alice endured. She tried not to listen to the grunts, the sighs, the slop of cock in wet tunnel. She blanked the rock of Amanda's body against her own. She ignored the slap of the hag's groin against her bottom.

Alice understood what he tried to achieve. She knew he tipped the erotic confetti hoping Alice would bite, betting that temptation would prove successful. Pride and bloody-mindedness screwed his scheming.

Body damp and sticky, the wicked witch used Alice's breasts to accelerate her climax. Bony fingers and sharp talons gouged the stressed knolls, her hips slapped as she rode in unison with her sexual cohort.

Legs spread, Alice pressed both hands to her pubic mound, fingers courting the clitoris, thrusting eagerly between the soft folds. She recalled Hughes, brought him to the fore of her thoughts, her tied so crudely, so invitingly. The ousting of the hag, to dress and watch, left Alice to the sole attention of that virile rogue.

He sliced through the rope that cut between her legs. He pulled the steel from her cunny. Then he pressed the mighty dome to that hungry gorge. To feel that piece slide back and forth between her sex lips drove her to distraction. Knowing what passed between her thighs, what swung between his legs, made her dizzy with frustration. The feel of his pubic hair against the bare flesh of her bottom instilled a yearning that endangered sanity.

He rode her like that for several minutes, the chaff of cockhead against her clit driving Alice into a frenzy. It was there, she was there, for the taking. Her arse was presented, stretched and tight, her fanny posed. *'Do it!'* flashed through her mind again and again. Hughes had manoeuvred and schemed, lied and cheated. He had won, but didn't seem to know, and Alice would not tell him. The man would have to take her without her

239

explicit permission. She could never consent, but she could suffer being taken.

The shaft slid back, then paused. Alice held her breath. Seconds, long seconds ticked by. Then she felt him, his bulb, his dome, his mighty plum. The glans opened her, stretched the walls of her cunt. It slid gracefully in, the pleasure consummate, incredibly satisfying.

An electric bubble expanded, filled her groin, inflamed her belly, before despatching its disabling troops the length and breadth of her body. Climax consumed her, implosion totally debilitating. Alice writhed, her body in rapture.

Hughes ignored, or failed to notice her reply to his coitus. Decided, he slowly pumped, his girth thrust and retrieved, plunged and withdrawn. Alice rejected thought, recrimination, regret. Instead she concentrated on what was, and the needs of. Her mind merged with her sex, rising sexual octave by sexual octave to ride the crest of an indomitable orgasm.

Hughes couldn't help himself. Deep down he would rather have left it for the irresistible carrot it was. He would sooner have left Alice on a pedestal, to worship and dream about. But earthy lust demanded sexual action.

The spark of masturbation could never hope to surpass the blast of sexual intercourse's climax. Disappointed with the damp squibs generated by her fingers, Alice turned on her side, her naked back aimed at the door.

'If he should come see me... if he should want... if he should... once bitten, the apple of Eden shall not relent its dominion.'

A sharp October morning. The window left ajar. Or was it the cold light of day that afflicted Alice? Not remorse,

240

nor regret, more an overload of guilt. She sat on the edge of the bed, eyes bleary, sleep not having proved an easy prey.

Her other hand lay defensively between her thighs, the horse having bolted. Or perhaps protective, comforting reminders, least she forget the fall from virginity. She lay her forehead to waiting hands. *Why?* hammered her conscience. Conviction deserted her, her confidence in tatters. Madness seemed a good excuse, suicide a remedy.

She reread the scrap of paper. The name brought back memories she would sooner forget; Malcolm, sex with Richard, the waking hours of her deviance. Other recollections tore at her heart; Kate, Jonathan. She had a day to make up her mind, the appointment she would either have to confirm or abandon.

What would she say? What could she tell a man of the cloth, a man revered by the church itself? It could prove to be death by a thousand cuts, or at the very least the most humiliating time of her life. But wasn't that what redemption was about? To flay the soul if not the body?

Did she want redemption? Did she need to be redeemed? Would she burn if soaked in holy water? Where did the truth lie? What is right and what is wrong, and where do the lines cross?

Her head ached with the complexities. Geoff was right. Jonathan was right. Kate was right. Richard was right. Father Cavenny will be right. Alice is wrong.

What the hell would Cavenny do? What could he do? He couldn't cure her perversion. He couldn't undo what's done. He could prescribe damnation. He could decree a lonely, loveless avenue. He could denounce her new life and condemn her to the sackcloth and ashes of ecclesiastical retreat and contemplation.

Months in the company of sisters did not appeal. Coarse linen, wimple and chaffed knees did little for her. There again, whoring for Geoff was not an option either. Somewhere the good turned to bad, and bad to good. Alice needed to know where, and where on the scale she stood. 'Looks like you win,' she whispered. 'But if you're a bloody Richard, then I'll not be stopping.

Alice checked her savings were where she had left them. She would need the fare to Edinburgh. She might need a B&B. An overnight bag should suffice, she couldn't make assumptions.

Davenport and Wisbeck stood humbly before Erin Roberts, heads bowed. They had not slept, Erin visiting each every hour. Required to kneel on a tray of marbles, their hands tied palms-up to a bar in front of them; theirs was a very uncomfortable night.

Six strokes of the cane were dealt ruthlessly to each hand and each foot. Every time the cell door opened it meant suffering twenty-four cuts.

By four in the morning both girls were dreading the key in the lock.

By six Erin had the names of all the other miscreants, the ringleader and who stole the keys. Davenport blamed Wisbeck, and Wisbeck Davenport. Both had eventually ceded defeat.

Alice stood watch on the assembly from the back of the hall, deep in thought. Hughes surprised her; she didn't hear the man approach.

'Told you I'd have you,' he whispered. 'Now tell me you didn't want it.'

Alice turned her back on him. 'Now you've notched me on your bedpost, will you leave me alone?'

'There you touch upon the heart of the matter. Normally I would. The conquest and all that. Trouble is, Miss Hussey, my feelings for you go far deeper.'

'What do you want this time, *Mr* Hughes.'

'You.'

'You had me last night. Remember?'

'Marry me.'

'Don't start with that nonsense again.'

'What do you want, candlelit dinners? Okay, I'll book us the finest restaurant in Chester for tonight. What else? Romancing? Flowers? I'll order the biggest bunch in Flint for you. Jewellery? Diamonds? You name it, Alice.'

'How about you jumping off the tallest wall in Flint castle? Oh, and to make sure of success, cut your throat first.'

'No good. You can't put me off. I'll book a holiday. Where do you fancy?'

'Skegness without you.'

'Do you want me to kneel? I will.'

'Don't be so silly.'

'I didn't sleep last night, thinking about you. I've never wanted anyone so much in my life. Come on, Alice, am I really that bad?'

'You're worse. You're unreliable, unpredictable and sometimes downright psychopathic. And if I said yes, it would take you one day to be unfaithful.'

He ran a finger down her spine, Alice shivering. 'But I get to you, don't I? I excite you. You know life with me would be a rollercoaster. You wouldn't have time to catch your breath.' He slipped an arm around her waist. 'How about trying it without the ceremony?'

'Live in sin, you mean.' She pushed his arm away. 'I might as well; I've sinned in every other way.'

'You mean it?' he asked, a thrill rising.

She shook her head. 'No.'

'Okay. How about dinner at the finest in Chester? Five pounds a head, plus champagne.'

'Trying to get me drunk?'

243

'Oh for fuck's sake, you're hard work.'

'So I've got to make it easy, have I? I thought you liked the chase?'

'Will you have dinner with me tonight? I will be the perfect gentleman. I will be witty, courteous and entertaining.'

'Juggling?'

'Eh?'

'The entertaining. I just wondered if you would be juggling. Maybe women. You know, Amanda, Sheila, Ruth, me.'

'I'll do the fucking rumba on the tabletops stark naked if it will make you happy.'

'Okay. It's a date. Just don't get us thrown out.'

'Is that a "yes I would love to come"?'

'The way your mind works, no. There'll be no coming. But I will permit you to take me out.'

Davenport was sobbing long before Hughes tied her over the back of a wooden chair. Stripped of every shred of clothing, she was roped with ankles to the back legs, wrists to the front.

The governor delivered the promised eighteen, Maureen's backside beaten to a purplish crimson, the woman screaming throughout.

Wisbeck faired no better. Similarly bound she tried to suffer in silence, but by the twelfth she sobbed and yelped to each subsequent explosion.

Both girls left over their chairs, Hughes delivered a message to the audience. 'Drake, Rachel Smith, Dawn Summers and Jane Catterall, attend my office at ten o'clock sharp.'

Hughes passed the strap to Roberts. 'Leave those two like that until after breakfast, then place them in solitary. We'll say for their own good for now. I have a couple of phone calls to make.' He smiled. 'I have a date to sort.'

Hughes left the stage, Erin mouthing, 'Bastard!'

'They grassed us up,' Catterall surmised.

'Expect they were persuaded,' Summers defended, uncharacteristically.

'Ain't no excuse,' Drake opined.

'Guess our arses will look like that come ten.' Rachel rubbed hers in anticipation.

'Notice,' Summers remarked, 'no Ruth O'Leary called out. Now ain't that a fucking surprise?'

Catterall lit a roll-up. 'What can we do about it?'

Dawn took the fag from Jane and drew deeply. 'You lot promise to stay out of it, and I'll take blondie in the bogs.'

'Don't know,' Drake said, unsure.

Summers looked the big woman over. 'What is your first name? No one ever says it.'

'Agnes.'

'Not surprising then is it, Aggie? I know Frankenstein made a fuck up with your grey matter, but please try to understand. Ruth is treacherous. Ruth is not trustworthy. Ruth needs a bloody good hiding. I intend to do more than bust her fucking nose. If you stick your great thick head in the way, I will break it.'

'Who's Frankenstein?'

Stress bred a needed release. The women burst into fits of laughter, Drake bewildered.

'You don't mind?' Hughes asked.

'No, of course not. I'm sure Hazel and I will get on famously.' Amanda handed Sweet's case to a taxi driver. 'Just look after my motorcycle until I come back.'

Hughes took Hazel by the arm and guided her to where he could talk in private. 'It's a simple deal,

245

Sweet. Once you're cleaned up Amanda will bring you back to the Hope. You will then reside with me. There will be an element of trust. I don't have the time to watch you every second, but there again I'm not going to end up red-faced over any escape attempt.' He paused to allow the words to settle. 'My house is secure, in as much as it is within the perimeter fence. I will trust you to treat that license with respect. Should you let me down...' Hughes smiled. 'Well, you don't want to go there. For every job you do for me I will deposit a sum in an account. That money will become available when your sentence expires.'

'How much?' Hazel asked.

'Bear in mind your position here. At best you could earn three shillings a week, and that would be in the sweatshop laundering clothes. Keeping a smile on my customers' faces will net you ten percent of the take, less overheads.'

Hazel scowled. 'Is that it?'

'It will amount to a tidy sum. Look upon it as an opportunity, and not one readily extended to the rank and file. See it as a chance to retire at a very early age, when other women are laying roots with husband and offspring, living in some grubby tenement. Or when they are working in a factory, doing time on menial and boring routines, you will be looking at... what do you want out of life, Hazel? Where do you want to be in say, ten years?'

'You know, or else you wouldn't be trying it on. Ten percent isn't enough, Mr Hughes, sir. I have eight GCE passes and three A-levels. I am not dumb, naïve or ignorant. I appreciate my position as it stands. I want twenty-five percent now, and fifty when I'm released. For that I will do anything you, or your customers, require. I don't have any hang-ups like Alice. It doesn't matter how disgusting or degrading the demand is, I will do it. And I will do it with a smile.'

'Okay, twenty, and an extra five for keeping me sweet, Sweet.'

'And does that equate to forty and ten when I'm freed?'

'Depends on how good you are.'

'Twenty plus five for now and fifty when I'm discharged.'

'Agreed.'

Ruth stood with her back to the door, arms folded, staring out of the barred window. 'What's this, Summers, a takeover bid?'

'You can take the easy way out if you like, O'Leary. I don't mind much which route we take. Thing is, we obviously can't trust you any more.'

'Is that you talking, or are you suddenly the mouthpiece?'

'I speak for us all. Strange ain't it? Names are called. Backsides will be pulverised, but it ain't gonna be yours.'

'Just shows the respect I have, that's all. You got grassed up cos you ain't worth a shit. Don't that tell you something?'

'What it tells me, tells everyone, is that you've done a deal. Whether it's with your bed-mate Scrubbs, or with Hughes himself, we ain't sure. Perhaps Sweet ain't the snitch after all.'

Ruth faced Summers. 'You think you can take me? You think the cons will follow you? Well, I will guarantee that within the next five minutes you'll be drinking toilet water.'

Dawn grinned. 'Guess what, O'Leary. You ain't got Drake to fight your battles any more. You're on your own.'

Skirt, blouse, underwear, stockings and a jumper lay folded and ready on Alice's bed, the girl searching beneath for a bag. 'Going somewhere?' dragged her rapidly back.

She stared up at Sheila. 'A day or two, that's all.'

'Does Geoff know?'

Alice shook her head.

'Do you want him to know?'

'I'll tell him, don't worry.'

'I'm not worried about him knowing, Alice. Just curious about you. Is everything okay?'

'Apart from the insanity, you mean?'

'You're not insane. You're just a normal confused teenager. Everything will come right soon, I promise.'

Alice sat on the bed. 'Geoff's asked me to marry him.'

At first stunned, Sheila then laughed. 'Oh God, that's a first. I assume every other line has failed. I suppose it's one way of getting into your knickers.'

Alice pulled a face.

'What? Oh, don't tell me he already has.'

The girl nodded.

'When?'

'Last night. I didn't say no. I let him.'

'And he still wants to marry you?'

'Why shouldn't he?' Alice took umbrage.

'No reason,' Sheila quickly assured. 'I didn't mean it like that. It's him. He's not cut for marriage. Christ, he couldn't keep his dick in his trousers for more than five minutes. He's been in fifty percent of the holes in this place, to put it crudely. I hope you told him where to go.'

'I didn't say yes.'

'Good.' She eyed the girl with suspicion. 'So what did you say?'

'That I'd let him date me.'

Sheila settled beside Alice. 'He's good-looking, isn't he, in a rugged sort of way.'

'Hmmm.'

'He's plausible and charming.'

'Yeah.'

'He's adventurous, exciting, masculine and horny.'

'He is.'

'And he will eat you alive then spit out the pieces when he's finished chewing.'

'I know.'

'So keep him at arm's length. I'd trust a psychopath more than I would Geoff.'

'I don't understand where he's coming from.'

'He'll want to own you. He hasn't the capacity for love. Possession, yes. And as his property, my guess is life wouldn't be bad, if one sets the expectations against a realistic base. Don't envisage love or tenderness. Forget compassion and kindness.'

Alice smiled. 'But when he looks at you in that way, you melt.'

'I get this fiery rush straight to the fanny. But there again I've been around a lot longer.'

'His smell,' Alice reflected. 'If it could be bottled it could make a fortune. Pure, virile man.'

'He can use what he's got to deadly effect. I've never seen a woman resist him permanently. And he can be *so* generous. Fuck it, marry him. You could do far worse. At least you won't get bored.'

Dennis Scrubbs strolled into the room. Folding his arms he leant against a window ledge. 'Air seems a bit tense.' Both women continued to wage a war of psychology. 'Tell you what, ladies. I'll let you resolve this difference in a time honoured way.'

'What difference?' Ruth demanded.

'Suspect it might be something to do with hierarchy.'

249

'Just go, Mr Scrubbs. Ain't nothing you can do here.'

'I think there is. Referee for one.'

'You'll let us sort this?' Summers asked, surprised.

'To my rules.'

'And they are?' Ruth stared at Dennis.

'You wrestle. The first to get the other stripped completely, wins.'

Summers accused, 'Just want to fill your eyes, don't you?'

'And the loser pays a penalty.'

Summers poured scorn. 'What, getting fucked by you, you mean?'

Scrubbs took a pound note from his pocket and lay it to one side. 'Winner gets that, her fiefdom and leave to chastise and humiliate her opponent. Worth fighting for?'

Ruth rubbed her hands together. 'Sounds fucking good to me.'

Drake stood alongside Smith and Catterall. 'Where's Summers?' Hughes demanded.

'Shits, sir,' Smith offered. 'Bad gut. Probably the lack of properly cooked food, sir.'

'Didn't that whip on your back teach you nothing, Smith?'

'Found out how much it hurt, sir.'

'Drake. You'll serve the remainder of your sentence in the laundry. Miss Roberts will see you re-housed in an adjacent cell.'

'I'd sooner take…'

Thunder crossed Hughes' face. 'I don't give a damn what you want! Think yourself lucky I don't have you removed and re-sentenced. You could easily find yourself facing another three years. You all could.'

'Catterall. Have you anything to say before I pass sentence?'

Ashen, the girl shook her head.

'You'll be birched before the Hope assembly. Date to be set.'

The young woman trembled.

'Now you, Smith. From the moment you set foot in this establishment you have tried to upset the status quo.'

Rachel smirked.

'You can apply the birch rod to your confederate Catterall. And every stroke I deem below full strength shall be reapplied twice and added to your tally, for when Summers birches you. In other words, if you try to go easy on Catterall by holding back on a stroke, she will receive two instead. And those two extra will be added to your sentence.'

'And Dawn?' Smith asked.

Hughes sighed. 'Drake, Catterall, you may go. Smith, you stay. It seems you still require some educating.'

Sheila took the bull by the horns. 'Why are you going away?'

'I need to resolve a few matters, that's all.'

'Is it anything to do with your mother?'

'A bit.' Alice nibbled her lower lip. 'Mostly it's to do with in here.' She jabbed her temple with a finger.

'Are you seeing a psychiatrist?'

The teenager shook her head. 'I'll be eighteen at the end of the month.'

'Oh. What date?'

'The twenty-eighth. Why?'

'Get you a card, of course.'

Alice smiled. 'No need. As I was saying, it's a religious conflict. So I'm going to see a religious seer. I hope he can help me sort my dilemma out.'

'Why not let me help.' Sheila chuckled. 'I know I probably haven't acted very professionally, but that's

251

only because I see you as a really good friend. I can analyse you far more efficiently than any church spiritualist. Believe me, Alice. Give me the opportunity and I will ensure you resolve your plight. I think you will see life from a new perspective.'

'There would be no drugs?' Alice asked, concerned.

'No drugs, Alice. I would hypnotise you, that's all. That way we can lower the drawbridges, the defences, find out who you really are, what you really want.'

'I have an appointment for the day after tomorrow. I either see Cavenny then or not at all.'

'Christ, Alice, I can't unravel your complexities by then.'

'I'll see Cavenny, then.'

'Okay, Alice, we'll have a session tomorrow.'

'Can you stop her?'

Sheila shrugged. 'Depends on the mess in her head. I've been fucking with her for a while now. Sleep therapy. Suggestions. Something in her drink to make sure she sleeps, and a few carefully contrived arguments. But I can't make her say yes to your ridiculous proposal. I can't actually make her go against her will.'

'The proposal isn't ridiculous. It's sound business. It would be like owning the rights to Alice-so-fuckable-Hussey.'

'What you going to do with Summers?'

'Haven't decided.' Hughes emptied his glass and poured another whiskey. 'Depends on what the outcome was between her and O'Leary.'

'Not heard?'

Hughes shook his head. 'I'll see Scrubbs later.'

'Smith?'

'The brat irks me. I think she's a weak link. Too much mind and grit. She could bring us down, Sheil.'

'I heated her butt again this evening, after I sentenced her, Drake and Catterall. Not many could take what I gave her. She didn't even flinch. Damned nice backside, though. Pleasure to spank. Firm and nicely presented.'

'Lamb?'

'I think so.'

'Wouldn't like to spank another girl with a well presented and fairly firm arse, would you?'

'What's it worth?'

'Fifteen positions after. If you're *up* to it.'

Hughes drew her over his lap, a hand lifting her skirt, uncovering her black lace panty-covered bottom.

Epilogue

Alice didn't take her eyes off the telephone. Hughes sat on the opposite side of the table, a piece of paper in his hand. Gravely he asked her again. 'Are you sure you want to do this?'

Alice nodded.

'I'm not concerned about my side. It's your future relationship with Rose I'm worried about. We're putting her on the spot. When you open this conversation it will be the first words her daughter has ever said to her.'

'Dial the number please.'

'Close your eyes.' He studied her, suspicious. 'You didn't argue. Stick your fingers in your ears as well. You're too smart for my good.'

A few seconds later Hughes placed the receiver in Alice's hand. 'Best of luck, girl.'

Alice listened to the ringing tone, hoping against all hopes she would answer the phone, and that her husband wouldn't.

For thirty-five long, interminable seconds no one

answered. Then finally Alice heard the magical words. 'Hello? Rose MacMahon speaking.'

Her mouth hung open. A million, trillion thoughts, feelings, emotions, heartaches, thrills and joys hit at once. The room spun, stars twinkling before her eyes. Hughes responded with speed. He caught the teenager as she slumped from her chair, the voice on the telephone saying, 'Hello? Hello? Is there anyone there?'

Chimera erotic books are available from all good bookshops, or direct from our mail order department. Please send your order and credit/debit card details, a cheque or postal order (made payable to *Chimera Books Ltd*) to: **Chimera Books Ltd., Readers' Services, PO Box 152, Waterlooville, Hants, PO8 9FS, United Kingdom**. Or call our **24 hour credit card hotline: 07012 906980** (Visa, Mastercard & Maestro).

We provide our customers with efficient and secure delivery, with all orders despatched in robust and discreet packaging. Since 1995 we have delivered our erotic books to thousands of customers in many destinations across the world.

We aim to deliver all orders as quickly as possible, with the majority being despatched within 24 hours of receipt.

And now we have simplified all our postage charges, no matter where in the world you are:

UK & BFPO - £1.25 per item
Western Europe - £2.25 per item
USA & the Rest of the World - £3.25 per item